A LOVE LETTER TO PARIS

REBECCA RAISIN

First published in Great Britain in 2024 by Boldwood Books Ltd.

Copyright © Rebecca Raisin, 2024

Cover Design by Alexandra Alden

Cover Photography: Shutterstock

The moral right of Rebecca Raisin to be identified as the author of this work has been asserted in accordance with the Copyright, Designs and Patents Act 1988.

All rights reserved. No part of this book may be reproduced in any form or by any electronic or mechanical means, including information storage and retrieval systems, without written permission from the author, except for the use of brief quotations in a book review.

This book is a work of fiction and, except in the case of historical fact, any resemblance to actual persons, living or dead, is purely coincidental.

Every effort has been made to obtain the necessary permissions with reference to copyright material, both illustrative and quoted. We apologise for any omissions in this respect and will be pleased to make the appropriate acknowledgements in any future edition.

A CIP catalogue record for this book is available from the British Library.

Paperback ISBN 978-1-83533-502-4

Large Print ISBN 978-1-83533-498-0

Hardback ISBN 978-1-83533-497-3

Ebook ISBN 978-1-83533-495-9

Kindle ISBN 978-1-83533-496-6

Audio CD ISBN 978-1-83533-503-1

MP3 CD ISBN 978-1-83533-500-0

Digital audio download ISBN 978-1-83533-494-2

Boldwood Books Ltd
23 Bowerdean Street
London SW6 3TN
www.boldwoodbooks.com

For Mum

1

NOW – JULY

My phone beeps with a text from my friend Émilienne that reads:

> I've been keeping a secret – I'm finally, madly, head over heels in love thanks to a little-known matchmaking website called Paris Cupid. Why don't you join? If anyone deserves love, it's you!

What Émilienne doesn't know is that I have a secret too.
I am Paris Cupid.

* * *

Six months ago

On a cold February day, Émilienne cups her head and cries. I give her shoulder a useless pat as we sit side by side at Café des Capucines in the 9th arrondissement. What can anyone really do for a heartbroken friend, except be there and listen? I've just returned from a holiday to London visiting my parents who moved back to the UK recently, so this is the first chance I've had to comfort Émilienne in person.

Dad is British and Maman is French. I've spent most of my life criss-crossing the English Channel because they could never make up their mind where they wanted to live before I settled for good in Paris in my early twenties. Truth be told, I went home to lick my wounds after a terrible break up too, but I'm at the stage I want to forget it, not rehash it. Besides, I'm here for Em today, not for me.

Émilienne's shoulders slump as she says, 'He told me I'm too intense. That my needs are too great – all I asked was if he wanted company at the gym, and suddenly I'm needy? Nothing ever goes the distance.' It's been a few weeks since he broke it off and Émilienne is still mourning the relationship. 'Is it me? Am I the problem?'

'*Non*, of course it's not you.'

'I'm *done* with men.'

'He wasn't the one for you, Em.' Time and again this comes up for my friend. If she's not being called needy, she's being called aloof, detached – it doesn't make sense.

The waiter arrives with our café crèmes, takes one look at Émilienne, and flees as if her sadness might be contagious. I encourage Émilienne to take a sip of her coffee as the waiter returns with a plate of colourful macarons. '*Excusez moi?*' he says. 'These are for you.'

Émilienne gazes at him, her eyes glassy with tears. 'But we didn't order…'

'*Gratuit.*' He dashes away as quickly as he came. Ah, Paris, the city where a broken heart is recognised and remedied by a hit of sugar. Temporarily remedied, at least.

'See?' I say. 'There's plenty of nice men around. Every day, I read the most heartfelt, hard-won love stories in the letters I sell at the market. Sure, true love can be elusive, but it's out there, I promise you. You can't give up.'

Émilienne gives me a weary smile. 'Your love letters are from another era, Lilou. While they're beautiful mementos of yesteryear, life isn't like that these days. Romances like those are a thing of the past.' She lets out a frustrated sigh.

'Maybe, maybe not,' I say as a murky idea takes shape. Could the lost art of love-letter writing and slow-burn romance be the answer?

Can you fall in love with a person purely by their words alone? According to the bundles of love letters I stock at my stall in the Marché Dauphine at the Saint Ouen Flea Market, you can. Those letters may be relics from the past but that doesn't mean that sort of love doesn't exist any more. 'You never know what's around the corner, Émilienne.'

My friend is usually a ball of energy, one of those early to bed, early to rise types who does yoga and goes on retreats to balance the days when she eats her bodyweight in *soufflé au fromage* and washes it down with a *demi-bouteille* of Sancerre, but this latest break-up has really done a number on her. It's hard to see her usually bright complexion so sallow as if she's given up on all the good things she does for herself. We've all been there. Eaten our way down a four-litre bucket of ice cream and chased it with a bottle of red wine to ease the hurt. But Émilienne can't seem to shake off this latest break-up. It feels more like she's blaming herself, rather than the fact they just weren't compatible.

I suppose it stems from dating a string of similar men, telling her a variation of the same sort of critique every time. And I get it. My dating history isn't exactly stellar. Are us unlucky-in-love types choosing the wrong men, or are we just going about this the wrong way? Maybe we need to change the method we use to find love since it's clearly not working for either of us. Could I match Émilienne with the perfect man? She always goes for the health nuts, men with regimented gym routines who wear too tight clothing and obsess over their green vegetable intake. These men don't seem to appreciate her, not the way she deserves. They're more likely to stand her up for an abseiling day or something equally crazy. Time and again she chooses the same type of guy. Are we all making the same mistakes with love, on repeat? I picture her with a man who is passionate not about his exercise regime but Parisian life. He's cultured but not pretentious. A reveller on occasion but appreciates waking early to watch a sunrise or two. Happy to humour early morning jogs when the mood strikes her, but equally happy to stay in bed late Sunday with a scattering of newspapers and a lot of lazy kisses.

Émilienne doesn't need platitudes about her lovability, she needs proof. More importantly, she needs to know she doesn't have to lower her standards to find her soulmate. But can I help her believe such a thing? It isn't like I have the best track record in relationships myself. Émilienne needs Cupid to shoot that arrow and snare her the type of man she'd never choose for herself. Could I make that work? Could I be Paris Cupid?

* * *

Later that evening rain lashes sideways at my apartment windows while I muse about my matchmaking idea. As I mindlessly scroll on social media I discover more posts about shock break-ups, speedy divorces, or awkward dating-app encounters. Why isn't love going the distance for some of us thirty-somethings? There's that overarching fear that all the best men are married by now and the clock is ticking to find whoever is left out there, being set up by friends or using apps.

Dating apps are the primary way in which my friends find love, and they work for a lot of people, but they're not for me. I tried them for a while but shied away in favour of meeting the one meet-cute style. A girl can dream, right?

From what I can see posted online there are others who find the rules of love just as mystifying. It's not exclusive to Paris either – some of my British friends are facing the same struggles.

What if there was another option? A matchmaking site for lonely hearts who have tried other avenues but want to take things slower? Really get to know one another by exchanging letters before they meet so they have a solid foundation that won't fizzle out within a few months. It *could* work. Matches won't exchange phone numbers, they'd exchange PO boxes. Instead of sending pictures, they'd send letters. All they'd share is their first names and what they do for work or a hobby to keep things mysterious as they get to know each other through words alone. They could fill out questionnaires about themselves which would help me find them a suitable match.

The idea needs fleshing out but what if it worked? What if I could singlehandedly help Émilienne and so many others like her find real abiding love?

I could develop a bespoke matchmaking service for those who have given up on love or feel that love has given up on them. Designed for singletons – like Émilienne, like me – who find modern-day romance tricky to navigate after one too many messy endings.

As I jot down notes, I use my own struggles in the dating world as inspiration for what I *don't* want Paris Cupid to be. I'm a heart-on-sleeve romantic and find myself weary having to constantly filter out the real from the fake. There's no such thing as old-fashioned courting any more. It's all a great big rush to meet, to remain non-exclusive, that it tends to leave one a little deflated, when time and again things end because they're not committed and only want a casual relationship.

In my other life I'm a merchant at a flea market. I sell love letters, diaries, ephemera from the past. That's where real love looms large. Men from bygone times who wrote sweeping promises in elegant prose, women who declared their mutual adoration. These couples from the past always fell in love, achingly slowly through words penned on thick parchment, the memory of them standing the test of time. Why can't I recreate that sort of romance for my matches?

It's always bothered me that we won't have love letters like these in the future because these days most correspondence is digital. Email doesn't quite cut it when it comes to looking back.

Paris Cupid will remedy that injustice by bringing back the lost art of handwritten love letters. My matches will partake in a slow-burn romance, with no need to swipe right, or Netflix and chill. My first goal will be to help Émilienne believe in love again.

I make a detailed list of everything I'll need to do to get the business up and running, including building the website, writing the question-naire, the rules and requirements for matches, and advertising to find clients. The plan is to make Paris Cupid exclusive and only accept those who are genuinely searching for the one.

Anonymously, under the guise of an advertisement for Paris Cupid, I email Émilienne with a free introductory offer and then set out to find others like her. People, who love had left bruised, wary and abandoned. People just like me. I'm a walking dating disaster story, so I happen to know a fair bit about what not to do in the course of true love. I'll have to keep the fact I'm Cupid quiet. I'm still reeling from *le scandale* at the market a month ago with the married man's wife. The man I was dating at the time.

2

SEVEN MONTHS AGO

Le Scandale

Hugging my jacket tight, I chitchat with acquaintances from the flea market while we wait in the queue at the outdoor café in the square. Soft rain falls as we huddle close. The queue grows steadily, as if almost every market vendor is desperate for a warm drink before their workday begins. It's a freezing January day but even the bitter weather doesn't steal my smile as I tell a work friend all about my date with Frederic last night, a man who *knows* how to romance a woman. I feel a poke on the shoulder. A rather forceful poke. I turn to find a pretty forty-something woman who shoots me a look that's so venomous I can't help but recoil. When I look closer, it's obvious she's been crying. Her mascara is smudged, and her eyes are puffy.

'Are you Lilou?' she demands, her voice so loud it draws the eyes of most of my market friends in the vicinity.

'*Oui.*' I can't place her. I'm sure I've never met this woman in my life but hostility radiates from her glare and is directed squarely at me.

'Do you enjoy sleeping with a married man? Did you think I wouldn't find out?'

My heart leaps into my throat. A married man? It can't be! '*Excusez moi*, are you sure you have the right person?' Frederic isn't married! We've been seeing each other off and on for months, including every second weekend when he stays at my apartment. A married man couldn't go missing for an entire weekend, surely?

Her face reddens. 'Are you or are you not sleeping with Frederic Beaumont?'

Humiliation cuts me to the quick as there are audible gasps around me. How embarrassing to have this play out in front of my market colleagues. 'Ah – I...' I close my eyes against the shock. I had no idea he was married. None. There must be some sort of mix up, a misunderstanding.

'Well?' The woman demands as she pulls her phone from her pocket and swipes until a picture of Frederic appears. That's him. Curled locks, crooked smile, playful gaze that makes me woozy. The woman flicks to another photo. There he is as a groom. How could I have missed this!

I cough, clearing my throat, wishing I could teleport myself away. My mind spins with scenarios and the dots suddenly join up. All those last-minute cancellations. The sporadic schedule due to his corporate job that had him flying all over France. He always switched his mobile off in my presence which I'd put down to good manners and a reprieve from business calls.

When I'd phone him late at night he'd whisper sweet nothings, his voice low and sweet. He wasn't talking softly because he was in bed and sleepy, he was whispering so he didn't get caught by his wife! I'm a fool!

And worse, this woman is as mad as hell and rightfully so. 'I'm so sorry. I had no idea. He said his marriage ended a year ago.' He'd told me they'd rushed into matrimony and realised soon after they weren't a good fit. He glossed over it as if it was a small speed bump on the road to finding real love. Opposites attract until they don't, kind of thing.

The woman lets out a bitter laugh that sends a shiver down my spine. More vendors stop to watch the show. 'Did he neglect to mention his children?' Her voice rises. 'All seven of them?'

Seven children! There are murmurs around me, and many shakes of the head. I'm never going to live this down. My reputation is ruined even though I had zero clue Frederic had a family. Not one. As much as this shameful public display hurts, I can *feel* this woman's pain. It's a hundred times worse for her. I soften my voice and say, 'I didn't know he had children.' That pig! That swine! Here I am believing I've finally found the one, and he's just as bad as the rest.

'Convenient.'

I swallow back tears. 'I *didn't* know.'

'You've destroyed my family. I hope you're happy with yourself.'

'*Non* – I—'

'Save it. I don't want to hear any more lies.' She spins on her heel, cursing me as she leaves. Colour races up my cheeks as the crowd eyes me suspiciously, including my market friend who I'd been reminiscing with about my date. Now she turns her back to me, but not before she shoots me a withering glare. Do I continue to voice my innocence? Will they believe me?

Just as I'm debating flight, Coraline, a slightly prickly woman in her forties, who has a flower stall near the entrance of the flea market, rushes over to me. 'Are you OK? I only caught the tail end of all of that.'

My tears finally spill as Coraline pulls me in for a hug. 'I swear I had no idea. I would *never* date a married man with a family!'

'Shush, shush. I know you wouldn't.' Out of everyone I'm familiar with at the market, Coraline is the last person I expected would comfort me. She's known for being a gossip and relishing in other people's misfortunes, but there are rare times when she shows a whole other side. I'm grateful for it today. 'Go,' she says. 'Go to your stall and I'll bring you a café crème. Shoulders back, chin up. You've got nothing to be ashamed of.'

I give her a small smile, trying to ignore the shake in my legs. How can I ever trust a man again? Not only has he lied and cheated but my hopes for finding the one are dashed again. Now I've got this woman's broken heart on my conscience. I scrub my face and look beyond the crowd to avoid their stares and somehow I manage to lock eyes with a tall mountain of a man who surveys me long and hard like he's trying to figure out a puzzle. 'Who *is* that?' I hope it's not the wife's brother or someone on her side ready to admonish too. I can't take any more today.

Coraline follows my gaze. '*Oooh la la,* he's got the looks and the body to match. All I know is his name is Pascale and he sells vintage typewriters in a stall in the middle of the market. Doesn't look like the approachable sort though, does he?'

'*Non*, he looks the exact opposite.' And why the intense stare? Has he never seen a woman being publicly humiliated before? There's something almost primal about the way he's locked his eyes onto mine. It's almost hypnotic. I find myself unable to look away even though the desire to flee is strong.

3

NOW

I'm woefully late to my day job after a long night of matching the lost, star-crossed and broken-hearted of Paris. The early July summer sunshine boosts my mood and makes the long walk to the market an enjoyable one.

I find myself thinking back to when my little side business came to life. That wintry day when I met with a despondent Émilienne who had all but sworn off love.

Her sadness felt like a plea for help. A call to arms. And it gets me thinking: why do we get punished when we set standards for love? It's not as though Émilienne was asking for too much. All she wanted to find in a relationship was kindness, monogamy and the hope of building a future together. And now she has, thanks to the art of love-letter writing.

Since that fateful coffee catch up, Paris Cupid has flourished although I've had to keep my role anonymous. My name is still mud after *le scandale*. Not everyone has forgiven me, despite my protestations of innocence. And it didn't help matters when Frederic recently visited the market and told me he still loved me. I had to resort to using my broom to drive him away and it dredged up the whole scandal again.

There were whispers that I must be secretly seeing him otherwise why would he drop by like that? The market is like a petri-dish when it comes to gossip, and left unattended it grows, multiplying until everyone hears an exaggerated version of the story that just isn't true.

Having Paris Cupid to pour my time into has been good for me in more ways than one, since men aren't exactly beating my door down to ask me on a date. Love has truly blossomed for a number of my matches, including Émilienne. Her kindred spirit is a man named Remy, who I found to be sensitive and soulful. He has a good understanding of healthy boundaries which, according to her application, had been an issue with men in her past. Émilienne is the type of woman who needs her space, quiet time to retreat and reflect, and Remy agreed that was important to him too.

It's been a whirlwind since start up six months ago and it warms my heart that future generations might one day unearth these Paris Cupid love letters, sit with a mug of tea, settle in and read a sweeping romance, just like in the books. The only problem is, these days my bespoke little matchmaking biz is taking a big chunk of my time and I'm finding it hard to balance both worlds, my market stall and my secret Cupid life, hence my lateness this and every morning.

Matching lovebirds also makes me yearn for my own love affair, but I still feel at odds with how to go about it for myself. Short of the universe throwing a man in my way, I don't see how it's ever going to happen now that I'm working more than ever. To get enough matches so I could faithfully promise people a chance at love, I've had to come up with all sorts of advertising campaigns for social media. It's where most of my clients have found Paris Cupid, and I've tried other avenues of advertising like letterbox drops, podcast ads, even a tiny little billboard at a Montmartre bus station and posters glued up around Saint Ouen Flea Market. Word of mouth referrals have been big as well. The income Paris Cupid is producing has really helped when I have slow weeks at Ephemera, so I remind myself the extra work is worth it when I'm feeling the pressure of keeping everything afloat. As I increase my pace, I pass *un kiosque à presse* and catch sight of a magazine headline that stops me in my tracks.

TV star Emmanuel Roux is engaged – thanks to Paris Cupid!

What! My heart leaps into my throat. I dig through my handbag for my purse and hand over some euros with a shaky *'Bonjour, Monsieur'*. Once I'm far enough away from the kiosk, I duck into an apartment doorway to read the article.

> Self-confessed 'Playboy of Paris' Emmanuel Roux from Twilight Dream TV fame has found 'The One' and proposed atop the Eiffel Tower. 'She's not from show biz,' he says. 'We were matched on a new underground site called Paris Cupid.' We asked Emmanuel why the Playboy of Paris would need to use a relatively unknown matchmaking site to find love. 'For anonymity,' he claims. We did a little digging into Paris Cupid, a small Parisian start-up that claims to find love for the lost, the lonely and those who feel they're unlucky in love. This is no insta-date hook-up site. Members commit to writing love letters and getting to know one another slowly by good old-fashioned courtship. 'My days as a bachelor are over,' Emmanuel says with a determined set to his jaw.

This cannot be! I vet every single member as assiduously as possible with the skills I have at hand. I search their social media accounts and their online presence. So it comes as a nasty shock to find that I've matched the so-dubbed Playboy of Paris without being aware of it.

I'd never approve membership to a man who dates and dashes like Emmanuel Roux famously does. Did he use a pseudonym? Photos can easily be doctored these days, but I wouldn't have paid much attention to his pictures anyway. I'm more interested in what they write about love than their physical appearance. Whatever social media accounts he'd given me must have appeared legitimate when I did my first round of checks.

My mind spins with worry. Who did he claim to be, and worse, who did I match him with? For all his protestations, I don't believe for a minute that Emmanuel Roux's playboy days are over. This is an unmitigated disaster for Paris Cupid, which I genuinely built for those who had given up on finding love. I also kept it exclusive so I could cope with the workload. I quicken my pace and head to Paris Saint Ouen Flea Market, to my stall Ephemera, where I sell my love letters, prayer books and scribed diaries.

4

I open my stall, switch on my laptop and glance up to make sure I'm alone. Satisfied there's no chance of being caught out, I search for Emmanuel Roux's pseudonym on Paris Cupid. As I scroll through the membership list, my frustration increases. I'm breaking a cardinal rule by working on Paris Cupid at Ephemera and risking my anonymity. Worse, I can't see a single man who doesn't appear real. Their stories are all so touching, I get lost down the rabbit hole, checking their statuses and making notes on couples I have to liaise with. Finally at the very end of the list, I see a potential and my heart judders to a stop.

Merde. How can I have made a mistake as epic as this?

There in bold is the name of the woman I matched Emmanuel Roux AKA Remy Tatou with. Émilienne Lyon. My friend, and the first ever member of Paris Cupid. I cup my face and resist the urge to wail. Émilienne, the unwitting inspiration behind the matchmaking site, now believes Emmanuel Roux of all people is her soulmate. The power of suggestion is a heady thing. Have I exposed her to a man who will break her heart and publicly humiliate her? So far, he's kept her name out of the press, but now the media have caught the scent it won't be long until they hunt down the newly engaged couple and splash their pictures all over the internet.

What have I done? *Emmanuel and Émilienne.* It even sounds farcical!

How did he persuade Émilienne that he's truly retired his Playboy of Paris status? It boggles the mind, but if the article's to be believed he must have convinced her well enough that she's accepted his hand in marriage. Or is it because *I,* playing my part as Paris Cupid, told her in no uncertain terms Remy Tatou AKA Emmanuel Roux is compatible to her in every way? The slippery snake has really done a number on me. I bring up his application and reread. It's poetic, heartfelt and honest (ha!). The lamentations of a man who claims to be ill-fated when it comes to love, despite his best intentions. The fraudulent application makes my teeth grind. But really, I'm responsible for any fallout.

There's nothing I can do about it at the moment, so I shut down my computer and distract myself with my morning routine at Ephemera. I wheel out my display tables and arrange stock. Water my plants. Give the rugs a quick vacuum.

Soon, the market is filled with shoppers; laughter, shouting, chitchat. Outside, horns are blaring, sirens wailing, the soundtrack of our market days.

Feather duster in hand, I make my rounds when I spot the arrival of one of my neighbours as he stomps up the stairs, his familiar scowl in place. I hide behind a postcard carousel and spy on prickly Pascale as he unlocks his stall. In the month or so since *la réorganisation du marché,* the big market vendor reshuffle, Pascale has managed to find fault with me numerous times. Allegedly my display tables are too wide and it's not fair to the others who share the hall. My rose-scented candles give him a headache. My lavender plants attract bees even though we're indoors and upstairs, and on and on it goes. Each complaint has caught me unawares. I'm not used to such criticisms. I've done my best to remedy these issues but then he comes back with another problem.

'Who are you hiding from?' A velvety voice rings out and manages to snare Pascale's attention. He looks over in my direction. I do the adult thing and drop to the wooden floor, hoping it will open and swallow me whole. The last thing I need is him storming over here again.

'Geneviève! Shush!' Glamorous Geneviève is one of my neighbours in Marché Dauphine and my very best friend, despite being twenty, or maybe even thirty, years senior to me. It's hard to gauge exactly what age she is as she has a timeless quality about her and is the least grown-up person I know.

'Lilou, honestly, that's no place to sit.' Geneviève shakes her head as if I've lost my marbles. Maybe I have. 'Get up this instant.' She's bossy at the best of times, but Geneviève has the sort of presence that commands a person to do as they're told.

I'm sure I can feel Pascale's laser-like gaze on me. Like the ultimate grown-up I am, I edge backwards on all fours like a hunted animal, which is surprisingly difficult, and take cover behind my desk.

I'd be mortified if he caught me spying on him. It would only give him more ammunition. He'd probably put a complaint to market management about me making him uncomfortable or something equally wild.

'Is he looking over here?' I ask as I duck my head and make a show of shuffling paperwork so she can't rebuke me again.

'Who?' She dons her bejewelled spectacles – Geneviève is so extra – and gazes across the hall. 'Ooh, is that the delectable Pascale? You should ask him on a date. This is a *clear* case of grumpy sunshine.'

I scoff. For the past month Geneviève has impatiently listened to my litany of complaints about the guy, and this is what she comes up with?

'I hardly think a relationship between us will evolve like it does in the books, Geneviève. Unless it's a true crime novel. Don't you always see this with warring neighbours? One ends up worse off. Or dead.' I massage my temples as a headache looms. I'm not usually so testy. I blame it on the morning I've had.

'*Non, non, non.* This is how they always start out! The couple can't stand the sight of each other' – Geneviève has a penchant for romance novels, the spicier the better. Most of her advice comes from such tomes – 'and then *voila*. Love hearts for eyes.'

'Well, lucky for me my life is non-fictional.' What I don't tell Geneviève is, I do find Pascale's abrupt unsunny disposition *slightly* alluring. And how ridiculous is that? Part of me wants to get to the root of why he's so abjectly *bothered* all the time. He's not much of a talker – why use a string of words when a grunt will suffice? But as a professional in the world of true love, I see it for what it is – an act. Those red flags are waving so hard they're impossible to ignore.

'Look at him. There's something almost wild about him. Purrrr.'

I roll my eyes. '*Really!* Did you just purr?' This is what she's like, absolutely man mad. Geneviève has a new beau every season, claiming her love is fluid and that she'll never be tied down to one man. Despite her fickle heart though, she remains good friends with all of her exes. Everyone wants to be in her spotlight as either friend or beau.

'What?' She reluctantly draws her gaze away from 'the delectable Pascale' and back to me. Geneviève leans close and whispers, 'You're a successful matchmaker, and yet you can't see what's right in front of you!'

'You make a valid point,' I agree, peeking over the top of the desk to make sure no one is eavesdropping on our conversation. Only Geneviève knows my secret, and I intend to keep it that way. 'For some *unfathomable* reason, my matchmaking abilities don't translate to my own love life. How is that fair?' It's a bone of contention, but who would I complain to? Truthfully, I've searched applications looking for a man who might be right for me, but it feels like it would be a breach of trust setting myself up. If it came to light I was Paris Cupid, it wouldn't look good, and after *le scandale* I'm not keen for the spotlight to be trained on me like that ever again.

Right now, no one suspects the quiet bookworm who sells quirky ephemera is the creator of Paris Cupid. It's my intention to keep Paris Cupid select, manageable and anonymous; to keep my secret safe.

I'm obsessed with love in all its guises, yet somehow real love eludes me. Another reason to remain anonymous. Members wouldn't have any faith in my abilities if they knew about my own dating history. I've been catfished, gaslit, stood up, friend-zoned, had my share of situationships, and most recently got caught up with married man Frederic with his rather large brood of children. That catastrophe has made me somewhat reluctant to dip a toe back in the dating pool.

You could say even my textpectations are at an all-time low. Besides, I don't have time right now. I'm too busy helping other hopefuls.

Geneviève shakes her head as if she too is befuddled by it. 'Such a riddle. You've set up so many couples, yet love remains elusive for our resident Cupid.' Her face softens with sympathy.

'You know what they say: lucky at cards, unlucky in love.' I shrug. Is it me? Am I too much of a daydreamer? Too caught up with work and Paris Cupid? If only the perfect guy would appear, like they do in the movies, where I'm walking along, head in the clouds, and oops, we bump into one another, my handbag goes flying and then we lock eyes and the rest is history. Or is that just romcoms giving me unrealistic expectations?

I'm debating whether to confide in Geneviève about the Emmanuel Roux development when Pascale cranes his neck my way. I drop my head to the desk, much to Geneviève's chagrin. 'Why would you *want* to hide from Pascale anyway?'

I drag my attention back to Geneviève. 'So I can avoid conversation.'

Her eyebrows pull together. 'What? Why? Because he complained a few times?'

'A *few!* He's intimidating. Look at that scowl, the fire in his eyes. I don't speak his language. Grunts, that is.' And after Emmanuel Roux taking advantage, I'm feeling a little more feisty than usual, so if he does stomp over here, I'm not going to be conciliatory this time. Geneviève lets out a string of tuts. 'Have a listen to yourself, Lilou. This is exactly the challenge you'd set for a woman on Paris Cupid, advising them to write and get to the root of the person's mind and soul before judging them. Yet here you are, bent like a pretzel, behind your desk.'

'I'm working, Geneviève, as you can very well see.' I vehemently shuffle paperwork so she can see the truth right before her very eyes.

She heaves a theatrical sigh and snatches the paperwork from my hands. 'This is nothing but a prop! Are you going to spend the rest of your natural born life hiding from him? A nice healthy response from someone who advises others on such matters.'

It's almost as if I can *hear* her eyes roll.

Merde.

She's right though. Why should *I* hide? I was here first before *la réorganisation du marché*, which brought this egotistical megalomaniac into my work life and made it infinitely worse.

***

A month ago
La réorganisation du marché

Geneviève arrives unusually early before the market is even open to customers, which is very out of character for her. She's wearing a swishy summery dress that's perfect for the mild June summer weather.

'*Bonjour*, Lilou,' she says, kissing me hello. 'Our new neighbours arrive today, so I thought it's best I am here to help welcome them.' The powers that be decided to reorganise the market, bringing together vendors with similar customer bases. We've said goodbye to our previous neighbours and await the influx of the new ones, feeling hopeful they'll be just as nice as the ones we had before.

'Aren't they lucky to have your attention so early in the morning?'

'Ha!' She opens her handbag and removes a compact mirror, checking her lipstick. 'You're right. I'm not a morning person. Is that a crime? But truthfully, I snuck in early to pop Paris Cupid brochures in the vendor pigeonholes to see if we can drum up some love around these parts. What do you think?' Geneviève is always thinking of new ways to spread the word about Paris Cupid and often helps delivering marketing material of her own accord.

'Great idea.'

I've set up around thirty couples since Paris Cupid began back in February. Of those, a handful weren't compatible, so I matched them again. A few people have decided it's not for them for various reasons, one said he found the process too slow, another woman said she found it dull. Not everyone will make it, or find true love, but I'm willing to help the ones who are in it for the long haul.

'Would you ever try Paris Cupid for a match?' I ask, as I'm genuinely curious. It's not that she has any trouble finding paramours, it's more that I wonder if this way of seeking out a partner intrigues her.

'*Non, ma Cherie*. It wouldn't be for me. I like my men with a bit of grrr. Those robust, take-charge types who keep me on my toes.'

'I'm surprised by how many men have signed up who yearn for

romance too. It's not that they're beta at all, it's more that they like the idea of a slow seduction. It's quite sensual this way of meeting someone and opening up to them.'

'Huh. I do like the sound of slow seduction. I must admit, French men can be deliciously romantic, and wildly poetic, so it makes sense this would appeal. That goes for men *and* women.'

'Oh, here's one of our new neighbours.' A mussed ginger-haired thirty-something guy bounds up the stairs, carrying bags and boxes that don't seem to weigh him down. He gives us a cheeky smile as he deposits his things before dashing over to us. '*Bonjour, je suis Felix.*'

'*Bonjour, bonjour,*' I say. 'I'm Lilou and this is Geneviève. What do you sell?'

Felix nods, acknowledging us both. 'Lovely to meet you beautiful ladies. I sell vintage printing press parts. And I design posters, cards and other paraphernalia using movable type to paper. It's a lost art form and using traditional printing methods is time consuming but a worthy endeavour, if I do say so myself.' He speaks fast and gesticulates wildly as if he has an abundance of energy that has to go somewhere. I like him instantly.

Felix the flame-haired printer is just the type of personality we need around here to bring customers up those stairs. We tell him about what we sell and about the amount of foot traffic we get in the Marché Dauphine, which is decent compared to other parts of the market but could always be better. He just might be the answer to that. I'd hazard a guess that he's the type of person who makes friends with everyone.

'I'm *thrilled* to have been chosen to move here,' he says, running a hand through his hair, which sticks up in all directions. 'I've been in the north corner, tucked away behind the maintenance office. A spot rarely visited and also difficult to find. This place is going to be much better for business.'

'Let us know if you need any help with… anything.' Geneviève gives him an exaggerated wink. She cannot help herself if there's a good-looking man in her presence.

Felix waggles his brow. Great, now we have two incorrigible flirts in our midst. Like Geneviève, Felix is a breath of fresh air, who I know will make market days just that little bit lighter. '*Merci*, Geneviève. Perhaps we can all share a drink after work sometime and get to know each other better?'

We chat for a bit until there's more footsteps on the stairs. '*Au revoir*, I better get myself sorted,' Felix says while looking intently at the newcomer.

'*Bonjour,* I'm Benoit,' the man says when he reaches the top of the stairs. He gives us a shy smile and continues to his stall, which is right beside Felix's and across the small hallway from Geneviève and me.

With eyes comically wide, Geneviève motions with her head in Benoit's direction in case I haven't latched on to the fact that he is rather beautiful in a bookish, intelligent kind of way with his neatly parted hair and spectacles, and his hot, introverted bookworm kind of vibe. Has the universe heard my pleas for love? Suddenly there are two very handsome men in my vicinity.

Just as I'm about to tell Geneviève to cool it, there's a commotion on the stairs. A mountain of a man speaks angrily into his phone as he takes the steps two at a time, shouting curse words in French. The quiet calm has been replaced by this hulk who has managed to get all of our attention yet is blithely unaware of us.

'Ooh, that alpha male energy,' Geneviève says, fanning her face.

'Seriously? *Non*.' How can she be taken in by a man like that? Is he really so self-absorbed that he doesn't know his bellowing might be considered rude in a workplace, and that he's really not making the best first impression with us, his new neighbours? I sneak a peek at Felix and Benoit to see what they make of it and find them sharing a small smile, as if they find the guy slightly amusing rather than rude.

'Lilou, that man is gorgeous, can you not see that?'

That surly alpha male energy is exactly the thing that Paris Cupid is designed to be the antithesis of, and for very good reason. Those highly combustible types who breathe fire are just such a cliché, are they not?

'Well?' she prods. I don't want to agree on principle, but I can't deny the man is rather… hot. 'If you're into tall, muscular bad boys, then yes, I suppose so, but I could never be into someone so lacking in manners like he clearly is. Who do you think he's yelling at like that?' I debate whether to politely inform him that he's creating a nuisance when he shoots a glare my way. My breath catches as I recognise him but can't place from where. Oh no. The man in the market square the day of *le scandale*. The one who locked eyes with me for so long I swear he could see into my very soul. Coraline, the florist, told me his name that day, but I struggle to recall it. 'Pascale,' I whisper.

'Why are you whispering?'

'He was there the day Frederic's wife confronted me.' How embarrassing. I'd hoped for a fresh start with new neighbours, ones who didn't know that particular rumour about me. Homewrecker. Destroyer of families.

Before I can break his gaze and turn away, he stomps over, glowering at me. 'Can you turn that music down? I'm on a phone call and can't hear a thing!' He turns away then stops abruptly and faces me again. 'Where do I know you from?'

'You don't.' There's no way I'm going to remind him. He narrows his eyes suspiciously. Surely he's not going to remember a passing look he shared with a stranger who had just been publicly humiliated? But *I* recognised *his* face, didn't I? Perhaps because every detail of that day is burned into my mind.

He presses his phone to his ear and resumes his call, albeit slightly less angrily. Why is he still staring at me? Ah, he's still trying to place me, so I spin on my heel and hide behind Geneviève, pretending to fuss with some trinkets on display.

'Ooh, he is a *feisty* one.' Geneviève grins. 'The perfect bad boy ready to set a heart aflame, but whose heart, eh?' She jabs a finger into my shoulder. 'You?'

'You can't be serious?' Does the woman not know me at all? 'Our very first conversation is him ordering me to turn my music down, music that is barely discernible, I might add. Not a single *bonjour*, not a single *s'il te plait*.'

Geneviève shrugs. 'Perhaps he's got sensitive hearing and he forgot his manners because he was in the middle of a phone call?'

'I hardly think so.'

While we're arguing about what makes good manners, Felix does more trips up and down the stairs, carting in more boxes. 'Do you need a hand?' I ask.

He shakes his head. '*Non, merci*. I have the heavy stuff coming by courier. There's only a few boxes left, but if you could watch my stall while I move my car from the loading bay that would be great.'

'*Oui*, of course.' Felix has one of those ready smiles and a boundless energy about him. As he goes back downstairs, I take a moment to see how Benoit is doing. He doesn't seem to have many boxes to unpack. Maybe he's waiting for a courier too. There's a quiet indifference about him, as if he's aware of his surroundings but separate from it. Lost in a daydream perhaps? I wonder what Benoit sells?

And as for Pascale, when I sneak a peek in his direction, he's staring at me with utter contempt and motions for me to turn down the volume of my music. I'm tempted to give him some finger signs of my own, but I won't stoop to his level. Instead, I roll my eyes and get back to work, feeling a strange sort of unsettled.

5

NOW

A month later our neighbours have settled in and set up their stalls which complement ours well with our literary and correspondence theme. Pascale manages to treat every workday as if it's an exercise in futility. The man is never happy. In fact he's downright surly. It bamboozles me how he stays afloat. For some inexplicable reason I can't keep my eyes off him because it's fascinating to see him behave so badly and get away with it.

It's got me stumped why so many customers flock to his typewriter stall despite his bad attitude. He acts as if he's doing his customers a favour if he takes a minute to stop typing to serve them. I push my display tables out to the common hallway and ignore his laser-like gaze. I'm well within my rights to use the area in front of my stall even though he's complained already about them taking up too much room. He glares at me as I trundle past – no surprise there, the man put the steel into steely eyed – and motions for me to move my display table back inside. I shake my head – *no*. I will not be ordered about by this tyrant. Still, it's a little thrilling and my heart beats erratically from these daily confrontations.

Once that's done, I sit behind my desk, taking a breath and willing my pulse to slow down. What is it about the guy that makes my body go so haywire? Anger, probably. I've never met a man like Pascale before, not in the flesh anyway. You read about these types of guys all the time, and I can never understand why women fall for men like that. Who needs that sort of conflict in everyday life? I'd much prefer a man like Felix, who brightens each day, or Benoit, who is introspective and thoughtful. Both drama-free and happy in their own skin from what I've learned about them over the last month. I risk one last look at Pascale, who has moved from glaring across at me to setting up his own display table out the front of his stall and is loading it with vintage typewriters. I'm incensed. His table is twice the size of mine!

As I'm fuming about his double standards, Geneviève sashays in, wearing a fitted three-quarter length dress that accentuates her curves.

'You just can't get enough of him, can you?' She peers down at me, tucked behind my desk.

'Of who?'

She scoffs. 'Pascale! Every time I get here, you're staring over at him like he's a nice juicy piece of *filet de boeuf*.'

I try to scoff but it comes out more like a gargle. 'You couldn't be more wrong! That man has no qualms badgering me about the size of my display tables and now here he is with his own that's at least twice the size of mine. Someone is *clearly* making up for a lack.'

Geneviève ignores me, gazes over at Pascale, her flirty smile at the ready, and gives him a fluttery little wave.

'Don't encourage him!'

She lifts a shoulder. 'I'm simply being a friendly neighbour.'

I huff and fold my arms across my chest. 'Does it not bother you that he's being a hypocrite?' The more I think about it the more riled up I get. 'It's not fair I've caved in to most of his demands, and he's put out a table that's so wide we'll all have to crabwalk to get around it.' I steal a glance and notice he's put candles on his display table. 'You're kidding me! He told me my candles were a fire hazard and I was violating the market code of conduct by having them, and now look!' I hiss. Annoyingly, Geneviève just gives me a smug smile. What is she smiling about?

I have to get the upper hand this time, so how do I play this? Demand he use actual words when he speaks to me? All that grumbling and scowling is not conducive to a professional relationship. After all, work is my happy place and if I'm confronted by his glowering face every day it's really going to dull my sparkle.

'I'll tell him he needs to lighten up if he wants to fit in here. Do you think that'll do it?' I pine for my former neighbours, a merry band of elderly men who were more like honorary *grandpères*. Well, except one of them who treated me differently after *le scandale*.

But they're gone and here I am. I mustn't allow Pascale to bully me. Internally I puff myself up and mentally prepare a script that will cut him to the quick and make him understand that I'm not to be messed with. I turn and run smack bang into a huge muscular chest. Specifically, his – '*Aie!*' – with my nose, which from the velocity of the altercation and the taut toughened muscles involved I expect is now broken. Tentatively, I touch the tip and am surprised to find the appendage intact and *not* gushing a river of blood. I must be stronger than I give myself credit for. I await a rash of apologies slung my way, but instead find myself staring up at him, his habitual scowl in place as if *I'm* the aggressor and not the other way around.

'Did you *plan* to march over here and strike my nose like that?'

His behaviour is escalating, this, this... Frenemy! Not even that – just plain enemy! Pascale scowls down at me. He is a lot taller when we're standing toe to toe. 'You struck *me*. I didn't expect you to turn around and launch yourself in the air like that,' he says with a loose shrug. How can he be so blasé when he almost knocked my nose clean off my face?

I jab my index finger into his chest and am surprised when it feels as though I've hit stone. He must work out. He's a veritable man mountain. Probably another intimidation tactic. 'You snuck up on me, Pascale.'

He casually leans against the door frame, as if he's visiting an old friend.

'Uh... are you going to apologise?' I ask.

'Apologise for what?' He lifts a quizzical brow.

'The nose?' I point to my appendage and bet it's bright red and not being painted in its best light. But what do I care? This man is trying to intimidate me, and for what reason?

He grunts.

Pascale is *clearly* not the apologising sort. I resist the petty urge to grunt right back. I will not stoop to his level.

I change tack to get myself back on the straight and narrow. 'I understand the market restructure has put quite a few, ahem... noses out of joint.' *Literally mine.* 'But we have to make the best of it. Geneviève and I shared an easy comradery with our former neighbours before they were sadly moved to another section. We hope we can have the same kind of relationship with you, but that means you'll have to stop ordering me about as if I'm an underling.' I try and fail to keep the bitterness from my voice.

Pascale blithely ignores every sullen word and turns his bad-boy head away from me. 'Geneviève, lovely to see you again.'

She lets out a girlish giggle. 'You too, Pascale.' Honestly, if there's a good-looking male at ten paces, Geneviève cannot control herself. It's usually charming but this is Pascale, gruff macho man, and it won't do. 'Looking as handsome as ever today, I see.' Seriously!

'Looks can be deceiving, Geneviève,' I throw into the mix.

Pascale throws his spotlight back on me with a slow smirk. 'Is that so?'

I fold my arms defensively, and then unfold them so he doesn't see I'm rather rattled by him. His smirk morphs into a wide smile. *C'est un miracle* his face didn't crack!

'Lilou, is it?'

Mon Dieu. This is, like, the tenth time he's double-checked my name. Passive aggressive or what? 'It is, as you well know.'

He takes a deep breath as if gearing up for another lecture. 'Li, you're right about one thing, at least. The restructure has been a nightmare. Now I'm stuck up these stairs in this dingy little hovel whereas before I was right in the centre of the action. It's ridiculous I had no say in it. I've got a screaming headache every day from your candles, your music and your laugh.'

Ouah. That's a lot of complaining to unpack. 'Firstly, it's Lilou. *Not* Li. And secondly, I wouldn't call this space a dingy little hovel. It's one of the most popular sections of the market and there were a lot of other vendors vying for it, so you should be more grateful. And as for this screaming headache of yours, how did you cope before when you were in the so-called centre of the action? Surely it would have been noisier there? And what on earth is wrong with my laugh?'

He sighs and scrubs his face. 'You talk fast. You throw questions at me like bullets. And your laugh, it sounds like chimes.'

What! This man makes my blood boil. 'And that's a bad thing?'

He frowns as if he's disappointed in me. 'Don't be like that. We can make it work.'

I screw up my nose. Is he gaslighting me? It *feels* like he's gaslighting me. I exchange a look with Geneviève but am met with some glassy-eyed rapture on her part. No help there then.

The bad-boy effect is real, but I won't be succumbing to his alpha-male energy. This act of his is a ploy, a gambit. None of this charade is real. I just can't get a handle on this. He swings the conversation around so fast I get whiplash. *My laughter sounds like chimes?* And that's offensive? 'You stay on your side, and I'll stay on mine. *Au revoir*, Pascale.'

The scowl returns and he stomps back to where he came from. He can't even stay in character long enough to fool me! I turn and am confronted with a suddenly stony-faced Geneviève, as if Pascale snatched the smile from her very face. Good! Now she can see what we're up against.

'That was a mistake, Lilou. A great whopper of a mistake.'

'*Quoi?*' My eyebrows shoot up. Is she not hearing what I'm hearing? Seeing what I'm seeing? He's got her under some kind of spell! 'You're supposed to be on my side.'

'I'm on *love's* side! Now that I've seen you two lovebirds interact in real time, it's blatantly obvious to me. This is your classic case of enemies to lovers. Open your heart *and* your eyes, Lilou, and let nature takes its course.'

Romance novels have ruined her! 'Oh, Geneviève, he's got you tricked! Did you not hear him insult me?'

Geneviève ignores me and stares off wistfully into the distance where Pascale is unpacking vintage typewriters and arranging his shop. 'Lilou, look at him! Trust me, there's more to him than meets the eye. What you've got is chemistry, that intensity in your eyes, the way you bounce back and forth off each other. It's wild to see it in action.'

'Yeah, it's a science experiment right before it explodes.' The woman is incorrigible! Chemistry! As if.

* * *

That afternoon, I keep catching Benoit's eye. It's almost like he's daydreaming, not actively staring over at me, but I realise I haven't really had much interaction with him compared to flirty Felix or prickly Pascale.

All I really know about him is that he peddles stamps and other philatelic keepsakes. When I catch his eye again, I give him a little wave and head over to his stall. The market is always quieter in the afternoons as locals and tourists alike take long lunches and enjoy the summery Parisian afternoons in bistros around the city, so it's as good a time as any to chat.

'*Bonjour*, Benoit.'

'*Bonjour*, Lilou. I'm sorry I haven't visited your stall yet. It's been so much work getting things in order here after the move.' He dips his head slightly as if he's shy. He really is adorable.

'By the looks of it, you're mostly sorted now?' Pascale's move was much quicker, having to only unload his antique typewriters and some antiquity books, same with Felix, whose main job had been setting up his vintage printing press. Benoit's move has taken a lot more time due to the fragile nature of his stock and having to install many cabinets to display his stamps and philatelic materials.

He pushes his specs up the bridge of his nose. '*Oui*, almost done. Although, I'm selling stock at a much faster rate here than I was downstairs, so I'm trying to source from new suppliers. As you can imagine, stamp collecting isn't exactly as popular as it once was so it makes it difficult to find new stock and still make a decent profit. That's why I've added calligraphy to my repertoire.'

'Oh?'

He gives me a quick smile. 'Customers give me messages, poems, birthday greetings and the like and I write them out in calligraphy on luxe stationery for them.'

His job is really rather romantic. Benoit seems like a sweet, shy, old soul.

'I love that idea.'

'It helps to offer a few things. Philately is my passion. Each stamp tells a story, not just with its design or provenance but imagining its journey around the globe, affixed to an envelope – that very stamp the reason correspondence can travel far and wide and end up in someone's grateful hands. Did that stamp ferry a love letter, a breakup note, support for a grieving widow, a postcard from sunnier climes?' His cheeks pink as if he's embarrassed he shared too much.

His love of stamps and their path around the world are just like my diaries and love letters. We'll never know exactly where they've been or who once held them, but it's fascinating to imagine just where these oft discarded bits of ephemera have been.

Our jobs are similar in that respect; we're treading water between the past and the present. The now and the then. We share that same sort of whimsy with our collectables. Most of the time, we'll never have all the answers about our treasures so we must fill in the gaps with speculation, wonder. There's a real gentle charm to Benoit; he's so markedly different from Pascale. In the past I've always chosen the happy-go-lucky kind, the cheeky, funny flirty type, like Felix. Perhaps I should go for a man just like Benoit. Quiet, contemplative and intelligent with the heart and soul of a poet. We lapse into silence and I find him hard to read. Perhaps it's his inherent shyness that stops him from saying more. I struggle to think of conversation myself, so lost in the idea of romance. Finally, I say, 'You should contact Guillaume. He might be able to source stamp collections for you. I can give you his number.'

6

A few days later, I cycle along Pont Caulaincourt, the only bridge in Paris that crosses over a cemetery. As usual, I'm running late. Guillaume will not be pleased. Summer is in full swing, and the heat is already slightly oppressive. I come to a stop and take a moment to catch my breath, leaning over the railing to wave at the tombs below. It's become a habit and I'd hate to disappoint any ghosts who await these impromptu visits. I may not be able to see any spectres, but I firmly believe they see me, thus, I say my *bonjours* and continue on my bike. Guillaume is an antiquarian dealer who scours the French countryside for rare and unusual collectibles for clients. When he returns from a jaunt, we hold our business meetings inside these Montmartre cemetery walls. It might seem a macabre location for some, but Guillaume suggested it one sunny day a few years back because it's close to where we both live and we've met here ever since.

It seems as fitting a place as any because to me, the dead are still very much alive. Not in a physical way, but in the essence of what they leave behind, the memories we hold fast to, mementoes that remind us of our loved ones. At the start, I only procured antique prayer books from Guillaume for my stall in the Marché Dauphine. They ranged from luxe editions with golden scrolled padlocks and monogrammed covers to delicate, jewel-like, illustrated pages from *The Book of Hours*.

There's a huge call for these rare books, but my favourites are those unpretentious beauties with plain covers and no adornment. Those with passages underlined and swollen leaves that have thickened over time as if their owner's love and very faith poured from their soul right into the parchment. They fire up my imagination. Who owned this prayer book? Why did that passage resonate so? How did this prayer book make its way to me?

Interestingly, at estate sales, personal effects are often sold in bundles though. So with the prayer books also come accoutrements like diaries and handwritten letters. The ephemera of those who came before, discovered when the next generation inherit a *maison* and empty the attic space, treating such paraphernalia as detritus of the past. Originally, only I would read these private diaries and correspondences, absolutely captivated, swept away, as if reading a historical novel. Afterwards I'd put them to one side, not quite sure what to do with them.

Then one day when a customer enquired why my nose was so firmly pressed inside a diary that wasn't my own, and begged to read it next, I realised the value of such things. There's a select group of collectors who covet these relics from bygone times, and my little flea market stall has become famous for them. Competition is fierce with my buyers, so I send out a newsletter when I get new stock so it's fair to one and all.

My clients don't care about trivialities such as proving provenance like one would with art; they only care about the story inside. A perk of the job is that I get to read each and every diary, letter or correspondence before I sell them on. Today, I'm hoping Guillaume has found untold treasures on his recent travels to the south of France. I find him sitting on our usual bench, sunlight making him squint. I lean my bike against a tree and join him.

'Bonjour, Guillaume.' We brush cheeks, the French custom known as *la bise*, before I sit beside him.

'Late as always, Lilou,' he says, his voice gruff. 'You're yet to make a meeting on time.' He makes a great show of checking his watch in case I haven't picked up from his words alone that my tardiness is an issue.

'Sorry, sorry. I got caught chatting to Luc from the *poissonnier*.' What I can't say is that Paris Cupid applications have come pouring in since the Emmanuel Roux article, which has only added to the pressure. I'm doing my best to weed out imposters and hook-up merchants. 'Luc gave me some tuna for the cats.'

Montmartre cemetery is home to around fifty cats. No one knows why they came here or why they stay. They stick to certain graves, sitting like sphinxes, guarding the gates to the afterlife. My theory is these foxy felines know exactly where their bread is buttered and are living the good life being fed by cat lovers. We could learn a lot from cats. A tabby feline we named Minou is the first to break ranks and slink over. He stops a few paces from our feet and sits, lazily licking his paw, as if showing us that, while we may be here to feed him and his feline friends, he will not stoop to grovelling in exchange for fish.

'They must be the most spoiled cats in Paris,' mutters Guillaume, who tries his best to hold on to his gruff reserve but fails when Minou bridges the gap and meows up at him. I hide a smile when Guillaume pulls a plastic container from his bag with fresh fish diced into small chunks.

Soon we're surrounded by a motley crew who stare at us through half-lidded eyes. They eat their fill and slink away without a backward glance. 'They act superior to us, even when we're feeding them,' I muse. 'There's a lesson in that, you know.'

'I don't have time to ponder it, since you were late.'

I do my best to appear contrite but fail. Guillaume shakes his head as if I'm a lost cause. 'Now to business.' He produces a folder and hands it to me. 'I found a range of prayer books and a few diaries, some love letters and a book of handwritten poetry from the early 1900s.'

'*Magnifique!*' My customers will be delighted. 'The diaries, are they special?' Some diaries are mundane, featuring shopping lists, a record of guests who visited, day-to-day matters. I'm looking for a needle in a haystack, the type of diary that reads like fiction.

'*Oui.* One of them particularly so.'

I flick through the binder, looking for the photocopied example. 'Ah.

This one.' I point to a page filled with loopy cursive. The inscribed date is 1964.

> Much to my parents' horror, I broke off my engagement with Elliott today. He's a great man with good prospects; however, he doesn't ignite my heart or soul. And shouldn't that be a priority? My maman says love goes from flame to a flicker eventually and that I'm making a terrible choice by abandoning a man who worships the ground I walk upon. She predicts I'll end up an old lady who lives alone in this crumbling chateau being gossiped about in the village. It does give me pause, only in that I don't see myself living here forever. I want to travel the world. Escape village life. Escape this prison of my maman's making. Why shouldn't I aim for such grand adventures? Why do marriage and children have to come into the equation at all? I'm not ready for such things, and some days I wonder if I ever will be. Love, Margot.

'Please tell me the diary continues.' Unlike fiction, sometimes the endings are ripped away, leaving us without answers. Another mystery in itself. Did they misplace the diary? Did ennui creep in and it became a chore to commit those words to paper each day? Why didn't their words continue? Not knowing how their life panned out is often bittersweet.

'It does, indeed. You will be pleased.'

'Where did it come from?'

He shades his eyes with the palm of his hand. 'A colleague in Carcassonne. She emptied a chateau for the new owners. That diary was found in a *chambre de bonne*.'

The maid's room? Could Margot have gone on to become a maid? Swapping her own life at a grandiose chateau to work inside one for another wealthy family? All I know so far is she had the desire to leave her stuffy, supervised life. So many diaries, so many extraordinary stories from ordinary lives.

Guillaume continues to squint in the morning sun. 'Don't you feel like you're trespassing on the dead when you read their most intimate and private thoughts, their secrets, their sorrows?'

I contemplate his question, searching for the truth. 'It could be seen as an intrusion but if so, then why leave the diary where it would be found? Why not burn it, shred it, throw it in the river? To me, this is the same as reading a memoir; the narrative of a stranger's life told honestly. These people live on, through the very words they've written. Their stories *matter* and if we were to discard them like junk, wouldn't that be a form of sacrilege? Why did they write them if they didn't want them shared one day?'

He shakes his head as if he doesn't comprehend such a notion. 'You're a hopeless romantic.' If only he knew about my alter ego.

I laugh. '*Oui*, I am. But Guillaume, these written diaries are often full of love in all its complicated glory. Unrequited love, like a punch to the heart. The devastation of lost love. The joy of second-chance love. First love. Love at first sight.' I've read them all, different decades, eras, in French and in English, and been swept away by real-life romance stories about people I'll never know or meet.

What a strange honour it is, to be able to become part of their story, an outsider peeking in for one moment.

As it's expected, we haggle back and forth over the price for his latest discoveries, but I trust Guillaume implicitly and appreciate the lengths he goes to in scouring the countryside for these marvels, when really there's a lot more money to be made for him in sourcing antique furniture for his other clients. We make arrangements for delivery for this coming Friday when the market is open to the public. The anticipation of what's to come is a heady thing indeed. Waiting for delivery is going to be torturous, but that's the way Guillaume works. Deliveries are on Fridays, no exceptions.

'Speaking of romance…' I say. 'Did you give any thought to trying out Paris Love or whatever it's called?' Guillaume is in desperate need of a sweetheart. *Widower finds love after loss.*

With a weary sigh he says, 'Not that Paris Cupid lecture again?' There's always a lot of head-shaking when we meet, as though I'm a pesky fly around his face. But if I don't encourage him, then who will?

'Lilou, I've told you a hundred times, love is off the menu. I'm old. Tired. Set in my ways. No one can replace Mathilde.'

Six years ago, Mathilde succumbed after a long illness. Before she got sick, she had a stall at the bottom of the stairs in the Marché Dauphine so we met for lunch often and got to be great friends over the years. I miss her still.

Loneliness has left its mark on Guillaume; it's evidenced in every line and plane on his face. His shoulders stoop with the heavy burden of grief. Love would lift his spirits *and* his shoulders, I'm sure of it.

Guillaume is special to me, and love *is* the tonic for what ails him. However, I must tread carefully so he doesn't suspect I'm Cupid. 'Why not give love a chance? You deserve it as much as anyone.'

He makes a great show of harrumphing. 'You're a busybody meddler whose brain has been turned to mush reading too many private diaries.'

'See, look at you throwing compliments around like confetti!' I bite my lip and hope I've managed to convince him.

Lost in thought, he folds his arms across his once ample belly. Without Mathilde, Guillaume has taken to eating convenience meals, avoiding the long lunches they used to favour, making him a shadow of his former self.

'Who would they find for tête-à-têtes, do you suppose?' He feigns disinterest but his eyes sparkle as if the possibility of sharing a conversation over *soufflé au fromage* appeals to him. No one will ever replace Mathilde, she was such a darling woman, but that doesn't mean he can't enjoy companionship and see where it leads.

I pretend to consider what Paris Cupid might offer when I clearly know very well. It strikes me that we're *both* doing a lot of feigning today. 'I'm not exactly sure on how that site works, but I'd expect there'd be some sort of application you'd fill out, to help match you with a companion who shares the same interests as you. From what I've heard from others who've joined is you write to your match first, get to know each other the old-fashioned way.'

Surprise dashes across his features. 'That's the way to do it. Everyone is always in such a hurry these days.'

I tip my head in agreement. Paris Cupid is designed for people just like him. A man who lost his twin flame, but still has love to give, who just needs encouragement. Needs reassurance that finding love after loss is perfectly acceptable.

'Once you've established a solid connection with your match you can meet in person. You used to love dining out, and long walks after your meal. Why not aim for that? No strings necessarily attached, just a friendly face over the dinner table?'

What he doesn't know is that I already have the ideal woman in mind. Clementine D'Amboise from the *fromagerie* on Rue Damrémont. Guillaume is a cheese enthusiast and Clementine enjoys simple pleasures, taken often. Her husband left her for his assistant a few years ago and she'd sworn off love until recently, when a friend suggested she try Paris Cupid, which she did with great reluctance. I've held off matching her because I feel it in my bones that Guillaume is the man for her, so now it's just a matter of convincing him to join.

I can already picture them sharing a wedge of *Brie de Meaux* and a bottle of Beaujolais. Basking in the sun on the bank of the Seine. Walking arm in arm around Luxembourg Gardens and taking a tour of the beehives. Humble pursuits with the sun on his face and a gracious woman on his arm.

He contorts his mouth into a moue. 'Well, I suppose if it's good enough for the likes of celebrities, it's good enough for a mere mortal such as me.'

'Celebrities?' I ask, my spine stiffening. Of all the people I'd expect to have heard about Emmanuel Roux, Guillaume would be the last.

A tabby cat we call Marmalade does figure eights around his ankles. Guillaume bends to tickle her ears. Marmalade is his favourite of all the cats with Minou a close second, probably because the ginger cat is affectionate and the tabby cat Minou prefers to be left alone – even if despite his frosty demeanour we've come to love him. Minou tolerates us and that's enough.

'Yes, that rather annoying man – from that TV series that never seems to end, despite every character dying in some unfathomable way. Last night he did an interview on the *Late Show*.'

Pas encore! I mute my shock and say, 'What was the interview about?'

Guillaume picks up Marmalade, whose meows turn into a purr when he rocks her like a baby in his arms. 'It was him gushing over an incredible woman he's met on Paris Cupid. He claims she's changed his whole outlook on life. Really, I detested the man before, but after watching his interview, my opinion changed somewhat.'

'Ooh, interesting.' I don't believe a word of it. Emmanuel Roux is many things, but faithful clearly isn't one of them. Is he using this latest tactic to stay relevant in the media? Anything to get more attention in the press. I'm stuck between a rock and a hard place.

I'll call Émilienne again and ask how she's going with her new love. Since she sent me the text confiding she'd fallen madly in love and encouraged me to try Paris Cupid, I haven't heard a word back. I've texted her a few times but she hasn't replied. She must know by now he's not Remy Tatou. There is no Remy Tatou! It appears this isn't going to blow over as quickly as I'd hoped. The next logical step is to reach out to 'Remy' as Paris Cupid and remind him of the clause in the application that says you must be honest about who you are.

A subject change is in order or else I'll be stuck on a mouse wheel worrying about Emmanuel Roux all day. 'If you were to choose, where would your first dream date be?' Marmalade spots her best friend Minou and springs off Guillaume's lap to play. They impishly swat at each other before somersaulting onto the grass in a messy heap, tumbling and turning like acrobats. Eventually they give up and stare into each other's eyes. Even the Parisian cats are in love!

'A simple bistro dinner. It mustn't be too noisy. The youth of today treat these outings as if they're performing for a crowd. Like they're on display. Taking photos of their food, those blinding flashes, those silly pouts they do. It's just bad manners, is what it is.'

I hide a smile. 'You should mention that when you join.' When it's time, I'll suggest La Maison Rose, an iconic bistro in Montmartre known for its pink walls. A famous haunt back in the day for the likes of author and philosopher Albert Camus and singer Dalida. Guillaume won't care a jot about that, but the seasonal food is well regarded and it's a charming, quiet spot to dine. The pretty pink façade is a popular tourist spot to take pictures, but rarely do they venture inside, so it should fit his criteria.

'Fine. If you insist, I'll join later today.'

'*Magnifique.*'

'I'm only agreeing to this so I can prove to you that I'm far too old for love.' He can lie to himself all he wants if that's how this is to unfold – gently like a flower blooming in the midday sun.

As we say our goodbyes and head out of the cemetery, Minou stares regally from his high perch, sunbaking on a tomb while Marmalade sleeps curled up beside him.

* * *

Later that evening, I log into Paris Cupid, curious to see if Guillaume has joined. I reel when I see membership applications have exploded. The Emmanuel Roux effect! I scroll through the many hopefuls, searching for Guillaume, and eventually find his application. He writes a heartfelt passage about his beloved Mathilde, how the world has lost all colour since she's been gone. It brings a tear to my eye, knowing my faux-gruff friend has been so lonely. I accept his application and tell him I'll be in touch with his match in the fullness of time. It can't be seen as too quick, or he'll doubt the process. I call Émilienne but her phone goes straight to voicemail. It's not unusual for her to have periods of quiet; if she goes on a retreat or is on a health kick, she often disconnects from technology for a while, but I find it strange it's happening now when all this has blown up. Perhaps the media have already found her so she's in incognito mode.

I send her a text:

> When can we catch up so I can hear all about your Paris Cupid match? I'd love to know more about it myself! Lilou x

Next, as Paris Cupid, I pen an email to Remy, AKA Emmanuel Roux, and ask him to kindly refer to his membership agreement which has a whole paragraph about being honest during the application process, which he clearly was not. I ask him to email me to discuss these rules once he's refreshed his memory. I remind him that Paris Cupid is a small matchmaking platform meant for genuine people who feel they're unlucky in love or wanting to up their romance game. It was never meant to become part of a media circus, which the small team cannot cope with. *Small team.* There's just me and my alfalfa plant and, between us, it's really not pulling its weight. I hit send.

7

On Friday morning, I lock up my apartment on Rue Tourlaque and head on foot to Saint Ouen Flea Market, ready for a bustling three days of trading. It's a thirty-minute walk, long enough to blow out the cobwebs after a long night of reading Paris Cupid applications. Still no reply from Emmanuel, but the influx of membership applications seems never ending because the man won't stop shouting Paris Cupid's praises. In any other business this would be a marketer's dream but it's the antithesis of what I want. Émilienne hasn't responded to the text I sent a few days ago. Perhaps she's in a love bubble and the rest of the world has faded to black, but I'd really like to find out how she feels about dating the Playboy of Paris.

I stop to buy some blooms from Coraline, the florist, outside the market. Every July she has the most amazing selection of summery flowers.

While I'm taking a great big sniff of a bouquet of wild roses, Coraline says, 'Did you hear about Emmanuel Roux?'

My heart sinks. If Coraline has heard, that means every second resident of Paris has too. 'Ah...?'

'You do know who he is, don't you?' Her eyes narrow as if not knowing who he is would be a sin. 'A singer?' It's best if I play coy with Coraline; she's a wily one. She lets out a frustrated sigh at my apparent lack of celebrity knowledge. '*Mon Dieu*, Lilou! He's only France's version of a Hollywood heart throb! Well known for performing his roles wearing very little, claiming that clothing is a construct and one he doesn't subscribe to?' She makes a show of scoffing and harrumphing to the point I'm about to ask her if something is stuck in her throat when she says, 'You don't *know* him?'

I cock my head, as if I'm trying hard to conjure this anti-clothes-wearing actor.

She rolls on the balls of her feet, jittery and hyper. 'The silver fox with the steely eyes?'

'Oh – uh, that sounds vaguely familiar.'

She waggles her thin Edith Piaf-style brows. 'He used some silly little site to find love! *Incroyable!* Now he's off the market for good, engaged, or so he says. But we all know what he's like.'

I frown. Silly little site?

She continues. 'It's more likely a publicity stunt...' Agreed! '...Now we're all trying to work out who the mystery fiancée is. But if she's not "in showbiz" how will we ever find out?'

Just how far will they go to find Émilienne? Lovely Em, who is not a fan of the spotlight and really only wanted to find a genuine guy who wouldn't try and change her. She will not appreciate being found, not like this. 'Best to leave them to it, is my advice.' If I didn't know better, I'd say this so-called scandal has given Coraline a strange energy boost.

With her tongue in her cheek, she gives an exaggerated shake of the head before saying, 'Impossible, not when it's news as tantalising as this.'

'Is it though?'

Coraline gives me a gleeful nod. 'It's downright scandalous!'

While my mind is in a furious battle figuring out some kind of damage control, I continue picking up bouquets, as if I'm having trouble choosing. I settle on a bunch of soft pink peonies and hand over some euros, doing my best to pretend this is any other day, but eventually curiosity gets the better of me and I ask, 'How is finding love scandalous?'

She makes a great show of rolling her eyes as if I'm too simple to understand such matters. 'Because it can't be real! He's probably being sponsored by Paris Cupid. That's the only scenario that makes sense to me.'

'Then why are you ruminating about who his fiancée is if you think it's simply a sponsorship deal and not actually real?'

Coraline reels back as if I've slapped her face. 'Because the fake fiancée is responsible for hearts breaking all over Paris right now! Real or not, we've been blindsided.'

Now I've heard it all! Poor Em. What have I *done!* 'What if his new fiancée is genuinely in love? A witch hunt would be well out of order.'

A frown mars her brow. 'Who said anything about a witch hunt?'

I cradle the bouquet close to my chest. 'It's best you leave well enough alone. Maybe Emmanuel Roux really is in love too. Have you ever thought of that?' Her mouth opens and closes like a puffer fish before she eventually says, 'Your peonies will need water, Lilou.' And she turns her back, dismissing me just like that. I shake my head and walk into the market, hoping Geneviève has arrived so I can debrief and ask her advice. This could well spiral out of control and truly leave broken hearts in its wake, the very opposite of what I'd hoped to achieve for Émilienne and so many others like her. My pulse thrums with worry, so I try my best to breathe through it so I can *think*. There must be a solution.

I wave to acquaintances as I make my way to my stall. The flea market is enormous. There are 1700 merchants spread over seven hectares, comprising of fourteen unique market areas. Locals and tourists alike can spend many a day hunting for bric-à-brac.

There are all sorts of eclectic shops here. Tapestry and carpets from Persia, Asia and Europe. Funky watches and vintage jewellery. There are art workshops to learn mediums such as ceramics, leather-working and upholstery. Stalls full of curios and *objets d'art*. Records. Pop culture. Recycled fashion. Whatever your heart desires, it is here somewhere. It's simply a matter of finding it.

In the middle of Marché Dauphine is Futuro House. The bright orange UFO landed here ten years ago and is a popular attraction for visitors. The flying saucer was one of sixty-three designed by Finnish architect Matti Suuronen who originally intended them to be used as holiday homes for skiers, because they were lightweight, easy to transport and small enough to heat quickly. However, things didn't go according to plan and now they're spread around the globe in the most unlikely of places. I take great pride in our alien craft, which is used for book launches, conferences and pop-up bar events.

I continue up the stairs. There's no sign of Geneviève at her antique furniture shop.

While we are all required to open our stalls at regimented times, Geneviève does not conform to such trivialities. Some days her shop remains completely shuttered. She plays by a different set of rules, and I envy her ability to not give a damn and get away with it. '*Bonjour*, Felix!' I greet the ginger-haired printer who is bent over his work, in full concentration mode. It's a painstakingly slow process to set a book, or pamphlet, which – as I've recently learned – is just about the only time you'll see Felix stand still.

'*Bonjour*, Lilou.' He steps back from his work with a devilish sparkle in his eye. 'Is your heart broken too?'

'My heart is just fine. Why?' While the market might be seven hectares long, gossip spreads faster than wildfire ever could.

Felix fidgets with a printing implement while tapping his foot, as if his body, mind and spirit runs on a higher frequency, a different bandwidth to most. 'Every woman under eighty seems to be heartbroken over the announcement that Emmanuel Roux is engaged. He's a bit of a *cause célèbre*, non?'

I shrug. 'I don't understand the appeal of the guy. Why would anyone fangirl over a guy who calls himself the Playboy of Paris?' His popularity has never made sense to me.

'Do you think it's real? I always figured it was just talk. One of those men who exaggerate every story for attention.' Felix shakes his head, dappled sunlight landing on his ginger curls, making them shine. 'The whole "look at me with my extra-large... *apartmente*".' He gives me a wicked grin.

I laugh. 'Could be. Do you think the engagement is real?'

Felix scoffs. 'Hardly. He'll never settle down – and who would want to? From what I heard, his life is a never-ending party.' There's an element of awe to Felix's statement. Is he too taken by the Emmanuel Roux persona: live and love, fast and hard?

'A never-ending party sounds exhausting.' I tuck a stray hair back. 'Are you saying you'd never settle down?'

'I'd settle down for you, Lilou.' Did I mention Felix is the flirtatious type? In the short time he's been my neighbour we've discovered a lot about each other during our morning catch ups. Felix is curious, and quirky. An over sharer. Really, he's a mood booster.

But he's also high energy and lives a high-octane life. I'm a homebody, whose nose is either pressed into a diary or else matching lovebirds behind a screen. We're as different as can be.

I shake my head. 'You would do no such thing.'

Felix places a hand over his heart as if it's broken. 'It's still a no then?'

I grin and shake my head. 'It's still a no.' At least once a day he asks me on a date, and I turn him down. He told me his idea of a fun night out is dancing under strobe lighting inside some club at all hours. Mine is being in bed with a book before midnight calls. I'm tempted to say yes, but I presume his invitations are made in jest so I don't want to look foolish by taking him up on his offer. Not to mention he's my neighbour now, so any fallout would be awkward.

He lets out a long sigh. 'But I love you and only you.'

'You don't mean a single word.' Felix doesn't take life seriously and everything is always a joke. Still, there are plenty of women who'd swoon in his presence. He's gorgeous in that distracted, just-rolled-out-of-bed way. The cheeky spontaneous type who makes you feel that adventure is around every corner.

He waggles a brow. 'I guess you'll never know, Lilou. Café crème?'

'*Oui*. Extra hot.' With a salute, Felix dashes off to buy coffee, while I stand there pondering where he gets his energy from. I'm tired just watching his brisk pace down the stairs. I open the door of my stall, inhaling the scent that sits heavy in the air. The musty, dustiness of times gone by. The perfume of inky secrets and hidden desires. I recently redesigned it with old-fashioned opulence in mind, furnished the space with replica Louis XVI gilded chairs, pink velvet chaises, thick brocade curtains and well-worn Persian rugs – all given to me by Geneviève at a criminally discounted price.

The space appears intimate, almost boudoir-like, in ode to the letters, the words, the thoughts penned in private so long ago. While I wait for my café crème, I take a duster and make my rounds. Righting prayer books and tidying shelves. By a collection of poetry books I find a pressed red rose. Did someone drop this here yesterday? It's just my sort of whimsical and I'm lost to wondering about it. Did it come from a secret admirer before being hidden between the pages of a book? Did it leave a rose-shaped imprint and scent? I'm saddened for whoever misplaced a rose that clearly belongs in a special book to be opened and reminisced over. For now, I put it in my own personal diary behind the counter to keep it safe.

Felix returns with two keep cups in hand and motions for me to join him outside. *'Mademoiselle.'* Felix hands me a coffee. 'Have a lovely day.'

'Merci. My turn tomorrow.'

'Make it a *vin rouge* after work, eh?' he says over his shoulder as he heads off to open his shop.

I give him a playful smirk. 'Don't push your luck.' As I turn away with what I hope is a playful hair flick, I run smack bang into a muscular chest. Pascale. The force of the altercation sends the lid of my keep cup flying and coffee ejects itself like a tidal wave over his shirt, which is of course white.

He lets out a blood-curdling scream that has me jumping out of my skin. *'Ca brule!'*

When my soul returns to my body after Pascale's terrifying screech, I take a breath and say, 'Of course it burns, it's hot coffee. Ah, extra hot.' How can one small café crème do so much damage? *'Pardon,* Pascal. I wasn't paying attention. I have some tissues inside.'

'Tissues?' he spits, his face devoid of all colour.

'Paper towel then?'

With a grunt he says, 'I'll have to change.' He pulls the sodden shirt from his chest, but not before I note the ripple of his muscles beneath the suddenly translucent linen.

However, muscles don't maketh the man. 'Would you like me to find you another shirt? Will that suffice?' There's plenty of clothing stalls in a different section of the market and it would be the least I could do so he doesn't hold this against me.

He continues grunting and groaning and making his displeasure known without using actual words. Honestly, he's acting like his first-born child ran away to join the circus.

'*Non.*'

And with that, he storms off. My morning is going to start without the requisite caffeine jolt.

'Did you purposely scald him with hot coffee?' Geneviève whispers in my ear, making me jump in fright as Pascale does some sort of Hulk stomp out of the market.

I gasp. 'Geneviève! Of course not.'

'Oh, shame. I thought it might be a very clever trick to get him half naked, and if so, I'm here for it.'

'I have no words. None.' I'd never waste my morning coffee on such an activity. 'Is that even a thing, scalding a man with a hot beverage to sneak a peek? Surely not!'

She grins. 'If the end justifies the means, why not?'

Srrieux! 'You don't think it'll result in permanent damage, do you?' He'll never forgive me if his tight, taut muscles are left scarred. Who would!

'Don't fret, Lilou. I'm sure it's fine.'

I consider my interaction with Pascale. He's so very different to Felix, who laughs and jokes as if all the world is a stage, whereas Pascale always appears hard done by. Clearly being drenched in scalding café crème isn't an ideal start to the day, but he could have at least thanked me for offering to help. I shake my head; some men are a puzzle with a few pieces missing. 'You do have to wonder why he's downright morose all the time.'

She tuts. 'Don't give up yet. The poor man simply has trouble acting on his feelings.'

I manage to contain my exasperation. *The poor man!* Seriously. If there *was* a guidebook about bad boys, Geneviève probably penned it.

'He doesn't *have* any feelings, except one – irritability. Just what has he got to be so moody about all the time? OK, his white tee is now coffee coloured, but it's not as if I threw it over him on purpose and, after his part in the nose debacle, he can't really hold it against me.'

'You're always going on about meeting a man meet-cute style and I can't help but think you've had two opportunities, the first of which smacked you right in your very face and the second in his very chest, and you *still* don't see it.'

'What? That's not exactly meet-cute style, Geneviève. Meet cutes are *cute* for one. My nose almost being sheered clean off my face didn't exactly feel cutesy. In fact, it felt downright painful, and I gather the extra hot coffee across his chest was up there in terms of discomfort too. A meet-cute is meant to be a charming interaction, not... an altercation with the world's moodiest man.'

'Moody men make the best lovers.' She gives me an exaggerated wink; her hooded eyes and long false lashes give her an aged Marilyn Monroe air.

I supress a sigh. 'And the worst boyfriends.'

'He's probably exhausted fending off women. He's almost *too* good looking.'

'Fending off women! Geneviève, you don't take anything I say seriously.' If you were into buff, hot, fiery-eyed men then I suppose he's attractive. In the past I've come to know men just like that, men who rely on their looks alone, never developing a personality, empathy, humility. Been there, done that, got the break-up text. His dominant macho-man energy is off the charts and I just wouldn't risk it with a guy like that. 'Firstly, we have no intellectual connection. He's not exactly friendly, and what's he got going for him except sex appeal? It's not enough, is it?' I want more than a sizzling sexual relationship. I want deep and meaningful conversations. I want romance to be front and centre. I want a man who is respectful and sensitive, and he is none of those things. Why am I even thinking about all his faults? It doesn't matter one bit to me!

Geneviève rummages in her iconic Fauré Lepage tote and soon brandishes her keys. '*Voila!* Follow me,' she orders in her usual haughty way. I can keep an eye on my stall through the window.

'Let me clean up the few drops of coffee that didn't land on Pascale and I'll be right there.' I dash to my shop and grab some paper towels and mop up the mess on the floor before joining Geneviève in her shop.

8

Geneviève's antique shop Palais is filled with truly exquisite antique furniture sourced from France and Italy. Gilded, golden creations that have lived on this earth longer than us both, and have a hefty price tag to match. Most of these luxe pieces come from chateaux or castellos. I lament that any person in their right mind would relinquish such beautiful antiques, but I suppose if they didn't we'd all be out of a job in the antiquities trade.

'Mimosa?' Geneviève asks.

'It's not even ten.'

'And?' Geneviève unwinds her gossamer-thin ruby-red scarf.

'OK.' I long for a cup of coffee but that ship has sailed. Geneviève takes a bottle of Taittinger and orange juice from a bar fridge behind the counter and makes two mimosas, heavy on the champagne.

'Now, I don't want to alarm you, but it seems that there's a bit of an investigation going on.'

I sigh and take a sip of my mimosa. 'Let me guess, Coraline told you?'

She frowns. 'What? No.'

'Then who?'

'The glossies, Lilou. I take it you haven't seen the *presse indiscrète* today?'

Not more tabloid press interviews with the man of the hour, surely! 'Emmanuel Roux is at it again?' He can't help himself! Is his star power on the wane? Did his PR team dream this up as a way to get his name in the forefront again?

She grimaces. 'No, it's about you! Wait a moment.' Geneviève sashays from the shop, champagne glass in hand, leaving me to ponder what she's on about. I'm anonymous when it comes to Paris Cupid, so how can any tabloid refer to me? Before panic sets in, I take a slug of my mimosa. It doesn't help. Anxiety looms large as I imagine the worst.

A few minutes later, Geneviève returns, waving the magazine. 'Normally, I don't pay attention to these trashy tabloids, but this one has me a little worried, I must admit.' She hugs the glossy tight to her chest as if she really doesn't want to expose me to whatever lies within.

'Show me.'

'OK, but I don't want you to be alarmed.'

'That is sweet, Geneviève, but how can I not be when you say something like that! It's like being told to calm down when you're in the middle of an argument.'

'Om...'

'Are we meditating now? There goes my blood pressure!'

With a sigh, she hands it over. The headline screams from the front cover:

Who's the mastermind behind Paris Cupid?

Mon Dieu! My stomach flips as I frantically search for the article, speed reading when I find it. They've taken information directly from the Paris Cupid website, saying it's a small affair dedicated to matching the lost, the weary, the broken hearted, or the just plain romantic, using the medium of love letters.

Then it goes on to say it's becoming increasingly popular as a new way to find the one, and it's being whispered about in Parisian bistros, and it's spoken about more widely after the site successfully found a match for actor Emmanuel Roux, who'd previously sworn he'd be a bachelor forever. Online groups have been created where conspiracy theories run wild. The secret everyone wants to know is, who is behind the site? Who is Cupid? Who came up with the old-school idea of a slow-burn romance for modern-day love?

My air leaves my lungs in a whoosh. 'Why! Why do they want to know who I am? Who are these people in the online groups?' I throw the magazine on Geneviève's desk as if it's tainted.

Geneviève lifts her palms. 'Nosy people. You know what these online sleuths are like if there's a mystery to be solved. The issue is, will they find out who you are? And if so, does that matter in the grand scheme of things?'

Does it? 'The scrutiny would be unbearable. If they dig into my background and discover I was named in Frederic's divorce, a married man with twenty million children – even *with* the caveat that I didn't know, it still won't look good. There are plenty of market vendors who saw *le scandale* unfold and would no doubt love to talk about it to these media types. If they kept digging, they'd find one disaster after another. Let us not forget the cryptomancer who I met in a café and exchanged numbers with (oh, yes, it's real and just as awful as it sounds) who had me fooled until he tried to seduce me into investing in crypto currency. I mean, why am I a magnet for all the wrong guys? Who would trust a match maker with that kind of relationship history? I wouldn't!'

Despite my own sketchy love life, Paris Cupid matches have been largely successful. Real love has blossomed for so many unlikely pairs. Getting to know one another by the written word has laid a strong foundation for them to build on when they finally do meet. And for those who didn't gel, I've rematched them and they've reported back that they're happy to have a new correspondent and another chance at finding love.

This new threat could change all of that. Take the mystery, the anonymity away.

'Pah! Surely they won't focus on any of that. If you do get outed, they'll probably want to quiz you on how you came up with the idea. It'll be a good plug for Paris Cupid.'

While her voice is upbeat, it's clear she's putting a positive spin on it to keep me from descending into panic.

'That's the thing, Geneviève. I'm already at capacity with members and what I can handle. By June I'd matched thirty couples. It's only mid-July now and I've matched a whopping twenty more. If I didn't need sleep, it would be in the hundreds, but I need to take my time when going through their questionnaires in the hopes of finding the compatible partners. Emmanuel Roux won't stop speaking to the press every chance he gets. It's been two weeks since his very first interview, and he keeps popping up all over the place. When he does, memberships go wild. But they're not the *right* kind of people. They're influencers, people chasing clout. LoveTokkers, I mean, what even is that? A few I looked into were already in relationships! It's becoming a circus.'

She nods wisely like a sage. 'Then it's time to double down. Pause all new applications for the last two weeks of July and possibly August? Let the furore dry up. Those insta-famous types will soon move to the next craze.'

While the idea is anathema to me, it might be the best way forward right now. I can't keep up with demand, and ferreting out fakes is a huge time suck. 'You're right. I'll do that. If they are serious about finding love, they'll wait. Or reapply, right?'

'*Oui.*'

My heart sinks at the thought of halting memberships, albeit briefly, even if it is the only option. But I'll honour those who have applied already, if they're in it for the right reasons.

'And what will you do about Emmanuel Roux?'

I blow out a breath. 'What can I do? He hasn't responded to my email. The phone number he provided isn't in service any more. I've reached out to Émilienne as myself, not as Cupid, but she hasn't replied to my texts and her phone is always off. She does that when she goes on retreats but the timing of it feels more like she's hiding, from the press, the scrutiny.'

Geneviève takes a long sip of mimosa. 'Reach out to her as Paris Cupid by email?'

I contemplate it. '*Oui.* Why don't I formulate a sort of... follow-up survey for her and Emmanuel, asking if they're happy with their match and whether they had any concerns, that kind of thing? Emmanuel will most likely ignore it, like he has with the previous email, but it will look legitimate if they both get the same survey if it comes up in conversation between them.'

'*Parfait.* You could add all of your membership rules again at the end of the document. It might jog their memories and she may just remind Emmanuel that the whole premise behind Paris Cupid was keeping the details of matches private and being honest.'

Paris Cupid has a handful of rules to protect members. First, they must use post office boxes for correspondence rather than give total strangers their home address. Second is to be truthful. I go further but it's all common sense advice spelled out so that everyone is aware of their responsibilities.

The rules clearly stipulate that every member must be honest about, but not limited to: age, job, name and relationship status. If members don't care to share that information with their match so early in the process, that's acceptable too, but they do have to share it with me, not only so I find them a suitable partner, but also because it's part of the background work I do on them to make sure what they say correlates with who they are. It's understandable if Emmanuel Roux has social media accounts under another name for relative anonymity due to his celebrity status, but he should have disclosed that information with Paris Cupid.

'Good idea, Geneviève. I'll do that tonight.'

In the hall, Guillaume arrives to deliver stock and greets Benoit with a wave and stops to chat. I presume Guillaume has managed to find some stamp collections on his travels after Benoit called and introduced himself on the phone two weeks ago. I hope it will work out well for both of them and I'm happy that Benoit has another source to help find stock for his stall.

He and Guillaume chatter excitedly about the finds from the south of France. Benoit's face lights up when Guillaume produces a stamp collection in an old binder. Really, Benoit is so wholesome.

'You know the quiet ones are also pretty good between the sheets.'

Geneviève nods towards Benoit. At least I hope it's Benoit she's alluding to and not Guillaume, who is at least thirty years my senior and about the same age as Geneviève. I've thought of setting them up before but Guillaume is much too traditional for her.

'Why is it always about sex with you!'

She shrugs. 'It's good exercise.'

I can only shake my head. I'm eager to take delivery of my own treasures, so I go to take my leave. 'Talk soon.'

'But your drink?' Geneviève is not one to leave a glass half full.

I take a long sip of my mimosa, suffering a rush to the head drinking alcohol in the designated coffee hour. '*Au revoir.*'

I give Guillaume a wave to let him know I'm ready to take delivery while Benoit pores over a stamp collection. He's lost in a world where those tiny rectangles of paper reign supreme.

They wrap up their conversation, and Benoit says, '*Pardon*, Lilou. I didn't see you there.' He blushes as if he's committed a terrible faux pas.

I wave him away. He's always blushing and mumbling. It's really rather charming. 'No need to apologise. I see Guillaume has found you some gems too.'

'*Oui*, thank you for connecting us. Selling these on will be the hard part.' He rakes his fingers through his light-brown hair. That same distracted gaze is back, as if he can't quite talk and dream at the same time.

'I understand. It's almost impossible to let them go.'

'Beauty comes our way but for a moment.' He stares just past me and I find myself lost for words as I so often am when Benoit says a phrase that's so startlingly poetic.

'I – I...' I fumble with a response, all at once lost in the deep intelligence of his dark eyes. He's not like other men. Not loud, not showy, not a rippled mass of muscles, which all adds to his appeal. Benoit's magnetising in a way I can't quite put my finger on. He moves his gaze to Felix who is in the hallway, chatting with a customer.

Guillaume glances at his watch with an impatient sigh. 'I really am pressed for time. Can you continue this chitchat later?'

I cough, clearing my throat, feeling unbalanced suddenly, as if the world tilted for a fraction of a second. The idea of finding love is literally making me woozy, which I put down to being surrounded by love in all its forms at Ephemera and with Paris Cupid. 'Oui. Sorry, Guillaume,' I finally manage.

Benoit nods *au revoir* and Guillaume follows me into Ephemera, hefting the small package of books with a grunt as if it's as heavy as a box of bowling balls.

Guillaume takes great care unpacking my wares and hands me a handwritten invoice. He detests the march of technology and will most likely never adapt to using a computer for his business. He did eventually capitulate and purchase a photocopier, but he only agreed to that in order to keep the stock safe in his office and to not cart valuable prayer books, first editions and other accoutrements around Paris to show his buyers.

'Did you sign up to Paris Match, Guillaume?' I say, pretending to be distracted, rifling through my new stock.

'It's Paris Cupid, Lilou. Must I keep reminding you?' He gives me a stern look.

I make a face at my obvious stupidity. 'Sorry, I keep forgetting.'

'I did, I'll have you know, but I'm expecting precisely zero from it. The more I think about it, the more I envisage this is a young person's game. It's not meant for old men like me.'

'Ah, but you're so very wrong! Love is a game for all ages.'

He purses his lips as if trying to stop scepticism leaching out. 'That's all well and good when it comes along organically, but not like this. A newfangled website, a matchmaker. I had to go to the Bibliotheque Nationale de France to use their computers to sign up to the infernal Paris Cupid site. I'm not sure this is the right course for me.'

The Bibliotheque Nationale de France is arguably the most famous of all Parisian libraries. The reading room features a glass domed ceiling and archways full of bookshelves. It's near the Place Vendome, home to the Ritz and quite a distance from where Guillaume lives and works.

'Why didn't you go to the library in Montmartre?'

'I didn't want any nosey friends to question me.' He lets out a long sigh as if all his friends converge at the library in Montmartre and question him relentlessly, which I'm sure they do not. He lowers his voice as he says, 'Those fandangle machines never work for me either so I knew I'd have to plead for the *bibliothécaire* to assist me, and the last thing I want is Kellie from Montmartre library knowing my business. You know what she's like, always hovering around.'

Kellie does no such thing but now is not the time to mention that.

Have I left it too late to send Guillaume his match? If his feet get any colder, they'll be blocks of ice. 'Give it a chance, like you promised, and if it doesn't work out, you can say "I told you so" for the rest of your life.' The sentiment produces a glimmer of a smile.

'That *is* tempting. Must dash.'

'*Au revoir.*'

Once Guillaume takes his leave, I make a note on my phone to send his match this evening. As I pocket my mobile, I notice Benoit across the hall, staring off into the distance as if lost in thought. Every now and then he glances in my direction with a faraway look in his eyes. What's on his mind? Probably his new stamp collection.

I turn back to my delivery, thumbing through my loot, hunting for Margot's diary that I'd read one tantalising page from the other day in the cemetery. The adventure-seeking woman who broke off her engagement with poor Elliott because he didn't set her soul on fire. When I find the diary with its worn leather cover, I peek outside. The market is quiet, so I settle on a chaise to read. When I gently creak the cover open, I'm assailed with a scent that takes me a moment to recognise. Lavender. It's as though clues are seeping out from the very pages themselves, exposing me to hints of her past.

Did Margot live in a chateau in Provence where lavender grows in abundance?

> *Maman has given me an ultimatum. I'm to rekindle my romance and marry Elliott or I'm to leave the village and give up my monthly allowance. I asked Maman, 'If Elliott's family weren't wealthy, would we be having this conversation?' and she didn't even have the audacity to lie! My dreams lie outside this village. Outside of these crumbling chateau walls.*

I'm not getting wed, having children and living a humdrum life because it's what someone of my station is expected to do. There's no other choice, except pack my bags and leave. Adventure awaits!

I close my eyes and picture her running her fingers along blooms of lavender as she made her escape from a life she didn't care for, the purple flower leaving an indelible mark on her fingertips and these very pages preserving the perfume. What a gift.

So she did pack up and leave? How did she support herself after relinquishing her monthly allowance? Guillaume mentioned the diary had been found in a *chambre de bonne*. Did she swap her upper-class lifestyle and lasso herself the life she wanted? Total freedom and the power to choose. I understand her need to be more than a wife, a mother. To explore the world and live on her terms, but just how difficult would it have been in the early sixties?

I read half of Margot's diary before a regular customer wanders in. With some reluctance I stash the diary in my desk and greet her. 'Bonjour, Giselle.' I give her a bright smile. 'Are you looking for anything in particular today?'

Giselle shakes her head as she picks up a prayer book and flicks through the pages. 'Just killing time before I meet a friend for lunch. I can't be this close and not visit Ephemera.'

I smile. Giselle is one of my favourites who has a keen eye and enjoys hearing a good backstory on her purchases. 'Take your time. On the shelf by the grandfather clock is a folder of new love letters. One of my suppliers sourced them from a small estate in Brittany a few weeks ago. They span decades.'

'And they haven't sold yet?' It's always risky knowing what to invest in. These beautiful letters haven't sold, despite being a one-sided sweeping love story told over a lifetime. *Forbidden love.*

'Not yet. The cursive writing is difficult to read, especially the letters towards the end. The penmanship is shakier then, but to me, that adds to the appeal. You can *see* the author age as the script changes. Once again, showing us the fragility of life...'

Giselle groans. 'I knew this would be an expensive lunch.' She laughs and goes to find the letters.

* * *

That evening, as Paris Cupid once more, I email Guillaume about his match. I don't give him many details, except her first name and that she runs a successful *fromagerie* in Paris. It's up to them to share their stories and get to know one another at their own pace. I explain that they're compatible in many ways and they have many shared interests, but I don't delve into what they are. When I hit send, I cup my face. I always want love to win, but I want it even more for Guillaume. I shoot up a prayer to the love gods and will them to make it so.

9

The next day, by some miracle I arrive at Ephemera early. The neighbouring stalls are shuttered. The halls are bereft of customers so I open my laptop and set about designing a feedback survey for Paris Cupid while no one is here to catch me. My set-in stone rules forbidding working on the site at the market are a thing of the past as I struggle to keep up with demand.

Ideally, I'd like to send the survey to all members – their happiness in the game of love is my main priority – but there's no time while I'm still assessing the influx of current applications and debating whether I will pause new applications for a while in order to keep a handle on it.

Last night, I didn't have the heart to close Paris Cupid to new applicants but I regret that when I open the portal to find so many more have come in overnight. I shelve the feedback survey for a moment and draft a statement explaining Paris Cupid will be suspended for a brief period of time because we're at capacity while our dedicated, but small, team work through current applications.

My chest tightens when I post the statement and disable the application process. Mostly, I worry about those types who have decided to give love one last chance, and I've pulled the rug from under them.

I return to the feedback survey. One of the last questions I type is:

Have you found the one? I add the Paris Cupid rules at the end and a gentle reminder they were made to protect all members and suggest they take a minute to familiarise themselves with them again. After a quick proofread, I send it to both Émilienne's and Emmanuel's emails and hope they'll take the time to fill them out. Truthfully, I'm intrigued.

What if Emmanuel has had an about-face so dramatic that he does really love Émilienne? For her sake, I hope it's true. But there's still that gnawing feeling in my gut that he has some ulterior motive. I pack my laptop away and tamp down my sadness about the suspension of Paris Cupid.

It's my turn to buy Felix a café crème. I text him to ask if he's close to the Marché Dauphine and he replies he's a few minutes away. I lock up and stroll towards the outdoor café. It's bustling with other vendors sitting down to hearty breakfasts before the busy work day begins in earnest. I wave to a few familiar faces. When florist Coraline shrieks '*Bonjour!*' and gestures to me to join her, I pretend to be absorbed reading the blackboard.

Coraline jogs over, frown marring her brow. 'Didn't you see me waving to you?'

'Sorry, I didn't. Can't chat long, I'm in a bit of a hurry because—'

She ploughs ahead, not listening to a word I say. 'Did you hear the latest news about Emmanuel?'

I let out an exaggerated sigh. Why is she so obsessed with him? She's like a dog with a bone. 'What now?'

Coraline makes a show of contorting her features as if she's about to impart some very grave news. She pulls up a website on her phone and says, 'His public relations team released a statement last evening, and I quote: "Emmanuel Roux is retiring from his acting career effective immediately. He intends to focus on his new great passion: spirituality." What have you got to say about that?' She pockets the phone and folds her arms, giving me the mother of all stare downs as if I personally had something to do with Emmanuel's retirement from acting.

I can't help it; I laugh at Coraline's overblown reaction. You'd think Emmanuel was someone important in her life and not a celebrity she's never met, the way she's dramatizing it.

'I would say: "Congratulations and thanks for the memories"? What else is there to say and what does it have to do with *me*?'

I can't help but wonder, once again, could he actually be in love with Émilienne? Is that what has made him reconsider his career, his celebrity status? My heart expands at the thought. Does Emmanuel truly want to leave the glitzy celebrity world for a more authentic life? Or is this all just a PR stunt? Who knows what the movie biz lifestyle is really like on the inside. It could very well be a soul-sucking shallow existence, a toxic environment that Emmanuel didn't know how to extricate himself from until Émilienne happened along. A girl can dream.

'*Allez*, Lilou! Don't you see what's *happening* in front of your very eyes?' Coraline's emphasis on the word is downright noxious. 'Parisians are in mourning today, and you're flouncing around like it doesn't matter.'

La vache! The flea market is like a small town, and like any small town there's the requisite local gossip who thrives on drama, and here it's Coraline. Furthermore, if rumours are sparse, like they are at the moment, she is clearly quite happy to jump on the celebrity bandwagon and embellish. 'In mourning – he's not dead!'

She inhales sharply. 'That silly little matchmaking site is to blame. He meets a... a *commoner*, and now he's renouncing his craft! You can't tell me it's not linked. It's obvious this mystery woman has her claws in deep to convince him to make such a terrible decision. *Everyone* is talking about it.'

It's impossible not to guffaw. 'A commoner? He doesn't have royal blood! Have you ever considered the facts, as boring as they are? *Twilight Dream* has been running for the last fifteen years – that's a long time for a TV series. He's done a number of movies as well. Could it be he's just exhausted?'

'You're not taking this seriously!' Her face reddens. 'And hang on, how do you know so much about him all of a sudden? The other day you had no idea who I was talking about.'

Merde! Miraculously I manage to keep my expression neutral. 'His face has been plastered across every tabloid in every newsstand in Paris, not to mention the amount of live interviews he's given over the last little while. I can't even turn on the TV without him popping up and, to be honest, I'm so sick of hearing about him.' I add just enough frustration to my voice in the hopes she'll believe me.

That was a close call. Too close. If Coraline had the merest hint that it's me behind Paris Cupid she wouldn't stop until she had proof, and then all of France would know. I soften my expression. 'I'm sure Parisians are going to miss him on their screens every evening, but perhaps he's retiring for his own sanity and we must support that.'

Mollified, she gives me a small smile. 'For someone retiring, he really has done a lot of media lately.'

That's what makes me so anxious about the whole scenario. Why does he constantly need to share his private life at every opportunity when he tells each reporter he's looking forward to leaving the spotlight, while he sits directly under one? It doesn't ring true.

'Going out with a bang.'

'Possibly. *Au revoir.*' Coraline spins on her heel, flicking her mane of black hair over her shoulder. I step towards the counter and order two café crèmes to go and can't help but continue to muse about the retirement announcement. Is it legitimate?

10

At lunch time the next day, I head to La Coquette, a bistro in the 7th arrondissement with a view of the Eiffel Tower and the verdant green of the Champ de Mars. As I get off the Metro, my phone beeps with a message. I swipe it open, happy to see it's from Émilienne.

> Sorry for the radio silence! I'm in love and all is well! I'll tell you all about Paris Cupid and my new man when I get back. Having a tech break but didn't want you to worry. Ém x

By the tone of her message, it sounds like Émilienne is taking one of her sabbaticals where she disconnects for a bit and usually goes to a retreat for a body, mind and soul break. I text her back:

> Who is the lucky guy? Can't wait to hear all about it!

Of course, I know exactly who the lucky guy is but I'm interested to see if she'll share the Emmanuel Roux name with me or not. Normally, she would tell me every tiny detail about her current flame, so this silence around it is odd but understandable if she's trying to keep her name out of the press.

There's no reply so I continue to the bistro, where I'm meeting Geneviève. Once a week we have lunch together on a day the market is closed. I arrive first and am seated at an outdoor table with a stunning view of the *la tour Eiffel*. As expected, Geneviève is late, so I order a bottle of *viognier* while I wait, knowing she'll arrive whenever she damn well pleases. It's just her way.

I look up at the sound of a commotion near the door and catch sight of Pascale, arguing with the maître d'. What is he doing here? Of all the places in Paris to dine, how have we managed to choose the same place? I take my menu and do my best to hide behind it while Pascale argues with the waitstaff. When he swings his head in my direction, I shrink lower in my seat. Why is he looking over at me? I let out a yelp when he walks to my table before it dawns on me. That crafty so-and-so. She's done the old bait-and-switch routine.

'You're not Geneviève,' Pascale says bluntly, standing over the top of me, drowning out the sunlight with his huge frame.

'You have great powers of deduction.'

He grunts.

'Are you going to stand over the top of me like that or are you going to sit down?'

'But...' He takes a seat opposite me.

'I agree, this isn't ideal. I was supposed to be meeting Geneviève too. More to the point, why were you meeting her?' Is he under her spell? She does tend to go for younger men, the broodier and moodier the better, so this wouldn't surprise me, but she's not here and I am, so I know exactly what she's up to. She'd make a great matchmaker herself.

'She wanted to order a typewriter.'

I laugh. 'You fell for that?'

'I did.'

'I suppose she wants us to sort out our... differences.' She wants me to fall in love with the guy or have some hot, lusty fling, but I don't dare educate him on that. The less he knows about her motivations the better.

'Well, I don't know about that but I am hungry.'

'I wouldn't expect anything less.' Talk about rude! He can't even admit he's at fault.

'Shall we order?' He picks up a menu. He's not big on small talk which isn't a surprise. The waiter returns with an ice bucket and bottle of Louis Roederer and two champagne glasses.

'*Excusez moi*?' I say. 'I ordered *viognier*, not champagne.'

'It's a gift,' he says, taking a small pad from his shirt pocket and flipping it open to a page. 'From Geneviève. She offered her apologies for not making it to meet you today and has settled lunch for you both.'

'Oh, has she now?' I'm quietly fuming. The meddler! Now I have to sit across from this surly dining companion for as long as it takes me to inhale a salad.

'She chose the degustation menu. Eight courses with wine pairings.'

Eight courses! I paste on a smile. 'That seems a little extravagant.'

'Don't worry,' the waiter says, giving me a smile while somehow also looking supercilious in that particular French way. 'They're small serves.'

'*Oui*,' Pascale says. 'I had a large breakfast…'

Contempt flashes across the waiter's face. 'It's been done.' His severe tone brooks no argument.

We lapse into silence as he unwraps the foil off the bottle of champagne.

'Congratulations,' the waiter says dully. I narrow my eyes.

'Congratulations?'

'Aren't you celebrating?'

'*Non*?' Pascale says. 'Can you hurry this up? I've got places to be.'

He can't even share lunch with me without wanting to rush off.

'You don't have to stay, you know.'

'I know.'

The waiter frowns. I'm sure this will make a great story for the kitchen staff later. Two eggheads get spoiled with a bottle of fancy French champagne and a degustation experience and can't stand the sight of each other.

'Then what's stopping you from leaving? I can manage sixteen courses. It won't go to waste.' I'll eat his and mine and drink every last drop of wine if that's what it takes.

'It would be rude when Geneviève had gone to all of this effort.'

The waiter sighs. 'Your first course will be out shortly.'

'Fine,' we say in unison. Pascale glares at me and I glare right back. If he wants frosty, I'll give him frosty.

* * *

The degustation is finally over and I'm a little tipsy from the wine. I leave a huge tip for the waiter precisely because he couldn't hide his haughtiness and disdain as lunch bore on. I wrap my summery scarf around my neck and fumble for my phone. As I trek to the Metro, I call Geneviève.

'How did it go?' she asks, excitement in her voice.

'You sneak, you...'

'Did sparks fly? Birds sing? Angels trumpet?'

'They did no such thing! The man is impossible. What were you *thinking*?'

'*D'amour!*'

'Of love! Pascale left as soon as he ate his last forkful, grumbling about his day being taken up and lamenting the fact he didn't sell an antique typewriter for all his troubles. Doesn't sound like love to me.'

She giggles, she actually giggles. 'What's amusing about this? You just spent a fortune on lunch for two people who can't stand each other. Even the waiter told us to stop glaring because we were frightening other customers.'

'What fun!'

'What?'

'Enemies to lovers, *ma Cherie*. You might not recognise these intense feelings because you've only ever dated those safe types who are always so accommodating and, let's be frank, boring. This is fireworks. Explosions! The clanging of bells.'

'Clanging of...?' My mind is muddled from the wine, the words. I'm having trouble understanding how she can possibly consider that man is the one for me. 'He's a belligerent fool.'

'Uh-huh.'

'Seriously?'

'You can thank me later.'

'Sure. You should have saved your money! Eight courses! You did that on purpose.'

'It's a good, solid investment into your future. Three courses wouldn't have been long enough.'

I sigh. I'm not going to convince her. 'I'm nearly at the Metro.'

'Alone, I take it?'

'Alone with only my frustration for company.'

'See? Already the love bug is working its way around your blood stream.'

'Then I should see a doctor about that. The only thing working its way around my blood stream is too many wine varietals.'

'No such thing!'

'*Au revoir*, Geneviève. Thank you for the meal.' After all, the food was spectacular.

I wobble off down the stairs to the Metro, my thoughts fuzzy from wine, from Pascale. Is she right about me having only dated safe boring types? Or is it that I go for men with more under the hood? That's probably it. My head might get turned occasionally by men like Pascale with that fiery-eyed overt hotness but I stop myself from feeling anything else because that sort of sex appeal might be good in theory, but it doesn't last and there's nothing else to build on. No, I need a man who can have intelligent conversation. A man who is considerate and thoughtful. A romantic at heart. And my lunch companion is none of those things.

11

On non-market days, I crisscross Paris buying stock for Ephemera. Today I zigzag along the left bank of the Seine, darting around clusters of tourists admiring the view. It's easy to spot a foreigner in Paris, not only because of phones and cameras held high but more so that they meander, whereas a typical Parisian walks at a brisk pace. Summer is peak tourist season and as July creeps closer to August, the crowds thicken.

I'm running fashionably late to meet Pierre, a *bouquiniste,* who sells second-hand antiquarian books and vintage posters from the ubiquitous tiny green boxes on the bank of the Seine. The Seine is the only river in the world with over two hundred and forty booksellers on its banks. Literature is hallowed in Paris and no book is ever left behind. Second- third-fourth-hand books will always find a home here or in vintage market and second-hand shops.

Pierre has a plethora of contacts in the book trade and calls me when he's found something that suits my line of work. We've been friends for years and he's just what you expect a bookseller to look like: windswept hair, obligatory cigarette dangling from his bottom lip, faded knitted jumper and distressed denim jeans; the whole ensemble screams bookworm. '*Bonjour*, Pierre. Sorry I'm late. But I have coffee and madeleines!'

'*Bonjour*, Lilou. *Mieux vaut trad que jamais.*' 'Late is worth more than never' should be my middle name. Pierre takes the proffered coffee and paper bag full of small shell-like cakes dusted with icing sugar. '*Merci bien.*' His life is what bibliophiles' dreams are made of. Most days, you'll find him nose-deep in a book, enraptured by other worlds that propel him far from here. The wiry bookseller has his regular visitors so well-trained that they bring him sustenance, so he doesn't have to move a muscle. While I'm deeply envious of his job, he does suffer come winter when the rain falls and the wind whips off the Seine.

We make pleasantries as I sit on a deckchair beside him and sip coffee. The wind from the Seine flutters the pages of the books as if they're waving a welcome.

'How did the market reshuffle go?'

I sigh. 'A little... rockier than I'd like. Do you know Pascale?' While there may be eleven million souls – not including the ghosts – in Paris, everyone knows everyone in the antiquity trade.

With eyes scrunched up, Pierre takes a deep draw of a thin hand-rolled cigarette as he contemplates my question. 'Sells vintage type-writers?'

'That's him. Inexplicably, he's taken a disliking to me. Yesterday, my music bothered him. Too loud and too tinny, apparently. And that's just one of many issues he'd found with me.'

Pierre frowns. 'Like what?'

I wave it away as if it's nothing. 'A few complaints about this and that. He's put my nose out of joint.' *Literally.* 'Geneviève arranged a surprise lunch for us to air out our differences and of course it didn't go well. By the eighth course I was ready to stab him with my fork. I've never met a man so disagreeable in all my life. But no point crying over spilt milk.' Or extra-hot café crème. 'I'm sure it'll settle down. The other two neighbours, Felix and Benoit, are lovely.' I don't go into more detail. I've already said too much probably, because Pierre isn't one to get involved in the minutiae of others' lives, not only because he doesn't like gossip, but mainly because he finds it not the least bit interesting. He'd rather find his drama inside a book.

Pierre smiles as if the situation is amusing and not annoying, which is something at least. 'I'm sure it will. He's probably put out having to move.' Pierre drops the butt of his cigarette into an ashtray.

'*Oui.* He wasn't happy being moved upstairs.' I glance at my watch. 'So what have you got for me?'

Pierre doesn't call me often but when he does it's always a sensational find. Love letters and cards, usually, the merest whispers of a stranger's life dashed across paper and secreted away in books, hidden for a passage of time until they reveal themselves once more.

'A letter. It's brittle like rice paper and has the most wonderful calligraphy that you can only *just* discern. Whoever buys it from you will possibly be the very last person to read it.'

Even Pierre seems excited about the find, which is unusual. He's always happy to save these trinkets for me but is usually more ambivalent about their charm and worth.

'May I see it?' He hands me a battered copy of *Madame Bovary* which I can't help but sniff. The perfume of old books: earthy, musty nuttiness with hints of vanilla and sweet almond is like a drug.

'It's inside the book, which was found in a bedside cabinet in an abandoned penthouse in the 4th arrondissement. You should have seen the apartment, Lilou.' He shakes his head at the memory. 'Stuck in a seventies time warp. I've never seen anything like it.'

'Abandoned? Who'd do that?' A penthouse in the 4th arrondissement is prime real estate. I can't imagine anyone who'd give a place like that up.

Pierre nods. 'It was eerie, as though they picked up one day and left in a hurry. There were coffee cups on the table, dishes in the sink and ashtray with the corpse of a cigarette that must have been left burning. The dusty cobwebby library room had books in many languages.'

I picture Pierre visiting the apartment to assess the library for its worth and finding the penthouse, stuck in the seventies like a living, breathing time capsule.

'What? Where did they go?'

He shrugs. 'No idea. The apartment sold recently, all done through some sort of trust. The new owners are gutting the place and want everything gone. A shame. You don't see places preserved like that.'

'Doesn't it bother you, the not knowing?'

'Nothing to do with me, but if I were a gambling man, I'd bet it was one of their many houses around the world and they left one day and forgot about their Parisian *pied-à-terre*.'

'Are there really people *that* wealthy they forget about Parisian penthouses?'

His weathered face dissolves into a grin. 'Hah – not us, Lilou.' For a moment he stares off into the distance, his eyes reflecting the sun off the Seine. 'We're the ones who preserve what's left behind.'

'The keepers of forsaken treasures.' Would they care, these invisible people whose mementoes we pore over then sell on? What might be rubbish to the new homeowners, another chore on their list, is our bright spot. Every person's history matters, not just those more notable among us. Why does a bundle of letters from a historical figure like Napoleon matter more than, say, a domestic worker who had big dreams and aspirations? Both are of equal importance and both ought to be preserved for history's sake.

'It seems fitting you should have the book and the letter since they were found together. But please, Lilou, don't open it in this breeze. The parchment is so delicate I fear it'll become confetti and then the words will be lost forever.'

I run my hand over the cover of *Madame Bovary*. Will this secreted letter explain why the people in the penthouse in the 4th left so abruptly and never returned? Like most letters, it will probably leave me with more questions than answers, but it's another thread to the past that will be cherished, instead of hidden away, lost and forgotten.

'What is it worth?' I brace myself. Pierre is always reasonable with pricing, but he's also usually more casual about his finds. This level of enthusiasm may be costly.

He waves me away. 'Nothing. It might not last long enough for you to sell it and the book is, shall we say, *very* well loved.'

'*Merci*, Pierre.' There's a sense of anticipation about it but I have other suppliers to see before the return journey home. I don't dare open the book and find the letter until I'm safely ensconced in my apartment where nothing can damage the fragile paper. I wrap my silk scarf around the book and place it in my handbag. I fight the urge to cancel my other appointments and dash home, but I can't let my suppliers down. Competition for collectibles is rife in Paris and while I may be a touch delayed from time to time, I always keep my word.

It's strange; it's almost like I can feel the letter beating from inside my bag, as if the words themselves have a pulse.

* * *

Once I've met with the rest of my suppliers, I turn in the direction of home. I dodge tourists holding phones aloft snapping pictures, their faces full of wonderment. Ah, Paris, the city of lights. Once you've been to Paris, you're never quite the same. It gets under your skin, like a long-lost love. It's in your heart forevermore.

With aching feet from so much walking, I arrive home, throw my keys on the kitchen bench and flick my flats off all in one movement. I say *'bonjour'* to my alfalfa plant that sullenly ignores me as usual. The letter thrums in my handbag. I gently unwrap the silk scarf from *Madame Bovary* and place the book on the table, as gently as if it were a newborn baby. On closer inspection, the book itself is weathered, its cover wrinkled, pages rumpled, as if it's been well read and had a long illustrious life. I find the letter snug between two middle pages. Careful with the delicate parchment, I gently unfold it. My heart drops. The ink has almost faded beyond recognition. It's hard to decipher the curl of the calligraphy in the stippled afternoon sunlight. I slip the letter back into the book and take it to the bathroom, hoping the bright lighting will help.

I switch on the light and the words appear as if by magic. It's a short passage written in formal calligraphy.

> *Late at night when I wander the streets of Paris, my thoughts turn to her. The woman who sees beauty where others do not. I walk alone.*

The only accompaniment is the echo of my footsteps while I conjure her in my mind. I see her pretty face, always adorned with a smile, her laughter that draws my attention. Everyone wants to be in her spotlight, yet she has no idea how special she is. It's a marvel. How do I tell her how I feel? Perhaps I need to show her...

I'd been expecting more of a clue as to why the penthouse in the 4th had been abandoned back in the seventies. Really, who leaves a grand apartment such as that, never to return? But this is all about love! *Unrequited love?* Or *oblivious to love?*

So many questions flutter in my mind. So many possibilities. Did he indeed confess his love to the woman and she didn't reciprocate his feelings? Or did he wait in the shadows and was left despondent when she chose another because he never spoke up? Maybe he never confessed his love as he waited for a sign to act. Why didn't he scream his love from the rooftops? Isn't love always worth it, even if there's a chance of rejection?

There's another possibility.

This mystery man confessed his love and romanced her in such a way that every other suitor paled in comparison. They were swept up in each other, and one day they spontaneously decided to leave Paris behind and go on a grand adventure to discover the world! They enjoyed a nomadic existence and, in their haze, forgot all about their fabulous *pied-à-terre* in Paris, because their love was tangible and the only thing that mattered.

At least, that's what I hope happened. Why shouldn't love win?

This letter, its ink slowly seeping into the atmosphere, is too delicate to sell. Too special. A fluttery sensation hits me and at first, I push it away as frivolous. But it returns.

Is this letter a sign meant for me?

A sign to stop living in the past and trust my heart to love again? I've spent too many evenings sitting here alone. Too many weekends cooped up and unsure. Paris Cupid has been my outlet for helping others find love, but it doesn't stop my own loneliness. That's always just below the surface.

I want a love story like the ones I find on the pages. Burning with longing and passion and an intensity that disturbs my very routine. And I'm never going to find that standing on the periphery, orchestrating the love lives of strangers while mine remains shuddered to a halt. Perhaps I *should* be more like Geneviève. She's never wary in the pursuit of love; in fact, she's the opposite and throws herself with wild abandon into it. There's something beautiful about a woman who doesn't let the past determine the future. I need to stop treading water.

I snap photographs of the letter before I find a picture frame and place the letter inside. I pop it on my bedside table, hoping that the glass frame will protect it and the words won't fade away completely. My heart thrums in my chest, as if the energy of the letter writer has transferred to me. The author of the letter said he planned to 'show her'. Perhaps I need to show myself I'm capable of love and being loved. Just like my Paris Cupid matches.

Who is my Mr Right? Annoyingly, Pascale's scowling face springs to mind. I shove the thought aside and Felix's flirty smile appears. Before long, Benoit's deep unfathomable dark eyes draw me in. It's a sad state of affairs when the only men I've got to dream about are my new neighbours. Unless… it means one of them is right for me.

12

I never expected I'd be the type to settle in one place. I've had too much fun roaming, taking work wherever I can and living frugally, with complete freedom. So, it's come as a bit of shock to find myself gloriously in love with a Greek man who only speaks snippets of French. I'm learning a bit of Greek, but our love doesn't need translation; it just is. And how can that be? I only know this feels different, like stars have exploded, a galaxy of light above showing me the way to him. And so I'm staying in this little whitewashed home perched on the side of a cliff, with my Greek God, his dog and a few donkeys. Who knows what the future will bring, but I feel like I've found my place and the person who I was always meant to meet.

I finish Margot's diary with a tear in my eye. What an energetic life she lived, for as long as the diary covered. Margot travelled all the way around France before moving on to Italy and then settling down in Greece with a man who worshipped her but gave her plenty of space.

If only I had more volumes of her life story. What came next for Margot? I like to think of her with the salty sea breeze in her hair, still wild and free. Her story has given me hope. Margot had been adamant she'd never stop roaming, but love caught her unawares and there she stayed. Who wouldn't want to live in a sun-drenched paradise like the Greek isles? I send up a thank you to the love gods for allowing me to be privy to Margot's diary and be alongside her for those chapters of her life. What a privilege.

When I look up, I'm surprised to note the market is swarming with people. It's been quiet in Ephemera but I haven't exactly been paying attention. Time to get to work before the day escapes. I'm expecting another Friday delivery from Guillaume. I check my watch, miffed to find he's running late. He's never late. Either I'll have ammunition for the rest of my days, or something terrible has happened. I peek outside and am relieved to see him chatting enthusiastically with Pascale, of all people.

Both of them are laughing and gesticulating as if they're long-lost friends reunited at last. What on earth? Guillaume's default personality is pernickety, and Pascale's is peeved, so to see them fully relaxed like this is somewhat out of character. What could they be so animated about?

'Guillaume?' I yell across the hallway. 'Didn't we have an appointment thirty minutes ago?' I make a show of checking a watch I don't wear in ode to all the times he's simpered at me.

A wrinkle mars his brow. '*Oui*, we did. But I'm talking to a potential new client. You won't begrudge me that, will you?'

Pascale gives me a mocking smile. 'There's a lot more value in typewriters than old letters, Lilou.'

That man! 'If you're talking monetary value, maybe, but isn't that a shallow way to look at the world?'

The mocking smile melts right off Pascale's face. 'What I meant was —' His words peter out as Guillaume picks up a box of stock and marches in my direction. Pascale says, 'Lilou, is this about the candles again?'

Guillaume stops midway between us, his eyes crinkling with suspicion. It's like a standoff.

'No, I've noted your sensitivities to candles, music, pot plants, my singing, and all the other things you've complained about. This is about you belittling me in order to feel better about yourself.'

Pascale's retort dries right there on his lips. Eventually, he manages, 'It was a joke...'

Guillaume shakes his head and takes a step towards me.

I fold my arms and lean against the door jamb. 'Which part was funny?'

'I'm sorry, Lilou.'

Oh, I see right through this amicable persona that's meant purely for Guillaume's benefit.

'You two can sort it out later.' Guillaume finally tires of our back and forth-ing. 'Now, Lilou, your delivery. The rest of my day is going to be a shambles if I don't catch up.'

We head inside Ephemera and, as I turn, I see what appears to be real worry on Pascale's face. Doesn't he understand that the show is over?

I drop my voice low and ask Guillaume, 'Any news about Paris Sweethearts?'

He grunts but fights a smile that plays at his lips. 'For the hundredth time, Lilou, it's Paris Cupid. You might want to write that down.'

I ignore the jibe and fight my own smile. 'Well?'

'If you must know, you busy body meddler, I've been matched with a certain Clementine. I happen to know of her. She owns the *fromagerie* on Rue Damrémont.'

'You know her? You've written already?'

'*Non*. You see, all I was given was her first name, and I was informed that she runs a successful *fromagerie* in Paris. It didn't take a genius to work out it was Clementine D'Amboise because of her first name and the fact her shop is around the corner from my apartment. I've stopped in on occasion for fromage but haven't personally made her acquaintance before.' I hadn't even considered he might know her, which is rather naïve of me considering he is a cheese lover and her *fromagerie* is in Montmartre.

'So you could cheat the system and go in and introduce yourself?'

He looks up, alarmed. 'That's not how this works, Lilou. I'm going to write her a letter this evening. Or maybe tomorrow. Or on Monday.

Wednesday at the latest.' This is a worry. He's had her contact details for a few weeks already and he hasn't written.

'Has she written to you?'

'*Non.*'

I take a moment to figure out how best to ease his nerves. 'Would reading a love letter here help, Guillaume? I have all sorts. Formal, informal, passionate, polite.'

He double blinks. 'Are you implying I don't know how to express myself?'

With an emphatic shake of my head, I say, 'Of course not! I'm confident you'll express yourself in the most articulate of ways. Only, I wondered if these penned letters might serve useful as inspiration.'

He looks up to the heavens as if he needs a miracle having to deal with me. 'If I don't agree, I suppose you'll keep harping on about me not trying hard enough and then I'll never hear the end of it. I'll have to speed read as I'm already behind today so only give me the very best. None of that purple prose, lovey dovey stuff either.'

As ever, Guillaume won't admit he needs help so I play along. 'You're a man who knows his own mind, a wonderful trait in a partner. Give me two minutes.'

'Two! I'll give you one.'

I shake my head as I find a selection of love letters that are a little more sedate, more Guillaume's speed. 'Here you go.'

As he settles in to read, I pretend to tidy, all the while surreptitiously watching the expression on his face changing from gruff to soft.

Love is a universal language. My lonely old friend just needs a little practice learning the fundamentals again. When he's finished, Guillaume grumbles about lost time and irate clients as he takes his leave. I can only shake my head as I watch him go, with a little more enthusiasm than when he arrived. The love letters touched him. You'd figure a man who procures these things would be well versed in such matters, but he insists he only ever gives them a cursory glance to check they're in good condition and aren't shopping lists before he agrees to purchase them.

I search through the latest delivery of treasures. There's an unusual prayer book. The tissue-thin paper has a mauve hue, the script itself bronze. I've never seen anything quite like it. As I gently flick through, I have the sense it belonged to a teenage girl.

I unpack the rest of Guillaume's finds. He really hit the jackpot with his latest trip near Neufchâteau. As I rifle through the goodies, I take photos for my newsletter as I go. At the bottom of the box is a typewritten letter that isn't familiar. Has Guillaume forgotten to show me this one? I double check his invoice; he hasn't charged me for it either. It's not like him to make a mistake. He's nothing if not meticulous. I snap a picture and text it to him.

> Did you forget about this one?

I take it from the plastic film.

> I've never believed in love. Or the notion that love conquers all. As for soul mates, give me a break – it's a ploy, marketing for gift card companies. That was until I met her. It felt like my world flipped upside down. Now my brain doesn't function the same around her. I say the stupidest things. I'm suddenly unsure of myself and my place in the world because I can only think of her. But I keep messing things up, trying to be funny, or trying to strike up conversation, and things go awry. I'm really not sure how to fix things. If I told her how I feel she'd laugh in my face. What to do?

Like a cliché I find myself holding my breath as I read. The honesty! I can relate too. I often stumble over my words or say the complete opposite to what I'm thinking when I like a guy. It's just that stupid sort of giddy that sometimes takes a moment to get a handle on.

As I fold the page, there's a notification on my phone from Guillaume.

> Non, I didn't forget. That's not one of mine.

How can it not be? Surely he's made a mistake.

> It was in the box, at the very bottom. If you're sure, then...?

Then what? Can I sell a letter that I didn't procure myself? But common sense says Guillaume has made a rare error and it's probably best to count it as a win and move on.

> Lilou, I pride myself on my organisational skills and I would never 'forget' a valuable item and I don't appreciate you implying such a thing.

Duly told, I grin at his predictable response and put the letter away, not quite ready to put it up for sale just yet. It reminds me of the beautiful brittle calligraphy letter. Two letters, both featuring men who love a woman they don't know how to approach. What are the chances? And what would the world be like if we didn't cherish letters such as these?

13

A market friend from downstairs rushes into my stall. 'Fair warning, a tour bus arrived an hour ago and they'll be making their way up here soon. It's a huge group and so far they've been buying up a storm, so get yourself ready.'

The market can be like one big happy family some days, where we all look out for one another. I suppose like any family, we can also have bad days, where certain sides aren't talking, someone's in a huff about something, a deal goes sour between two stalls, that sort of thing.

I thank my friend and rush over to tell Felix and Benoit, who are standing in the hallway chatting to each other. 'A tour group is on its way up.'

'*Merci, merci*,' Benoit says.

'Let's hope they aren't those destructive types.' Felix sighs.

Big tour groups can be hit or miss. Sometimes they do more damage than they're worth with an influx pouring into our small spaces and taking photos and moving stock around without buying a thing. Other times, they spend up big and find our unique stalls a marvel. It's always a little stressful having so many people arrive all at once but it's part of Parisian life, and without tourists our businesses would struggle to survive.

'I hope so too.' I give them a wave and go to tell Pascale. 'A big tour group is on the way.'

He groans and cups his face. 'Should we close up, pretend we're not here?'

I shake my head, as always slightly baffled by him and the way he actively avoids customers. That doesn't stop them buying though, even if he treats them appallingly. I just don't get it. He spends more time bashing at his typewriter than anything else.

'Are you joking?'

'Should I be?'

'Don't you need to sell a typewriter or two to survive?'

'I sell plenty.'

'You could probably sell more if you didn't ignore customers all the time. Yesterday, I saw a woman hovering behind you for a good ten minutes before you finally acknowledged her.'

He leans against the door frame and folds his arms, his biceps bulging all over the place like he's some kind of muscle man. Urgh, that's probably why he draws so many people in – that animal magnetism of his. While I admit it is *slightly* alluring, it's also obvious to me that he's the type of guy that would stomp all over a heart and not have a care in the world about doing so. He's just so one-dimensional with his gruff exterior and fiery temperament. I can't see Pascale ever wooing a woman, and as for romance, I bet it's not in his vocabulary.

'So...? I was busy.'

'You were typing?'

'And?'

I take a deep breath. Why is he so monosyllabic with me? 'So, don't you think you should have stopped typing for a moment and helped your customer find what she was looking for? Your customer service reflects on us all.'

He screws up his face. 'How?'

'We all get lumped together when tourists post reviews like "Upstairs at Marché Dauphine" so it would be nice if you were considerate of our businesses and the fact that while you might not care about turnover, we do.'

'I care, just not enough to stop working when I get a bunch of customers asking me every little thing about vintage typewriters and then they go off and buy them online anyway. If they're serious buyers, they'll get my attention.'

I shake my head so hard I get dizzy. 'How can you know that for sure? What if they're shy, or hesitant to interrupt you while you're typing?'

'Then they miss out on my sparkly personality and witty repartee.' He grins and it transforms his villainous face and makes him seem affable, but it doesn't last and I suppose it's not genuine since he was being sarcastic.

'What are you typing, by the way? Your memoirs?' I try and fail to hide my smile. He's just the right sort of egotistical to pen a whole book about himself.

'Something like that.'

'*How To Offend Customers and Get Away With It.*'

'I'll take that title into consideration.'

Our chat is interrupted as a horde of smiley-faced shoppers thunder up the stairs. They're wide-eyed and walking fast with that whole just-arrived-in-Paris energy I see so often.

'*Mon dieu.*' The fiery facade is back. 'This is not going to be fun.'

'That's the spirit.' I shake my head and jog back to my stall, greeting the influx of customers with a cheery '*Bonjour!*'

* * *

Later that afternoon, I'm tidying Ephemera after the whirlwind of visitors from the tour group. The money they spent more than makes up for the mess they left behind. Mostly, stock has been put back in the wrong spot, and there's a few discarded water bottles and empty takeaway coffee cups. Not too bad considering. I've got a spring in my step after a busy day serving customers who were really taken by the idea of old diaries and love letters and purchased them as keepsakes of their time in Paris.

'I found out something interesting just now.' Geneviève slides on to the chaise longue.

'Oh?' I say.

'I was just doing my usual drumming up of potential business for Paris Cupid.'

She knows very well that Paris Cupid is on hold for new matches at the moment while I catch up. I narrow my eyes at her. 'Drumming up business for a matchmaking site that's on hiatus, or putting your nose into other people's love lives because you can't help yourself when it comes that sort of thing?' Honestly, Geneviève would make a fabulous matchmaker. When it comes to romance and, let's be frank, sex, she is invested. She only wants everyone to be as content as she is in that department and doesn't mind poking and prodding to get information out of people.

'OK, fine, it's a bit of both.'

I raise a brow.

'So after the tour group left, I innocently glided over to that devilishly handsome Pascale and asked him if he'd heard of the site and what he thought of joining.' She gives me a coy smile.

'*Innocently glided?* I'd like to see that! You only did that to find out if he was single, didn't you?'

'*Oui.*'

'And...?' Not that I'm the least bit interested. It's only if he is in a relationship, I'll be very surprised. He doesn't seem the commitment type to me.

'He said he wouldn't ever use a matchmaker and it didn't matter anyway as he's already met someone recently he has feelings for... What do you make of that?'

I glance over towards him. As usual, he's at his desk, typing away. I didn't have a moment in the rush to see if he was engaging with the tour group or ignoring customers as usual, but I can hazard a guess it was the latter. I'm intrigued as to what sort of type he'd go for. But I don't dare admit that to Geneviève or she'll be off and running, taking my interest as a sign I like the guy, which I do not.

'I suppose everyone deserves love, even alpha males,' I say with some reluctance.

'What sort of answer is that?'

'A truthful one.'

She guffaws. 'Well, I also asked Felix and Benoit if they'd heard about Paris Cupid and if they liked the idea of writing love letters to woo a new flame.'

I perk up a bit. I'm keen to know what they thought. There's something rather sweet about both men. I can't quite put my finger on it, but I feel a real sense of ease around them. Felix the cheeky flirt, and Benoit, shy and handsome. 'What did they say?'

'They both said they've got feelings for someone they've recently met.'

'All three men said the same thing?'

'A version of it, *oui*.'

'Interesting.'

'I found their use of "recently" *very* interesting indeed.'

'What do you...' I study her expression to see what she's getting at. 'Oh, Geneviève, only you could put two and two together and wind up with ten.'

'What?' She puts a hand to her heart. 'Think of the market reshuffle. Suddenly they work across from two very beautiful women, and while I'm all for dating younger men, in fact I prefer it, I don't sense they're attracted to me, more's the pity.' She gazes lovingly over to Pascale and gives him a saucy wink when he catches her looking. He laughs and sends an exaggerated wink back. Why is he so laid back when it comes to Geneviève and always irked around me? It's infuriating.

'You're reaching, Geneviève.'

'I'm not. I'm telling you now, I can feel the sexual tension in this place and eventually something is going to go *bang*.'

I can only laugh. Geneviève is desperate for me to find love that she'll magic it up if she can. Still, while I clean around Geneviève, I think of Benoit, the man with the soul of a poet, and wonder who he's crushing on. Perhaps Geneviève could do a little more digging in that regard...

14

August arrives, the last of the summer months. Part of me pines for autumn. I love the cooler weather, the crunch of fallen leaves and the cosiness reading a good book in front of the fire. I briskly walk to Saint Ouen Flea Market, having overstayed feeding the cats at the cemetery on my way to work. Blame Marmalade, who curled up on my lap like a baby. I didn't have the heart to move her as she primped and preened.

I avert my gaze as I pass the flower stall, but Coraline clocks me. She never misses a thing, that woman, and she practically chases me as I dash past her with a look on my face that implies I've got places to be. Her footsteps quicken and she yells for me to stop.

Honestly, she's a menace to society. There's no getting away from her. 'Are you actually *chasing* me, Coraline?'

'What? No!' Spots of pink appear on her cheeks.

'What is it? I have to open Ephemera.'

'Emmanuel has left Paris, gone to an ashram in India. I'm guessing whoever this new fiancée is, she's really bad news. What do you say to that?'

'Namaste?' While I'm teasing Coraline, my mind is reeling. Émilienne regularly goes on retreats to India and takes them very seriously. There's no way she'd invite Emmanuel if he wasn't the genuine article.

The retreats are a religious experience for her. Even his celebrity status might have given her pause as she wouldn't want to create any fuss at an ashram.

'Very funny, Lilou.'

'How did you find out?'

'The tabloids – how else? He did another interview about finding enlightenment. Do you think they're paying him for the interviews and that's why he's doing so many?'

'Probably.' How can Émilienne be buying this? The woman I know would recoil at her significant other sharing to the world their every movement. Just what is going on? And why haven't they completed their feedback survey? Perhaps there's no internet at the ashram, and she usually switches off, unplugs from society for a while. But wait... How is he still doing interviews then? Her brief text about switching off for a bit was a week ago, so they must have left then. The frustration of not knowing how Émilienne really feels builds. 'Why do you care?'

Coraline's face falls. 'You think I'm an overzealous fan, and maybe I am, it's just that Emmanuel Roux has been on my TV screen for the last fifteen years. How strange it will be coming home and not seeing his face. It's a comfort to watch him being flirtatious, charming, using all those funny one-liners only he could get away with.' There's a sag to her shoulders as if her body has deflated alongside her mood. 'It's like losing a best friend, a friend you can never ever speak to again. I feel a sense of abandonment...' At that confession, she flushes deep scarlet.

It all clicks into place. This is a clear case of an imaginationship: a crush that develops in your mind and builds up over a long period. Ah, how I've misjudged Coraline's motivations. Emmanuel's character on TV is the Emmanuel she adores from afar, a fictional man who she has grown to love. But haven't we all done that? I've fallen for many an author of letters from the past because of the way they wrote about love and desire. I'm annoyed at myself for not seeing it sooner – Coraline is lonely, just like the rest of us.

I give her arm a useless pat. 'Oh, I get it now. It makes sense you feel the way you do, and honestly, I think we've all been there.'

She gives me a wobbly smile. 'Now he's chanting "om" instead of learning his lines. I'll miss him. Miss him more than is probably healthy.'

I don't dare say, but it won't be long before they're back in Paris, eating buttery creamy foods and drinking carafes of wine. My friend Ém is happy to escape every now and then for healthier pursuits but it's more of a circuit breaker, a detox from life for a bit. I toy with an idea, not sure if I should suggest it or not. After all, Coraline is still a gossip aficionado, and I'm opening myself up to all sorts of issues if she finds out about my alter ego. As I survey the sadness in her eyes, and can almost hear the breaking of her heart, the choice is made for me. Everyone deserves love, and this type of bruised heart is exactly what Paris Cupid caters to. We've shared a confidence, a secret of hers that has changed my opinion of her in some significant way.

'Have *you* ever thought about signing up to this Paris Cupid? Perhaps getting to know someone else in a slow, gradual way might be a nice distraction?'

'Replacing him with a pen pal? Not my style.' Her words are heavy with sarcasm. Why do they always fight it?

'It's not for everyone, I guess.'

'Have *you* thought about joining?'

I give a loose shrug. 'Why not? What's not to love about getting to know a stranger in a slower way? Remember when you'd tell each customer of yours that each flower tells a story, to be careful what they bunched together because they all have meanings? You could write about what they mean to you, and how you came to be a florist.'

She folds her arms. 'Floriography, the language of flowers. It used to fascinate me what each bloom meant and that you could send a message in the most secretive of ways. And then I just lost interest… after my worst break-up to date.'

'What happened?' I can't recall ever seeing her with a significant other.

Coraline gives me a sad smile. 'I helped him when he needed it and once he was back on his feet, he left – just like that.' Her lip quivers as if she's battling to rein in her emotions. 'It feels like an abandonment each time, like I've served my purpose and whatever we had together had no real depth, for them at least. It's a bit of a pattern in my love life.'

'Maybe joining Paris Cupid might help change that pattern?'

She takes a moment to contemplate it. 'Why am I holding on to the past so hard? I need to get back out there and find love, rediscover the hidden language of flowers again.'

I give her an encouraging smile. 'So you'll join Paris Cupid?'

The light in her eyes dims. 'Paris Cupid is closed for new members. Maybe it's closed for good? That would be just my luck – to get excited about something and have it taken away from me.'

'Why don't you email them about your passion for floriography? They might make an exception? After all, that's a truly romantic topic to be able to share with a potential match. It's worth a shot.'

'*Oui.* It's worth a shot. I'm not saying I can't find love myself. But I do like the idea of changing the pattern.'

'Makes total sense to me.'

'Oh… I forgot. Guillaume is waiting for you at the pâtisserie, Maison du Croquembouche. He said it was urgent.'

'Coraline!' Just when I think we've mended bridges, she spends ages chatting to me while Guillaume is tapping his foot waiting impatiently for me. We never meet outside of Ephemera or Montmartre cemetery for business meetings, so this is strange. I hurry along, hoping it's nothing serious.

* * *

The display window of Maison du Croquembouche is full of colourful macarons and mouthwatering gâteaux. In pride of place is a breathtaking croquembouche tower, made up of profiteroles laced together with gossamer-thin strings of spun toffee.

Peering in, I see Guillaume chatting to Désirée. Guillaume's other great love is canelés and while Maison du Croquembouche is famous for its profiterole towers, it's also known for making the best syrupy rum-infused caramelised crusted canelés.

'Ah, Lilou!' Guillaume calls, and I enter the shop, assailed with the sweet scent of cakes. I search his face for clues for this out-of-the-blue meeting but find his features amiable.

'*Bonjour*. Is everything OK?' Guillaume appears healthy and happy. I relax my shoulders and say, 'Coraline said it was urgent.'

He frowns. 'Lilou, don't you ever answer your phone? Really, you're impossible to do business with.'

I grin at his usual gruffness. It's just his way. He likes order in a disorderly world and unfortunately, I'm a shambles in that regard. 'I didn't hear it ring.' I search my handbag and come up empty, remembering too late that I put my phone on charge before I took a shower this morning, and there it's stayed. '*Désolé*, I forgot my phone. But here I am, in the flesh.'

'Late as usual.'

'Well, we didn't have an appointment for a business meeting, and if we did we always meet at Montmartre cemetery, and then I take your deliveries on Fridays, so you'll have to give me some leeway, *non*?'

'*Oui, oui*. You're probably right, but still, I haven't got all day. And I did call you many times, and you didn't answer…'

I cut him off before he continues highlighting all my foibles, of which there are many according to him. 'Don't keep me in suspense. What did you call me for?'

Désirée interrupts, order pad in hand. '*Bonjour*, Lilou. How are you?'

I've always liked Désirée. She's the one person who never sticks her nose in anyone's business and always has a smile on her face. I put this breeziness down to the fact she's surrounded by sugary sweet treats. Who *wouldn't* be joyful surrounded by the art of patisserie all day long? It's the perfect type of workplace where you can eat your feelings if you're down. And from the range of gâteaux on offer, you wouldn't be down long. There are rows of *éclair au chocolat*, *tarte au fraises* with ruby red berries, millefeuille, which means 'a thousand sheets' in French, alluding to the delicate layers that make up the pastry, and *crème pâtissière*. Pâtisserie is an art form and one that is highly regarded in France.

'I'm well, thanks, Désirée.' I get lost for a moment, starting at the delights in the display fridge. 'What's good today?'

She lifts a thick and lustrous brow. 'May I recommend the chocolate ganache cake with Amarena cherries? It's a new menu item and proving very popular.'

'*Oui.*' My stomach rumbles, drawing a frown from my conservative dining companion. 'And I'll have a café crème, please.'

'Won't be long.'

'*Merci.*' I face Guillaume. 'She's always so jovial. It's like she absorbs the sweetness in the air.'

As usual, he disrupts my musings with an impatient sigh. 'Honestly, Lilou, if you poured half the effort you use to wonder about people into your business, you could expand your shop and get into the antique furniture trade.'

I reel back. 'I couldn't think of anything worse. Why would I take on all that work? Not to mention selling antique furniture doesn't interest me in the slightest.' Did Pascale's throwaway comment about there being more value in other antiques get to Guillaume? The profit margins on the ephemera I sell may be markedly less, but it's more valuable in so many other ways.

Guillaume does the obligatory head shake, making his disappointment known. Sure, there's a lot more money in other avenues of antiques, but if they don't inspire me, what's the point? There's no need for expansion. I'm happy in my little stall at the Marché Dauphine. Like most people, Guillaume presumes I have a lot of downtime as we're only open three days a week in the market, but clearly that isn't the case when I spend the other days hunting for stock and spending my nights working as Paris Cupid.

Désirée appears with my coffee and cake and my stomach rumbles its thanks. '*Magnifique!*'

'*Merci.* Guillaume, your *crêpe au jambon* will be along shortly.'

He lets out a weary sigh. 'The bane of my life, always waiting, waiting, waiting.'

Désirée shakes her head and doesn't play into his grumbling. 'You'll survive, Guillaume,' she says as she walks away with a laugh.

He clears his throat and says, 'You're curious as to this unexpected visit.' He has a faraway look in his eyes. It's almost as if he's talking to himself.

'*Oui.*' While I'm eager to know, Guillaume is not the type to do business over crepes and café crème, so I presume it's a personal matter. I don't rush him; I let the silence sit between us until he's ready to share.

I'm halfway through my café crème when he speaks. 'I wrote a letter. But I can't send it.' He casts his gaze to the table. Gone is the amiable façade of the Frenchman enjoying café life. This is a worried man who can't meet my eye.

A wave of guilt washes over me because my urging him to join Paris Cupid is making him doubt himself like this. His melancholy is almost palpable, and I struggle with how best to support him in this moment. I pat the top of his hand while he gathers his thoughts.

I truly believe female companionship is what he needs most. A friend to dine with, attend the theatre with. All he does is work, and that's not the French way. The workaholic ideal is abhorred here. There's no balance, and Parisians enjoy *après* work more than anything.

'So you wrote the letter but you couldn't send it because…?' He nods and averts his gaze once more. I take a moment to decipher why he can't look me in the eye. Ah. 'You're feeling guilty about Mathilde?'

'*Oui*,' he says, his voice cracking on the shortest of words.

I swallow a lump in my throat. It's difficult to see the sadness return to his eyes as if it were just yesterday Mathilde left. This new situation has clearly reawakened a lot of memories of his beloved and reopened wounds that were once closed. What can I say to appease his guilt? When the end neared for Mathilde, she and I had many a chat about what would come next for Guillaume, and she did suggest he find a companion when he was ready. But will he believe me? She couldn't tell him herself. She tried, but he wouldn't listen. Talk of her impending death he outlawed completely. The head-in-sand approach was his way of dealing with it. And I understood. Death is so final, it was easier for him to pretend it wasn't drawing near.

I take his hand across the table. 'I don't have to say it, do I? You already know.'

Slowly, he lifts his glassy eyes and meets mine. 'What if she didn't mean it?'

Is there anything more beautiful than a man who wants to keep his promise about loving her eternally for both their lifetimes? I fight back my own tears, as his fall. For a moment, we sit in these roiled-up feelings. Love and death. The cornerstones of life. I don't want to dole out platitudes because they just don't land in situations like this. Mathilde *was* a rare gem and he will always love her, but that doesn't mean he can't hold another in his heart too.

'You know, Guillaume, that you can't keep living life this way. You're only half here. You subsist on work, and that's no way to be. When you're not working, or travelling for work, you hide away in your apartment. You don't ever dine out in the evenings any more, you don't go to the opera, the theatre, and you loved doing those things.' I've invited him often enough, but he always refuses.

It strikes me, I've been doing the same thing. Sure, I can use the excuse that Paris Cupid is stealing my nights away, but if I'm honest, I was hiding out in my apartment before then too. *Le scandale* made me feel that a bit of hibernation was in order and then I just stopped going out in the evenings altogether. Eating out alone gets a little tedious and while I have plenty of friends, I tend to catch up with them during the day when I'm crisscrossing Paris meeting suppliers.

Guillaume's lip wobbles as he recognises the truth in what I say.

'Hiding away is not honouring Mathilde.' He tries to compose himself, so I continue. 'We get one life, a short time on this merry-go-round. You've been incredibly lucky in love until Mathilde was called away, but that doesn't mean that *you* have to stop living too.'

He nods. 'She wrote me a letter, you know, and left it inside my pillowcase.'

I smile. That's so Mathilde. 'And?'

'She said I was a stubborn old man.'

We share a burst of laughter. Mathilde was not one to pull punches, especially when it came to her husband. 'She got that right.'

'She said there'd come a time when I was ready to find love again. I'd feel it. But how do I know that this is the time? What if I'm wrong?'

'What if you're not?'

'I'm too old for this caper.'

'Just think of this like having a pen pal. A friend to correspond with.

I'm sure Clementine has all the same reservations as you. There's nothing here suggesting there's any expectation except friendship to begin with.'

'Can I write that in my letter, do you think?'

'Why not? Honesty is the best policy.'

'Thank you, Lilou. A new friend wouldn't be so bad. Forgive an old man his tears.' He takes a handkerchief from his top pocket and scrubs his face, while I send Mathilde my thanks. I bet she's orchestrated this from wherever she is. She was the type of woman not to let death stand in her way.

15

After meeting Guillaume at the pâtisserie, I head to Ephemera. When I get upstairs, Felix calls me over, cheeky smile at the ready. 'A courier left this for you.' It's a box of stock from a new Parisian supplier.

'*Merci!*'

'Do you ever write love letters, Lilou?'

I stop short. I have never written a love letter and that fact has gone unnoticed by me until this very moment. 'I've been so focused on finding them that it's never occurred to me to write one myself, even with a previous flame. Why is that?' I'm not going to tell Felix that I've been single since *le scandale*, and before that my relationships were so short-lived that I didn't get to the pining-for-them stage where I'd have felt comfortable pouring my heart and soul out in love letters.

'Ah, because they haven't been the right man for you! What you need is a ginger-haired prince of men, one who will...'

'What? Make me stay out until the witching hour and drink far too much champagne?'

'Now that sounds like a fun night!'

As always, I don't quite know how to take Felix's flirtatious nature. It comes across so jovial that it's impossible to take seriously. But is that his way of showing me he's interested in me? He can't be though; he flirts with everyone just the same, men and women alike. It's just his bubbly, fun persona. 'Thanks for this.' I hold up the box. 'Maybe we can get that glass of wine after work soon?'

He makes a great show of clutching his heart as if in some sort of rapture. 'You'll make all my dreams come true.'

I cock my head. 'You're simply a showman.'

'I'll take that as a compliment.'

'*Au revoir.*'

'*Bonne journée.*'

I unlock my stall and wheel out the display tables, taking great care not to look in Pascale's direction. I don't bother to light candles or play music, not because I'm conceding to him but because I'd rather open the box of my new treasures.

As I'm going through it, a greeting card falls out of the bundle. I pick it up to inspect it. It has a pressed picture of Cupid on the front. Inside is printed too, with a phrase that reads:

> To the woman who makes my heart sing. I wish I could tell you how I feel.

My pulse quickens. Has someone figured out I'm Cupid? If so, the message inside doesn't make much sense.

Just as I'm mulling it over, Geneviève sashays in, a cloud of perfume following in her wake. 'What's that?' she asks. 'If you keep frowning over your work you're going to age before your time.' She attempts to smooth the furrow between my eyes with a fingertip. 'Tell me what's got you daydreaming like that?'

'I've got a stack of new letters from a Parisian supplier, and this card was in the box. Do you think someone knows I'm Paris Cupid? This wasn't part of my order...' It's so *specific*. It has to be. 'The supplier – it can't be her.' I barely know the woman. We chat via email and aside from a few pleasantries about the weather, we only talk shop.

Geneviève takes it from my hands and dons her spectacles. 'This looks like the type of personalised hand-printed cards Felix makes.'

'He accepted the delivery because I wasn't here!' The card is like one of Felix's made on his vintage press with his luxe paper and traditional font. 'But there's no way he could know that I'm Cupid, is there?'

Geneviève frowns over the top of her glasses. 'Do you think I've made it obvious it's connected to you when I've visited market vendors and tried to spread the word about Paris Cupid? I hope I haven't blown your cover.' She massages her temples as if the idea gives her a headache.

'*Non*, Geneviève, I don't think so. You're always prying into everyone's love lives, so that's not out of the ordinary for you.'

She laughs. '*Oui*. I love love. So perhaps it's just coincidence that Felix took delivery of the card and the card just happened to have a Cupid on it.'

'Doesn't that seem like one too many coincidences? Felix is funny and flirty, but maybe that's a cover and his plan is to... extort me, or something nefarious.' His open nature could be a sham. 'It's always the ones you least suspect, isn't it? The ones who hide in plain sight.'

Geneviève's eyes widen as if she hasn't considered such a thing before. She probably needs to lay off the romance novels for a bit and read a thriller every now and then. Her face dissolves into laughter. When she finally composes herself, she says, 'And the gold medal for jumping to conclusions goes to Lilou!'

I shake my head. 'It's not out of the realm of possibility.'

'It makes no sense. If he sent you the card, it's because he's got a soft spot for you, not because he's aware that you're Cupid and wants to toy with you. You watch too many of those true crime documentaries.' My guilty pleasure. 'Don't forget he said he'd met someone recently he's got feelings for – could it be that our flirty happy-go-lucky neighbour is taken with... *you*?'

If I was matching myself on Paris Cupid, I would choose someone like Felix. He's a bright light and would make every date fun, but there's just a niggle there I can't quite figure out. It's probably because we all get the Felix treatment – mega-watt smile, jokes and laughter as if he doesn't take life too seriously. Or I'd match myself with Benoit, a deep thinker, quiet and studious, who I sense would have a really romantic side to him. Often I suggest to my matches to step outside their comfort zone and allow me to choose them a type of person they claimed they'd *never* choose for themselves; so then shouldn't I be following my own advice? That would mean taking the risk with a man like Pascale who just clearly isn't the one for me. Is there anything under that gruff exterior, except hardened muscle? I think not.

'It's just an odd way to go about it, stuffing the card in a delivery, don't you think?' I ask Geneviève.

'Odd or *romantic*?'

'Wait.' I'm reminded of the letter I found in the earlier delivery from Guillaume. Written by a man who didn't believe in love – until he did. Why are these strange missives appearing out of the blue? Are they connected?

'Geneviève, have a look at this...' I go to my desk and find the typewritten letter and hand it over. Geneviève takes a seat at my desk and reads.

'Typed. Abrupt. A different tone to the card. They can't be connected.'

I lean over her shoulder and read it again too. It strikes me that the letter isn't written *to* anyone. It's more like a journal entry.

'So, let's take stock for a minute. We have what we think is a handpressed card. A frankly written, typed letter. These can't be accounted for with your suppliers? Have any others appeared like these? A man yearning for a woman but doesn't have the courage to tell her how he feels?'

I frown. 'I do have one! Pierre, the bookseller by the Seine, gave me a *Madame Bovary* book. The letter tucked inside it was tissue-thin, and the parchment was so delicate with age. The calligraphy writing faded almost beyond recognition. The letter was written by man who walked Parisian streets alone at night, contemplating a woman he loves from afar. Wait, I have a photo of it on my phone.' I find my phone and pull up the picture of the delicate letter.

Geneviève reads it and says, 'There's a theme here then! A connection?'

Ah, she's a real romantic at heart. She wants to believe there's a mystery here but there isn't. A few misplaced letters, or mixed up deliveries. It's bound to happen when I'm buying from sources all over the place. 'Not really. I buy letters just like this all the time.'

'Full of unrequited love?'

'All types of love.'

'I don't know, Lilou,' she says, tapping her chin with a finger. 'It just seems so strange to suddenly have these little... gifts appearing, and they have the same premise. They love a woman and can't tell her. Don't you think?'

I think of the pressed rose I found a while back. I'd presumed it had been misplaced by a customer. 'There was a flower here too, but it's probably nothing. Left behind. Forgotten in someone's haste.'

Geneviève gets that preoccupied look in her eyes that I know all too well. It means she's not listening and is off in fairyland dreaming about romance.

* * *

That afternoon, I'm tidying up after a flurry of customers when there are raised voices from downstairs. I strain to hear who it might be and what they're arguing about. Pascale stops typing and looks up before locking eyes with me.

'What are they saying?' I ask as their voices rise, but they're too garbled for me to untangle.

'He's saying her display table is far too wide.'

I roll my eyes. 'He is not.'

Pascale shrugs. 'He *could* be saying that.'

'Only a *roi des cons* would say such a silly thing.'

'Are you calling me the king of idiots?'

I lift a shoulder. 'Who can say?'

He shakes his head. 'Why do you want to hear what they're arguing about anyway?'

'Why do you?'

'Makes the day go faster.'

The voices quieten down. 'Guess we'll never know.'

16

I'm meeting Geneviève on the left bank of the river to hunt through a nighttime antique market held in mid-August. Under the guise of searching for stock for Ephemera and Palais we spend time shopping at various market and vintage shops across the city, searching for curios and all sorts of weird and wonderful. You never know what you're going to find. Some days we come away empty-handed, other days rich with spoils.

I walk under the shade of horse chestnut trees as I spot Geneviève. She stands out in the crowd wearing a scarlet wrap dress, looking every inch a movie star while she chats to a vendor who we befriended a while ago who keeps an eye out for love letters and diaries for me.

When I get closer, I note the stiffness in Geneviève's posture. Outwardly, she's chatting and laughing away, but inwardly something is amiss. When I get to the table, I make pleasantries with the vendor while I scheme up a believable way to get Geneviève away from here so I can ask her what's wrong.

'Sorry, Lilou,' the vendor says. 'I haven't come across much this month.'

I wave her apologies away. 'Thank you for keeping a look out. Geneviève, would you mind joining me for a drink before we peruse the market? It's been one of those days…' I make a great show of appearing frazzled and fraught but must have overplayed it because Geneviève narrows her eyes ever so slightly.

But really, it has been one of those days. I made the mistake of checking Paris Cupid as soon as I woke up only to find a number of complaints about the sudden hiatus. There were also a tonne of enquiries from journalists pushing for interviews and asking for the inside scoop on Emmanuel Roux. Not all of them believe he's legitimately in love either. The press messages ranged from friendly enquiries to downright threatening.

'Of course, Lilou. We have all evening so there's no rush.' Geneviève links her arm in mine. We walk along the path as boats chug along the river. Mostly they're dinner cruises. Guests stand on the deck, champagne glasses in hand, fairy lights twinkling above them. I often wonder what it would feel like to be a tourist in Paris. It must be magical to visit the beautiful city and try and take in all the sights, the history, and the culture.

'What is it?' I ask as I turn my head to her, moonlight reflecting off the inky Seine.

Geneviève glances behind us before she says, 'So, I joined a few of those Paris Cupid online groups.'

I wrinkle my nose. I've figured it's best to ignore those types of sites; they can only be full of speculation and gossip. 'Which groups? The ones mentioned in the tabloids?'

'*Oui*. It intrigued me. I've been checking these groups sporadically, keeping an eye on what they're saying about finding out the mastermind. Mostly they were positive posts. There were a range of Parisians chatting about Paris Cupid helping them find true love, so they were there to share their story and encourage others to join.'

'OK, that's good news. I've matched over one hundred couples now so it's still going strong, even though new sign-ups are suspended. I'm just not sure who is genuine and who isn't now it's been exposed like this.'

'You can only do your best, Lilou. And if the match doesn't work then you try again, just like you've been doing so far.'

'So the groups weren't saying anything else? It all seems rather tame.'

'There are a few members pushing the group to find out the identity of Cupid. At first, the majority were adamant about the importance of keeping Cupid's identity a secret. Lately, more are switching sides. It *seems*' – she exhales an angry breath – 'that since applications have been suspended, it's roused their suspicious nature. That or they're just some really convincing online trolls who are set to get as many other converts as possible on board. I feel terrible, Lilou, because it was my idea to put membership applications on hold.'

Poor Geneviève really does look like someone took the wind from her sails. She leans heavily against me as we walk. I want to reassure her, even though the idea of them trying to find me is a worrying one. 'It's not your fault. I'd have done the same thing *without* your advice. There's just no way I can handle all those applications alone. I'm still going through the influx after the very first Emmanuel Roux interviews. It's a lot of work so I dread to think how many more would have come in if I didn't shut it down.'

She nods, her lips pressed in a tight line. I haven't convinced her.

'Geneviève, seriously. Without your guidance I actually might have pulled the plug on the whole thing, and I'm so thankful I didn't. There's definitely a future for Paris Cupid, but it's going to take some planning, some restructuring to keep it exclusive and manageable.'

'You're being very kind. Perhaps you need to read some of the posts. They really want to find you. And really, is that so bad?'

I try to hide my worry, but I'm sure it's evident in my eyes. 'If only my dating history wasn't such an unequivocal disaster story.' I can see the headlines now and know just what they'd lead with. It doesn't bear thinking about, especially as I don't want Geneviève to stress further. 'Let's not worry. Maybe they'll get bored and move on?'

'Maybe you need to take control of the narrative?'

'How?'

'Tell them to stop searching for you or it will take the magic away. Tell them you're only doing this if your anonymity is guaranteed.'

'Would that not provoke them further?' It's not that I'm ashamed of my dating history, it's only that how can they trust in me to find their perfect match when I can't find that for myself? What sort of matchmaker is single at the prime of her life? And being that my last relationship was with a married man will surely not come over well, no matter how much I protest my innocence.

Concern lines her face. 'It might. It's so hard to know what the best course of action is, Lilou. It bothers me they speak about you in such a way. Some of the posts are nasty and I just cannot fathom why.'

'It's the online world, Geneviève.' None of the nastiness surprises me. Not in the slightest. It's why I went with the love letter angle for my matches. 'People act differently over a keyboard.'

'You're right. I'm sure they'll soon move on to the next thing.'

'I'm certain they'll soon get bored. Don't they always with these things?'

17

The next day I head toward the Marais to visit the Musée des Archives Nationales housed inside the Hôtel de Soubise. It's a museum full of words, of history, and the place I go to when I need to reconnect and remember that I am just one person trying to make a difference in this great big world. The national archives are a good reminder that there have been many a conflict greater than mine. I'm taking a self-care day. A full twenty-four hours where I don't think about Paris Cupid or Ephemera. A battery recharge.

Inside I make my way around the displays, as always so grateful for those who preserved these relics from history. There's so much to see, and the exhibits are regularly changed. Today I find the diary of King Louis XVI. I read Mary Antoinette's last letter written only hours before her beheading. It highlights her strength of will, her love for her family and the hopes her children wouldn't avenge her death. I'm not sure if she truly had no inkling her children were at risk, or if she was simply hoping for the best. Either way, her letter gives me chills and brings her to life right in that very room.

While it's fascinating to view Napoleon's last will and testament, more exciting to me is a coded love letter that only the two lovers could decipher. Why did they write in code? Were they forbidden to be together? Did their love endure? I'm taken with the idea that they devised a plan to write in code so their romance was kept private. Did they end up together? Did someone stand in their way?

I'm stuck in dreamland about two strangers from hundreds of years ago as I turn and bump into a man who is bent at the waist reading a plaque. 'Sorry,' I say, embarrassed to have knocked into him from behind and forced him forward. When he stands, I stifle a groan. What is it about this guy and my spatial awareness? If only I could meet-cute a man I'm actually interested in!

'Li, do you think you might need glasses?'

I roll my eyes. 'It's Li*lou*, Pascale. And why would I need glasses?'

'So far you've run into my chest, thrown hot coffee over me, and today you've walked directly into my... *derriere*. If I didn't know better, I'd say things are escalating.'

Mon Dieu. I scrub my face. '*Excusez-moi?* I think the real issue here is you manspread all over the place and making it impossible for people to move around your... your enormous frame.'

'Are you suggesting my physique is... too big?'

There's not an ounce of fat on his body as I'm sure he well knows. He must stare at himself in the mirror as he lifts weights or whatever fit people do in order to bulk up like that. It's not from eating croissants, that's for sure.

I cock my head. 'I'm doing no such thing. Yet again, you're trying to turn this around, making me look like the bad person.'

'*Moi?*' He plays the innocent by widening his eyes and raising his brow. This guy is next level.

'*Oui, toi.*'

'Look—'

I hold up a hand. 'Don't.'

He bites down on his lip as if to stop a smile and it's really rather distracting. 'Apologies, Lilou. I seem to have trouble communicating with you and I'm sure it's all my fault.'

Is he being sarcastic? This is his way, always confusing things. 'Well, I won't argue with that.' He grins, putting me off balance once more.

Why do I never feel quite right around Pascale? It's like he interferes with the energy around me.

'What are you doing here?' he asks.

'Are you joking?'

'Right. Stupid question.' He rubs the back of his neck as an awkward silence falls between us. 'What I should have said was, did you see the coded love letter? It reminded me of you.'

'Oh?' What does he *mean* by that?

'You sell love letters, right?'

A blush creeps up my neck. Why am I having so much trouble talking to him? I'm reading into things that aren't there! It's hot in here, or I'm feverish. Perhaps I didn't eat enough breakfast and my blood sugars are all over the place.

Pascale stares into my eyes with so much fervour I almost forget what we were discussing. Eventually, my mind reboots and I remember. 'I did see the coded love letter. It's a shame that men aren't as romantic in modern times.' I shrug as if it's not a big deal that romance is almost dead, dead, dead. For me, anyway.

He folds his arms across his muscular chest. I do my best to avoid dropping my gaze but I am really quite intrigued by the way his biceps bulge out all over the place. I've never dated a man who is quite as athletic as Pascale. Not that I intend to, either. More time building muscle is less time reading, unless he got his physique from lifting hardbacks, and that I highly doubt. He doesn't seem the type who'd spend a lazy day in bed with a book. And really, that's vital in a partner. But if he's not a reader, why is he at the national archives?

'You have a low opinion of me, or of all men?' His voice is softer, as if he wants an honest answer, not a sarcastic rebuttal, which is the way we usually seem to communicate.

I contemplate the question. 'It's more that I don't understand how as a society we've graduated from writing coded love letters, sending bouquets of flowers with their own unique language, to picking up a handheld device, squinting at a thumbnail-sized picture and finding love that way. I mean, if that works then great! But it hasn't worked for me. I want a love story like the letters I sell.' Why am I being so honest!

'Not just me, obviously. There's plenty of other singletons who want what I want.'

People brush past us, paying no attention to me, but Pascale receives many a double take. Really, can they not see he's not interested? He's more inclined to fall in love with his own reflection.

'Why do you think you can't find a love like that? Is it because you got burned by that guy?'

'Ah...?'

'That day in the market square. I heard the wife yelling at you. You looked so startled, so shocked. I really felt for you.' So he does have a heart under all that muscle? And he remembered me from that small slice of time, like I remembered him. I suppose it was memorable; it's not every day you seen a scorned wife berating the unintentional mistress.

'He – he really broke my heart. He'd ticked all the boxes. The most romantic man I'd ever dated and it turns out it was all based on a lie. It definitely hurt. Perhaps that's why I've sought refuge in other eras, other worlds with love letters and diaries from the past. They give me hope when I feel like there is none.'

Why am I even telling him all of this? By the unsurety in his eyes, he's not romantic in the slightest and its evident now as another silence between us descends.

'I suppose I've never thought about it like that before.'

'It's just one of the things that keep me up at night.' I laugh, trying to lighten the mood.

'Would you like to get coffee?' he asks.

It occurs to me that maybe Pascale isn't as intimidating as he pretends to be. Times like these, it's almost as if he's unsure of himself, or maybe it's more that he doesn't know how I'll react to his invitation since we haven't exactly been friendly with each other.

'Sure. We can take a walk past the Stravinsky fountain too if you like?'

The Stravinsky fountain is a masterpiece featuring sixteen colourful sculptures that move and spray water. There's a surrealist ornamental air to it. It's close to the Centre Pompidou, an architectural phenomenon known as the inside-out building. Paris really has something for every taste.

'*Oui.*'

We head to the fountain, Pascale with his hands deep in his pockets, me trying to keep up with his long-legged pace. 'Are we in a rush?' I walk Parisian fast, but Pascale goes at Olympic walk speed.

'Sorry, I'm used to walking alone.'

'No love interests for you then?' I want to slap my own forehead. Where did that come from?

He gives me the side eye as if he's also surprised I went there. 'Why? Do I seem so unlovable?'

I make a face. 'Erm…'

He lets out a bark of laughter. 'It's OK, you don't have to answer that.'

'Are you sure? Because I can if you want?'

'No, thank you. I've learned quite enough about how I'm lacking today.'

'*Touché.*' There's a current between us at times. He stares at me like he's about to impart a secret or wants to know mine. It's unusual and it sends a jolt through me.

We lapse into a companionable silence. I'm not sure what it is, but opening up to Pascale and him being truly interested in what I had to say has slightly changed my view on him. *Slightly.* Perhaps his gruffness is a defence mechanism? Could it be that he's not as confident as I pegged him for?

When we come to the fountain, I offer to buy coffee. He checks his watch and says, 'Sorry, Lilou, I just remembered an appointment I've got to keep. Let's do this another time?'

And there goes whatever progress I sensed we'd made. The old 'I forgot an appointment' charade. Really, does he think I'm that dense? 'It's fine.' I give him a blustery wave as if I'm too caught up with the stunning kaleidoscope of colour of the sculptures in the Stravinsky fountain.

'No, I mean it. I really am very…' He makes a show of lifting his watch again, as if he's got somewhere to be.

'It's fine. I'm going to grab a coffee. *Au revoir.*' I spin on my heel and join the queue for a nearby coffee kiosk, glad to be away from his unnerving gaze so he doesn't see the hurt in my eyes. Really, how ridiculous am I? Suffering a slightly bruised ego because my work nemesis gave me the brush off. Why then was he the one to suggest a coffee only to change his mind? I suppose it fits with his fickle nature and I remind myself to be on guard around him. While there's something intriguing about him, he's just a walking red flag. Alpha males are off the list no matter how convincing they can be. Why does my brain compute that but not my subconscious?

18

It's a blindingly sunny Wednesday when I take the funicular de Montmartre and disembark at the Sacre-Coeur Plateau. Right next to the Basilica is the famous Sinking House of Montmartre. It's an optical illusion, helped by the position of an opportune grassy knoll so that when the camera is tilted just right it gives the appearance that the great big orange house is sliding into the earth. Well-informed tourists converge in the outdoor space to tilt their cameras to capture the shot, but I come here for the fresh air and the remarkable view over Paris. Most Parisians enjoy the parks and gardens around the city. While there are plenty of exceptions to the rule, most apartments are somewhat compact, so we live outside as much as possible when the weather is fine. As we're coming to the end of August, I want to soak up as many summer days as possible.

I spread out a picnic blanket on the lush green grass and sit, taking in the view from the high vantage point. I've lived in Paris for a big chunk of my life but there's still so much to explore. Today the outdoor area isn't too busy but come sunset that will change. It's a great spot to watch the blue sky change colour as the sun sinks over the sprawling city below.

Now, however, work beckons. I open my laptop, tether it to my phone for internet connection, and commit a solid hour doing Ephemera bookwork, reconciling accounts and answering customer emails and social media queries.

Once I've caught up, I log on to Paris Cupid to work through previously uploaded applications. I scroll through the emails and so many hopefuls who've sent their unlucky-in-love stories that really tug at the heart strings. There's a couple of people who don't want to join but are emailing to say after hearing about Paris Cupid, they've been writing love letters to their husbands or wives and it's given their relationship a boost. I feel a pang of regret as I come to many an email pleading for a chance to get matched even though applications are closed.

How can I steal the chance of real abiding love away from lonely hearts such as these?

Emmanuel Roux might have made my life ten times more difficult by shouting Paris Cupid's praises, resulting in me having to weed out the genuine from the not, but surely I can figure out a way to manage it. But how? I don't want to rush choosing matches. I want them to work, and when they don't, I want time to find them another match.

I feel a renewed sense of purpose this morning because, according to Geneviève, chatter in the online groups has quieted down. Have they become bored of the hunt? I hope so. I hope I can continue doing what I love without worrying about my identity being exposed.

I open one with the subject line: *Paris Cupid: Aide Moi!*

I've been completely obliterated by love. Destroyed. Demolished. Yet again, I fell for a pseudo-heart who disappeared with no explanation. Why do I keep choosing the wrong men? Is it me? I resolved to give love one last chance with Paris Cupid only to find the site closed for applications. If you'll accept one last application, I volunteer! Kiki.

Gah! Kiki is the perfect candidate for Paris Cupid. My fingers hover over the reply button before I stop short. What if Kiki mentions this to others and it creates a furore? Especially if it was shared on one of the online groups. I must be fair to one and all and remember to tread carefully while things are so uncertain.

Which reminds me – I encouraged Coraline to email and plead her case. What was I *thinking*?

I scroll through looking for an email that could belong to her and find it.

> I send this appeal with a tender heart. A friend – actually 'friend' is too strong a word. She works in the same vicinity as me, but I digress. This acquaintance reminded me that as a florist, that I used to care about the language of flowers, their hidden meanings, their secret stories. What could be more enticing than learning by bouquet alone what the sender feels for you? A heliotrope is an expression of eternal love. A Carolina rose warns that love is dangerous. A spider flower is an invitation to elope. But it's so much more than that. You can share your innermost desires with a colourful posy without having to say one single word.

I shake my head at Coraline's description of me but she's right, we're not exactly friends. I get swept away in the evocative language of flowers. I read on:

> Exactly two years, one month, and eleven days ago, I lost the love of my life. He vanished and all he left me was a note to say things weren't working out. He wasn't the first to do this, but I vowed he'd be the last. But still, it crushed me. Looking back, that's when the language flowers speak also went silent. Work became a chore, life became bleak. It's almost like the sun switched off and I slowly shrivelled without that warmth on my face. Without love, what's the point? I'm missing a key nutrient, and that imbalance is causing bitterness to leech into my soul. I'm wildly envious of customers who visit my flower stall, choosing bouquets for their lover; excitement shines in their eyes, radiates from their smiles. It's like a gut punch every time. Romance is alive and well in Paris for those in the light, but not for us

left in the dark, wilting, drooping, becoming brittle. Is there any hope for me, or is this it?

Matches always write a brief history about their love life and give reasons why relationships haven't gone the distance. Reading those is one of the hardest parts of the job – I *feel* their sadness, I relate to it. Usually, they lay the blame at their own feet, their confidence at an all-time low. While Coraline and I might not be the best of friends, my heart still goes out to her. For all her gossiping, I never knew she'd been ghosted in such a callous way and, by the sounds of it, more than once. She's suffered in silence, turned inward. Don't we as humans need solace in times such as those? Why do we attach a sense of shame to it? Outwardly pretend everything is fine, when inside we're crumbling? Everyone deserves love, including Coraline. I might not agree with the way she tattles, but that could very well be a coping mechanism, and who am I to judge?

I'm in a bind. How can I say yes to her and no to the other enquiries? What to do?

'Hello, stranger, you use this place as your office too?'

I snap my laptop shut and paste a smile on my face. '*Bonjour*, Felix.' I shade my face with a hand and gaze up at him, as his red curls blow about in the breeze. '*Oui*, I like the view over Paris.' Did he see what was on the screen? I survey his features for any sign he did, but he's just smiling that same impish grin of his.

'Are you meeting a friend?' I ask. Felix has a laptop bag in one hand and a picnic basket in the other. He shakes his head. 'Figured I'd need stamina to get through all my invoicing while I eat my body weight in camembert and then maybe read a book, all under the guise of working outdoors to soak up some vitamin D.'

'Late night?' I ask as he unsuccessfully stifles a yawn.

'Always. Actually, I went on a literary treasure hunt! One which resulted in finding a hidden speakeasy in the 10th. We then had to solve a riddle to gain admission.'

'Wow, that sounds incredible. What did the treasure hunt itself involve?'

He points to my blanket.

'Sorry, yes, sit, sit.'

Felix takes a corner of the blanket. 'We started at the bookshop Shakespeare and Co.'

Shakespeare and Co is the most famous English language bookshop in all of Paris. An eccentric by the name of George Whitman opened the shop in 1951 and invited all sorts of literary enthusiasts into the fray. He was well known for inviting aspiring writers to work and live in the bookshop. They'd sleep in beds crammed between shelves. These guests were called Tumbleweeds and could stay as long as they liked on the condition that they'd help customers, read a book a day and write a short biography to be filed away with all those who came before. A beat generation, bohemian enclave where all were welcomed as long as they pitched in and loved the written word. The disorderly charm is still evident inside, with double-stacked books and hidden nooks and crannies. Even now you might pull out a book that's been signed by a literary great, hidden in the stacks for all those years.

'We had to find a clue inside, one word that would lead to the next literary venue and the next clue. Harder than first thought, when a bookshop is *full* of words.'

'Sounds like so much fun! Where did you find the word?'

'One of the floors has the tiniest alcove with a desk and a typewriter that had a piece of paper in the reel with only one word: *Procope*. I only found it because I can't see a typewriter just sitting there and not have a go on the keys. As I squished into the small space, I came face to face with it. That word led us to the next place, Café Procope, a café rumoured to be the oldest in Paris, that famous writers such as Voltaire frequented. There we found *his* desk on display and another word. We trekked to the apartment F. Scott and Zelda Fitzgerald first lived in near the Arc di Triomphe, and on it went. Let's just say, I have a new respect for all the plaques around Paris. I've never paid any attention to them before.'

Paris is a joy to discover on foot. There are many plaques that show where literary greats, artists and the like lived and worked. From what I've gathered about Felix, there's always a new adventure on the horizon.

Today is the first time I've seen him suffer any aftereffects in the way of fatigue. Usually, his energy is off the charts, so it's nice to know he *is* human.

'Sounds incredible. So what was the final riddle?'

He arches a brow. 'Why? Do you want to go?'

'Ha!'

'My spine is stiff, my body pale, I'm always ready to tell a tale. What am I?'

'Ah!' I hold up a finger. 'That's too easy. A book!'

Felix leans back on one arm and grins. 'Yes! I guess they were eager to sell the literary cocktails and didn't want guests to fail at the last hurdle. Be warned though, if you do go, they change the riddle every night.'

When was the last time I went out like that? I shudder when I recall attending a night at the Palais Garnier with Mr Married. We'd spent a wonderful night at the opera having a late dinner at Panasia, a fusion restaurant, before walking around the 9th arrondissement stopping every few paces to kiss under the moonlight. Mr Married did things like open doors for me, pull out my chair in bistros, that sort of old school chivalry that I'd thought was dead. After the opera, he stayed at my apartment – I never wanted the night to end. I'd been so swept up in our burgeoning love that my mind drifted to wedding dress styles and venues because I'd been convinced he was *the one*. The love bubble burst early the next morning when his wife confronted me.

I'm lost in thought when Felix taps my knee. 'Earth to Lilou.'

'Sorry, I was a million miles away.' Down the same old rabbit hole of what was not to be. It occurs to me that all of us singletons are facing the same battle, albeit emerging with different battle scars. Why haven't I gone out? Why have I holed up in my tiny box of an apartment and found love for others and not myself? A therapist would have a field day with my predicament. Really, what sort of hypocrite doesn't attempt to find love herself? Sure, I dream about it, but I don't ever actively pursue it for myself.

While Felix fiddles with his laptop, I surreptitiously observe him. Did he send the Cupid card, or is that wishful thinking? If so, is there a spark between us? He's so lovely and flirty and makes me feel adored, but is that just his energetic persona?

'Now...' He catches me staring at him, so I pretend to be gazing just past his shoulder at the sinking house. 'The big question remains. Do we work or do we feast?' He opens up the picnic basket, displaying a range of mouth-watering temptations. *Brie truffé*. *Terrine de Lapin*. *Rillettes*. Served alongside juicy herbaceous olives and a fresh crusty baguette.

'Do you even need to ask?' I joke.

'If I'd known you'd be here I would have included a bottle of wine.'

I laugh. 'It's your lucky day, Felix.'

'It sure is.' He grins, coy smile at the ready.

From my tote, I take an insulated bottle bag. 'Don't judge me, but some workdays are better with a bottle of rosé. But I only have one glass.'

He holds up a finger. 'I have glasses in the picnic basket.'

A man who is always prepared. I wouldn't have pegged Felix for the organised type. We spend the afternoon chatting while intermittently working, but mostly our screensavers bounce around as we get to know each other better. Felix is an open book, and steadier than I'd first thought. When we're silent, I return to pondering about the similarities between Coraline and myself. It's never really hit me before that by shunning love I'm allowing Mr Married to have won. But what's the remedy? Failure to launch is usually a young person's issue, but that's what it feels like in my situation. Would a night out with a flirty friend be just the tonic, or am I setting myself up to fail? Before I can overthink it to its inevitable death, I blurt out, 'I've always wanted to go to Musee des Arts Forains.'

It's a museum full of vintage carnival rides and other antiquities, including the personal collection of Jean-Peal Favand who was an actor who traded in antiquities, just like we do. 'You can even ride on the Manege velocippedique, an historic bicycle carousel that will only move if we cycle hard enough.'

'That sounds just like my level of quirky. I'd love to go. Tonight? Dinner first?'

'Tonight. Dinner would be lovely.'

We make arrangements to meet later that evening.

There are some big decisions that have to be made for Paris Cupid, so reluctantly I say my goodbyes to Felix and head back to my apartment to work in private.

19

Back home at Rue Tourlaque, I'm surprised when I catch a glimpse of my sun-kissed reflection in a small gilded mirror in my living room. My eyes are brighter than usual. Felix has the unique ability to add buoyancy, liveliness, to a person's day. Between grazing on charcuterie and imbibing fruity rosé while we gossiped about market life, the day slipped away. I fill a glass with water and sit at my dining room table with my laptop. I'm easily distracted recounting the easy afternoon with the ginger-haired printer. When did I last have an outing like that? Too long ago. The spontaneous nature of it took any pressure away and it had just been good old fun.

I shake the memory away and log in to Paris Cupid. All fuzziness evaporates when I check the portal and find responses from both Emmanuel Roux and Émilienne Lyon. Not only have they completed the feedback surveys, but they've also both sent private messages. I quickly scan Emmanuel Roux's first, most interested to see the answer to the question: Have you found *The One*?

Emmanuel Roux:

Oui! And she is perfect in every way. I knew I needed change, but I didn't know in what form until Émilienne's words appeared in my life.

We started slowly, achingly slowly, when I'm used to a faster pace in life and love. Émilienne refused to meet in person for the longest time. I had months and months of waiting and hoping she'd eventually agree. I presumed the letters would eventually peter out; after all, I'm more of an instant gratification kind of man, but what surprised me most is that waiting only added to the anticipation of a possible meeting. Our letters grew more fervent; we wrote more often. When we finally met face to face…

I quickly scroll to the next page.

Stars collided, invisible orchestras trumpeted. I swear there was light surrounding her. It was one of the most incredible moments of my life. As if all roads had led me there, to that very moment, and I knew with utmost certainty my life was about to change for the better. She could have said she wanted to move to Timbuktu and I would have said, 'May I carry your bags?' We haven't quite made it to Timbuktu, but we're on a holiday in India and that's been another great gift. I'm trying hard to leave the past behind, but I want the world to experience what I have with Émilienne. I want to sing Paris Cupid's praises, because I know deep inside my heart, if we hadn't started slowly, writing like we did, this would have ended the way all my previous relationships did: quickly, because we wouldn't have had such a deep connection, developed over all those days and months writing about our lives, our hopes, our dreams and all the ways we'd failed. I'm sorry if I've broken so many rules, but I'm hoping you can forgive me. I only meant to show my gratitude and give others hope on their journey on the path to finding true love.

My pulse hammers loudly in my ears as I finish reading Emmanuel's message. Can it be true? I take a moment to reflect to read between the lines and all I can come up with is that it's a message written from the heart, and he means every single word. Why I'm struggling with such a notion is strange. Shouldn't I be overjoyed the slow burn method worked? Why do I still have lingering doubt? Perhaps I need to hear

Émilienne's side for my mind to be at rest. Aside from her short texts assuring me she's happy and in love, I have no real details from her. In writing to Paris Cupid itself, she might be more forthcoming.

Émilienne Lyon:

I've found the man I've been waiting for all this time. Oui, I fell in love with a man named Remy. A man who had a messy romantic history and a lot of regret about his past regressions. Regrets are such a waste of energy. Mistakes are a way to learn but not if you keep making the same ones. That is then a pattern of behaviour, not an error in judgement. Remy then did the work, facing himself in the mirror and owning his past. It's a journey of forgiveness, and that work can only be done internally. But he did it. It wasn't easy but he knew how important it was. There could be nothing romantic between us until the slate was wiped and he was ready to start fresh. For his benefit, not mine. He had a lot of soul searching to do, and so did I.

Over the course of our correspondence, we fell in love in the most organic and natural way. When he finally confessed in a letter to being Emmanuel Roux, that didn't bother me. We'd worked on our past selves and I felt like we were both coming into this with open hearts. What came before is dust in the rearview mirror. I love him for the man he is now. Thank you, Paris Cupid, for putting the perfect man in my path. I wasn't ever going to settle for second best, and I felt that my standards made me unlovable, but now I know better. Staying true to myself has been difficult at times but the payoff is worth it. I'm blessed beyond belief and know that he is my life partner, the man who will stand beside me when inevitable storms come, and be there for the rainbows too.

I'm blown away by how honest they are with me. They've shared their vulnerabilities, their flaws, and worked through them together. This is proof that love-letter writing can really be the answer to finding real and lasting love. If a man called the Playboy of Paris can find love and settle down, anyone can.

I've always believed in the power of the written word and this gives me a real sense that Paris Cupid might just be as successful as dating apps are, and offers another method for those who want to find love at a slower pace.

I'm proud of Émilienne for sticking to her principles, for remaining true to herself. For not becoming starry-eyed at his celebrity status, and conversely not running away from that when the truth came out. If they make it work, there's real hope for all of us.

If I'm to continue matchmaking, I'll need help. Geneviève is a possible candidate. She's the only person who knows my secret, and I can trust her implicitly. She's already had a hand in drumming up business and spreading the word because she genuinely loves romance and hearing about happy ever afters. She will think outside the box when it comes to matching couples. And that's what I've been trying to do all along. I often choose them the exact opposite of who they'd normally go for, because why not try to find someone different if what you did before kept failing time and again?

When it comes to matchmaking, I don't have an exact formula. I don't key in their heights, their weights, what they look like. I don't ask for their non-negotiables, a checklist written in stone. Instead I focus more on what they felt went wrong in the past. They always become more honest the more they write. It's like the floodgates open and they share and reflect on the past, including *their* flaws and faults.

Before I get back to applications, I call Geneviève.

'Lilou, to what do I owe this great honour?'

'Would you like to help me with Paris Cupid? I mean, really help me as an employee.'

There's noise in the background, laughing, talking, like she's at a bar. 'What made you decide this?'

'I heard from Emmanuel and Émilienne. They're in love. I sort of knew how Em felt from her texts, but I wasn't sure about him. What they wrote was so heartfelt and honest. There is no question it's real. Whether it goes the distance is another issue, but I'm hopeful it will.'

'I'm happy for them, for you. I'd *love* to help with Paris Cupid. What do you need me to do?'

'Become a matchmaker extraordinaire!'

'I hoped you'd say that! It's like a romance novel coming to life! What fun we shall have!'

Geneviève's enthusiasm is contagious. I get the feeling Paris Cupid might just have a solid future. 'When can you start?'

'Is tomorrow soon enough?'

'Perfect. I'm going out with Felix tonight.' If I don't mention it and she finds out, she'll wonder why I kept it to myself.

'Felix? He's lovely of course, but...'

'But what? You were certain he sent the Cupid card the other day.'

'It's not that. It's more, isn't he the type you always go for?'

'He's similar, but clearly nicer. Anyway, it's not exactly a date. More just two friends catching up.'

'OK. I just don't see fireworks between you two. Not even a little flicker of a flame.'

'Well, I guess we'll see.'

After we end the call, I reply to both Coraline and Kiki, advising them that Paris Cupid is once again open to matches, if they'd like to formally apply, but with the caveat we cannot guarantee a timeframe, and I ask them to be as patient as possible as we work to find them a most suitable match.

20

The humid August morning has me dragging my feet to meet Guillaume at Montmartre cemetery. It's nearing the end of the month and soon it will be autumn. I'm torn between rushing to make it on time and slowing my pace so I don't arrive a sweaty mess, weighing up whether the lecture will be worth it. I'm keen to quiz Guillaume on where he's at with his letter writing after he admitted he was grappling with guilt. I stop on the bridge to wave – as always – to the ghosts who I'm sure hover below and then continue on, hoping today I'll see Minou, who has been absent the last couple of visits. While the cats are wild, often locals fall in love with them and catnap them home, to live a safer more luxurious life in a Parisian apartment. I can't begrudge them this, but the idea of not saying goodbye and never seeing him again hurts more than it should.

Inside the cemetery gates, I search for Minou, calling his name while I shake a container of cat biscuits. A few other darlings come running, but not the one I most want to see.

I find Guillaume on the bench and drop my handbag beside him. '*Bonjour*,' I say, spreading the biscuits on the soft shaded grass.

'*Bonjour*, Lilou.' He gives me a wide smile while I wait for him to remonstrate me for not being punctual. I wait and nothing comes. Curious. Perhaps he too is distracted about our missing tabby friend.

'No sign of Minou?'

He wrinkles his brow. 'None. I dropped past yesterday and the day before too, early morning before they'd have a chance to be fed by anyone else, and no sign.'

A wave of sadness hits me. It's silly, I know, being attached to an animal who roams free, but I've come to love him after so many visits. Without a goodbye, how will I ever know what fate he suffered? I'm embarrassed to find myself choking up when I go to reply.

Guillaume gives my shoulder a pat. 'Don't worry, Lilou. He'll return. That cat has many a hang up about people. I can't see anyone spontaneously adopting him because he'd make his displeasure known.'

'*Oui*, that's why I love him so. He's not a lap cat, and he won't bend his will for anyone, not even when there's fresh fish on offer.'

Guillaume shakes his head. 'He's probably hiding from us on purpose. Revenge because you only brought biscuits again.'

The idea of a such a thing produces a small laugh because it rings true. I gaze around, expecting to see his furry face peeking out from a headstone. 'That wouldn't surprise me. Tomorrow I'll stop by the *poissonnier* for some tuna. That's his favourite.'

'That ought to do it. And we'll laugh about how worried we've been, you'll see.'

Guillaume is trying to lighten the mood, but if Minou isn't here, and most likely hasn't been claimed by a local, where could he be? My mind goes to scenarios I don't want to contemplate. If only his feline friends could speak and reassure me he's just on an adventure elsewhere in the cemetery and will be back soon. I swipe at my eyes.

'What have you got for me today?'

He takes a folder from his briefcase. 'A range of decorative prayer books. One is written in Latin. A diary from the village Colmar, Alsace, known as the little Venice of France. Such a pretty town, with colourful cottages along the canals, like something out of a storybook. I've also got a postcard collection. If they don't interest you, I'll ask Benoit.'

I take the proffered folder and flick through photocopies of the range. The prayer books are exquisite. But it's the diary I'm searching for. I find the passage he's photocopied and I read it.

1988. How do you know when you're in love? How do you distinguish it from general admiration for the person? There's this new guy in my maths class, gorgeous, dreamy, utterly mesmerising. When I go to talk to him, my voice dries up. My knees go weak. I stutter and stammer, trying and failing to find my equilibrium. Try to make my mind catch up with my body. Is this love? And if so, how can I love someone without exchanging a single word with them? Is that even possible? I can't see how I can ever find out unless my useless voice decides to work in his presence. My wobbly knees manage to hold me up long enough. What is wrong with me?

Puppy love! 'This is adorable. Tell me, did her voice eventually work long enough for her to speak up?'

I'm expecting his usual faux gruff response, but he surprises me when he says, 'I'm not going to spoil the surprise for you, Lilou. You'll have to read it for yourself.'

'Aha! You *do* read them, even though you claimed you don't!'

He smiles. 'I do no such thing. However, in this case, I'll admit to being intrigued. When I photocopied that page, I needed to know so I skipped to the end and found my answers there.'

I gasp. 'You skipped to the last page? Sacrilege!'

'How did I know you'd say that, Lilou?'

It's then I notice a marked difference in Guillaume. His shoulders aren't as stooped as usual. There's high colour in his complexion. Even the hollow in his cheeks isn't as pronounced as it once was.

Could it be the first blush of romance? 'You sent your letter, didn't you?'

The obligatory head shake is back. 'An old man gets whiplash the way you dart from one subject to another.'

I grin. 'Ooh la la! I'm right, aren't I?'

He hugs his arms around his middle section as if trying to stop the secret spilling out. To see his eyes sparkle with happiness is a huge relief. I wasn't sure if he'd go through with the plan, and if he chose not to, I would have understood.

'Fine, fine. I'll tell you only because I'll never hear the end of it, and here we are at a business meeting, discussing everything but business.'

I smother a smile. 'Stay on track, Guillaume! You sent the letter when…?'

'I sent the first letter a month ago, almost. That very day we spoke at the pâtisserie.'

'And she replied?'

'I got one in return within a couple of days. I wasn't sure how my correspondence would be received as I told Clementine in no uncertain terms that I'm very sorry but I had already met the love of my life.'

'Brutal, Guillaume!' My shoulders spring up somewhere around my ears. Should I have given him more pointers?

'Let me finish,' he says, holding up a finger. 'I didn't want to give the woman unrealistic expectations. I explained Mathilde was the love of my life, and I miss her terribly still and always will. If that didn't discourage her then I'd be open to becoming acquainted with her slowly via letter.'

My shoulders relax. I do tell matches honesty is always the best policy, so perhaps he's expressed himself well. 'What did she say back to that?'

He chuckles and I almost fall off the bench. Not once since Mathilde died have I heard such a sound escape his lips. 'Clementine wrote in great detail, describing her ex-husband, and I only laugh because it was the polar opposite of what I wrote. She called him a snivelling crackpot of a man who has been going through a mid-life crisis for most of his adult life. While written in jest, I felt it was cathartic for Clementine to write about what unfolded, and how it had stopped her opening her heart again. It's understandable that she would have reservations trusting in love, so I have reassured her I'm only a letter away and she may use me as a sounding board as long as she wishes.'

My heart explodes. It really does. This is exactly what I hoped would happen. Guillaume has so much love and support to give *and* to receive in turn. Having a special friend to converse and confide in might just be their ladder to love…' 'That's so lovely, Guillaume. I bet she really could use a friend like you. Often it's easier to confide in someone who is a stranger to the situation. There's a real freedom in being able to express those pent-up emotions and receive support in return.'

'True, true. I felt it would be unfair to continue singing Mathilde's praises when Clementine's marriage was so different, but sometimes it's hard not to. Mathilde's always with me.' He pats his heart but doesn't choke up this time. The guilt has been replaced with a quiet confidence.

'I'm sure Clementine understands and will be just as respectful when you reminisce about Mathilde, but it's nice that you're hesitant to make it the focus of your letters.' Marmalade, the ginger cat, saunters over and springs up on Guillaume's lap, letting out a plaintive meow. The sound is so sad it gives me goosebumps. Is it because her best friend Minou is missing?

I don't mention this to Guillaume because I don't want to tear up again, and I'm sure he's noticed the difference in Marmalade's nature too.

While I gaze around the cemetery for Minou, I ask, 'How many letters have you sent and received?'

'Oh, who's counting? There's been a number of them, going back and forth as fast as the post service can keep up. I'm expecting a reply today. It's made leaving work rather exciting, stopping to check my PO box in the hopes there's a letter waiting for me.'

'That really is beautiful.' I can picture his face as he stops to check for a letter, his wide smile as he carries it home where he pours a robust red wine and sits on the sofa to read.

'I'm so glad Paris Cupid found Clementine for me. She's a wonderful person and seems to be at the same stage of life as I am. It's not that we want some torrid love affair, it's more that we want to build a friendship based on trust and mutual affection. Having someone in this big bustling city I can write to about my day, my work, my pain, my joy, breaks up the monotony of those long dull evenings.'

'I agree. Clementine seems a good match for you and I'm so happy to hear the nights aren't as lonely. Do you have a timeframe in mind to meet or will you take things as they come?'

He absently pats Marmalade, unaware that she's gazing up at him with such rapture in her eyes, as if his presence is easing the loneliness of missing Minou. The cats here love Guillaume, so much so that when he's here I become almost invisible to them. Perhaps I need to invest in fresh tuna more regularly.

'As a gentleman, I think it's best to follow her lead in that respect. There's no need to rush. I'm enjoying the letters far more than I can say.'

'You really are a gentleman, Guillaume, and you've made me very happy giving this a chance.'

'I really should thank you for encouraging me, but I don't want any praise to go to your head and give you any more crazy ideas.'

I laugh. 'Probably wise.'

'Anyway, let's talk business. Which of these suit you?' He points to the folder.

'Benoit can have the postcards, but I'll take the rest.'

'*Merci*. Now, price?'

I rattle off a figure, ready to counter.

'Fine,' he says.

My jaw drops. 'But – Guillaume, we always negotiate.'

'No time! I'll deliver them on Friday.' If I didn't know better I'd say his mind was busy with thoughts of a certain Clementine…

Guillaume says goodbye to Marmalade, packs his things and strides away with great purpose. I spend the next little while traipsing through headstones and ornate graves, looking for Minou, but have no luck finding the tabby cat.

21

The market is hectic the following Friday as shoppers are out and about enjoying the start of autumn. There's an influx of tourists on holidays and the halls are awash with many an accent. Guillaume waves as he delivers my latest purchases, but I'm too busy with a group visiting from Australia to chat to him. The Sydney ladies pepper me with questions about the handwritten diaries, having never seen such a thing on sale before.

'Where do you get them from?' a woman named Janet asks.

'All over! Estate sales, auctions, other flea markets. Friends in the trade keep an eye out for me.'

'I want to read them all!' Janet's friend says. 'And the love letters. I wish I could read French.'

'I have some English love letters. My father is British and spends a lot of time attending car boot sales and the like in England hunting for me.'

'This has to be one of the best jobs going,' Janet says.

I laugh as I show the women around Ephemera and point out diaries, prayer books and love letters that are written in their native tongue. Tourists like these always brighten my day. Not everyone understands the importance of what I do, so when people like this step inside and are so invested in learning about my more niche antique trade, it's makes it feel so worthwhile.

'Letter writing is becoming a lost art form, so it's my mission to bring that back. Remind people that emails aren't going to cut it when the time comes to looking to the past.'

Janet shakes her head as if she's annoyed with herself. 'It never even crossed my mind, and now I can't think of anything else. I'm going to start writing letters again. Who knows, it might rekindle that stagnant part of my marriage. I love my husband, of course I do, but after thirty-two years together, there's a certain complacency there...'

'I understand. Is he here in Paris?'

The trio of women laugh and Janet says, 'No, we left the husbands at home.'

'Why don't you write to him *from* Paris?' I'm off in fairyland, dreaming about Janet writing to her husband, pouring out rich descriptions of our wondrous city, the sounds, the sights, the colour that's all around. 'I have some beautiful letter-writing paper. Or...' I look across at my neighbours. 'Another option, my neighbour Benoit writes letters in the most beautiful calligraphy.' I point to his shop. 'And next to him is Felix, who makes hand-pressed cards on a vintage press. You could get a card from Felix and have Benoit write your message in calligraphy for you – it could be a lasting memento of your visit here.'

Janet's eyes light up. 'That would be lovely. Can I also take a look at your letter-writing paper?'

'*Oui*.' I show Janet and her friends the range of thick, lush papers I have. She chooses one with that has an embossed Eiffel Tower in the corner. I'm not surprised; every tourist chooses this one. *La tour Eiffel* is always fascinating to our overseas guests. The Australians choose some love letters, a diary written by a woman who felt trapped in a marriage of convenience, and pads of letter-writing paper. 'Would you like me to introduce you to Benoit and Felix?'

'Sure, and – ooh – what does *that* guy sell?' Janet points to Pascale.

Pas*cowl*, more like.

'How do you get any work done with him around? I'd spend all day staring at him!'

'Ha! He's OK I guess, if you're into the sullen broody kind of guy. He sells vintage typewriters. Or, they sell themselves. He doesn't seem to put a lot of effort into his sales. He mostly ignores his customers.'

'Does he type out love letters too?' Janet is not listening to a word I say. She's got her gaze locked on Pascale, and there it's stayed.

'He doesn't seem to be the romantic sort. He's more likely to type break-up letters.' I might be a little more bitter because of his abrupt departure after the visit to the national archives.

Her eyebrows shoot up. 'Is that a thing?'

I usher them to the counter to break the spell. 'I hope not!' I ring up their purchases and place them in an Ephemera tote.

'Well, let's meet the neighbours, eh? My husband's going to love getting letters in the mail, rather than only electricity bills.'

I smile, knowing I've converted one more soul, keeping the lost art of letter-writing alive. Once I've introduced Janet and her friends to Felix, I dash back to my stall to unpack my delivery from Guillaume. Sitting atop the unopened box is an unfamiliar prayer book. I frown. Where did it come from? Did Guillaume forget one? Again? He has been rather distracted lately. I open the box and check the stock against his invoice, but it's not there and I haven't seen this one before in his photocopies. I take a picture and text him. His reply is instant:

> Not one of mine. Should I be worried about how forgetful you're becoming?

How forgetful *I'm* becoming? He really is the limit. I shake my head as I gently prise the prayer book open. It's a simple sort, leather bound, yellowed paper. My favourite kind. On each page, a French word has been underlined. Only one word per page. Why? *Keeper. Of. My. Heart.* It's a message written in code. Did two star-crossed lovers swap prayer books to communicate in secret? *Will. She. Ever. Understand. The. Weight. Of. My. Feelings. For. Her? Shall. I. Confide. In. Her. Or. Keep. This. Ache. Of. Longing. To. Myself?* I want to rush across the hall to show one of them how romantic this is, but Felix is chatting away with Janet, and Janet's two friends are with Benoit. Pascale is the only one alone, as he sits scowling behind his desk, not paying an iota of attention to his surroundings. I don't want to show him; he'll probably make light of it. We haven't spoken since he left me at the fountain. He hasn't even complained about me lighting my candles today. I'll have to show Geneviève.

It's after lunch and still her shop remains shuttered. Our Paris Cupid work has kept her late at my apartment most nights, and I'm worried it's affecting her business, even though she insists it isn't. Like I've summoned her from sheer will alone, she strides into the hall, a riot of colour in a fifties-style swing dress with a thick white belt. How does she effortlessly pull off such looks? She gives our neighbours a fluttery wave and blows a kiss to Pascale. Honestly, she has no shame. Not even a little bit.

When she turns to face me, I wave her in. 'Geneviève, you're so late!'

'*Oui, oui.* I had the most amazing idea!' Outwardly, Geneviève is well put together, but on close inspection, it appears as though she's put her make-up on in a rush. Her lipstick is slightly skewed and the sweeps of taupe eyeshadow uneven.

'Do tell.'

She ushers me further inside and lowers her voice to a whisper. 'The Coraline predicament. I've solved it!'

'*Quoi?*' When I told Geneviève about what had transpired between Coraline and me and the confidences she'd shared about being used and then dumped, she still wasn't convinced we should allow her to join Paris Cupid, possibly risking our anonymity. Coraline has burned a number of bridges with her penchant for gossiping, so this about-face is interesting.

'I know, I know, at our first meeting I was of a different opinion. I had a good long think about what you said about everyone deserving love. And what I came up with is that maybe Coraline is a scandalmonger because she's lacking in other parts of her life. The woman needs sex, no two ways about it!'

'Geneviève! It's always sex with you!'

She waves me away as if I'm a bug. 'Intimacy is everything, Lilou!'

'Romance is everything.'

'And intimacy falls under that heading, *non*?'

'Fine. So who do you think is right for someone like Coraline?' While I feel she needs a strong man, she doesn't necessarily need a take-charge sort because in the past those types have tended to manipulate her. But conversely, she can't be with a pushover either because she can be a little domineering too.

'I spent this morning on the Paris Cupid portal, searching for that elusive guy, the type who is sensitive yet strong, supportive but not controlling. A man whose romance game is on point. After all, to woo a florist you need some skills, especially a florist who knows the language of flowers intimately the way Coraline does. From reading her dating history a hundred times, I deduced a pattern!'

I bite down on a smile. Geneviève has become enamoured with figuring out the psyche of matches. 'And...?'

'Coraline goes for men who take advantage of her kindness.' Without discussing any of this together, we are both of the same opinion. 'For example, she wrote that her last beau, the one who really did a number on her, moved into her apartment after they'd been dating mere weeks! I considered that for a bit, wondering why she'd allow that to happen so quickly. When he didn't need her any more, he vanished, leaving only a note. The boyfriend before that, she employed at her flower stall even though he didn't know a thing about floristry. She wrote that he needed a helping hand. And on it went. Coraline tried to save these men from whatever problem they faced and in return they broke her heart. What Coraline needs is a man who is self-sufficient and ambitious and successful in his own right. The type who won't take advantage of her but won't be bullied by her either.'

'Wow, Geneviève, you're a natural at this!'

'Right? I've missed my calling.'

'And so humble too!'

She laughs. 'That's me, the whole package. But wait... there's more! I found the man for her. But I want your take on it first.'

'Ooh who is he?'

Geneviève goes behind my desk and logs into the Paris Cupid portal and brings up a photograph of a man. Gone are the days I kept the two worlds separate. I double check no one is watching us before I scoot closer to the screen. 'Is that Pierre, the bookseller from the Seine?'

'*Oui!* His application came in late last night. Can you believe it?'

I double blink. 'I'm not surprised actually. He's a word nerd so finding love this way would suit him. But he hates gossiping with a *passion*, Geneviève.' I don't even know much about his private life; we only ever touch on it and move on to the business of books and letters.

'*Exactement!*'

'Well... isn't that going to be an issue for them? Coraline might draw a line between work and play, but at her core, she does love telling tales.'

'Because she's *lonely!* Sad people do silly things because their mood drives those behaviours. I'd bet that Coraline in love is a whole other person.'

I consider it. Coraline certainly used to be a sunnier sort until a broken heart robbed her of that, its dark cloud hovering in her wake. For a long time, her stall was popular with Parisians because of her personal touch, educating customers about the language of flowers with such passion and fervour you couldn't help but be swept away by the notion of it. I'm still not convinced Pierre is the one for her though. 'This match... it's so left field.' I'm not sure Pierre would have the patience if Coraline's true colours were on full display. And that doesn't mean she needs to change; if that's her default setting, then that's up to her, but are they a good match?

'Opposites attract! Trust me, I've read a million romance novels with this very coupling.'

From that viewpoint, it does make more sense. Maybe Coraline's forthrightness will suit Pierre's more reflective nature? They both enjoy the art of storytelling, Coraline with flowers, Pierre with books. He's also definitely not the type to take advantage of a woman. He's softly spoken with just the right amount of French flair and has a stubborn side that I've witnessed when customers try to bully him over the price of his books.

'Actually, Geneviève, the more I consider it, the more I do see the appeal of such a match. Love might just bloom if they form a connection through letter writing, and then eventually decide to meet in person.'

That's the part we can never really gauge. On paper they might be a wonderful match, but in person, if the chemistry isn't there, there's nothing we can do about that. It's just one of those things.

'Shall I send them the details then?'

'*Oui*. I'll visit Pierre next week and see if he mentions it.' He's notoriously private so I don't like my chances. I've got a lot more chance hearing from Coraline, but I'll have to be careful and let her lead any talk of Paris Cupid. I'd also like to find out more about the letter found in the *Madame Bovary* book.

'OK, I'll do that later. What's that book you're holding tight against your chest?'

I glance down. 'Oh, another mysterious arrival that turned up. But have a look.' I flick through and point out the underlined words.

Geneviève's eyes widen. 'A love letter in code! These must be meant for you, Lilou. You can't keep explaining them away.'

'I would love to believe that, Geneviève, I really would, but this was in a delivery from Guillaume and it's more likely he's making mistakes because he's distracted by you know who.'

'But they haven't *all* come from Guillaume's deliveries.'

'Right, and he's a stickler for organisation, so if he can make the occasional lapse then so can other suppliers.'

'Lilou, I think it's someone from the market. They could easily pop in one of these treasures when a box is delivered by your door or dropped to a neighbour.'

'Maybe...'

'I wonder if it's Felix? That Cupid card. This is just his kind of quirky. He's the type that would do something like this, don't you think?'

It is sort of reminiscent of his literary treasure hunt. It would be just like Felix to go out of his way to romance a woman.

'I'm not sure, Geneviève. When we're together I feel like a different version of myself. More spontaneous, more willing to try new things, but it's more like a friendship than a real flirtation. I adore him, but like you pointed out, there were no fireworks. I don't feel a spark...' Our museum meet up had been a blast but didn't feel romantic in the slightest.

Geneviève considers it for a moment and then says, 'I've changed my mind about him after seeing this. Maybe deep down he's shy and this is his way of wooing you. You need to take your own Paris Cupid advice and give someone a chance. Let things develop over time.'

There's a mutual respect there with Felix but is it enough? Shouldn't it be more than that and more obvious? But Geneviève is right; I advise others to let that spark build and here I am wanting the thunderbolt. The weak knees. The arrow to the heart that shows me he's the one I've been waiting for. The one I'm ready to risk my heart with. Is it Felix?

* * *

I head downstairs to grab lunch, a sandwich to eat at my stall because the market is so busy today. I order at the counter and, while I wait, I scroll on my phone when a Facebook friend suggestion for Pascale pops up. Intrigued, I click on his profile and am surprised to find it unlocked. And that he has friends – lots of them. Maybe outside of work, he's the life of the party? I click on his photos. There are a lot of arty travel pictures taken around France. There are many featuring bookshops with disorderly piles on double-stacked shelves. I suppose if he's writing a book, then it makes sense he enjoys reading them. Maybe he is the type to spend a lazy day in bed reading? A picture forms of him in my mind, shirtless, a sheet wrapped around his large frame, novel in hand. It's appealing for some strange reason. I'm lost in thought as I flick through his albums and almost die, literally die, when a voice says, 'Find anything interesting?'

Pascale smirks at me. I hastily pocket my phone, but it's clearly too late; he's caught me looking through his profile.

'Nothing. I'm not sure why the algorithm suggests certain people and not others. It's a mystery!' I let out a gurgle of laughter that sounds forced even to me.

'Is that so?'

'Uh-huh.' My face is aflame and I feel a little unsteady on my feet. He's surely going to think I'm secretly obsessed with him or something.

'Oh look, here's my order.'

I hurry away. When I get back to Ephemera, I do my best to hide behind my desk. A few minutes later, my phone pings with a notification. A friend request from Pascale. I click accept, unsure how else to play it. As soon as I do there's a message from him that reads:

> You can stalk my profile much easier this way.

Mon dieu! It makes total sense that he would react in such a way. He probably thinks every woman on planet earth is in love with him!

22

On Thursday when the market is closed to the public, I'm at Ephemera catching up on paperwork. Paris Cupid work has been so much fun with Geneviève on board to help, but I've let things slide here. I have new stock arriving and need to shuffle things around to make room. I love working in solitude like this when the place is deserted and there's only the faint hum of electricity. Once the bookwork is done, I shut down the laptop and survey the stall, wondering how to move the cabinetry around to fit a new glass display cabinet that will house my more valuable prayer books. I don't get many shoplifters, but I also don't want to tempt fate, and a collection of rare prayer books I have are worth thousands of euros.

I'm about to move a small shelf when I spot what looks like a rolled scroll. It's bound with red ribbon. I unwrap it and read the beautiful calligraphy writing.

Why is love so difficult to share? I almost told you. I was so close to sharing how I felt and asking if there was any chance between us. Instead, I froze in the moment. Driven by fear that you'd laugh in my face. Fear you'd think I was joking. That you wouldn't take me seriously, or worse, you would take me seriously and still say no. I write to you now and wonder if anyone has captured your heart like you've captured mine. If I knew how you felt I could act on this impulse. But I don't know how you feel and I don't want to make things awkward.

My pulse thrums as I roll the letter up and re-tie it with ribbon. Is this meant for me? And if so, who is the author? Is it Felix? The reference to joking makes me believe it must be him. But then it's written in calligraphy, so could it be Benoit? I can't see it being Pascale. It could be anyone from the market. The more these arrive, the more I can't deny they're being left for me to find. It's wildly romantic. I can't wait to show Geneviève and get her take on it.

* * *

'Geneviève!' I yell when I see her coming up the stairs.

'I know I look fabulous for my age, *ma Cherie*, but these stairs require some careful manoeuvring on my part.'

She's as spritely as they come. It's more likely her killer stilettos are the culprit to Geneviève navigating her way up the flight of stairs.

'What is it? You're flushed. If I didn't know better I'd say you finally got over your sex drought.'

I laugh and roll my eyes. 'Not exactly a drought, Geneviève. Just a pause. I was here yesterday working and found this scroll. Have a read and tell me what you think.'

Geneviève takes the proffered letter and rummages in her handbag, vintage Hermès today, for her glasses, before settling on the chaise to read. 'It looks like we have ourselves a love... square.'

'A what?'

She lets out an impatient sigh. 'Like a love triangle but with more players. You have Felix sending you the card, a couple of calligraphy letters which must be Benoit, and there was a typed letter too, wasn't there? That's Pascale, for sure. Then all the other trinkets and the beautiful prayer book; we'd have to figure which man sent those. Don't you see?'

I rub the back of my neck as I contemplate it. As usual, Geneviève puts two and two together and makes about five hundred. 'Oh, Geneviève, as if! This is too fanciful even for you to dream up. You're expecting me to believe that all *three* men are interested in me and instead of admitting it, they're going to these great lengths?'

Geneviève's face dissolves into a smile. 'That's exactly what I'm saying! They know your love language is letters! I'm not sure they know they have competition in each other, that part remains a mystery, but as for the rest, I'm convinced it's all three of your new neighbours – who, might I remind you, *all* told me they had feelings for someone when I prodded them about joining Paris Cupid.'

'I just don't see it. It's not all three. Pascale can't even stick around long enough to share a coffee with me. Though I think it could well be Felix.'

'It could be. But Felix doesn't have a gift with calligraphy. Leading me to believe they're all wooing you with their specialities.' She stares me down. I feel a lecture coming. 'You're in the business of love and yet you doubt yourself every step of the way.' She shakes her head so vehemently I worry she'll rupture something. 'Why wouldn't they all vie for you? You have that French fragile beauty about you, with your pixie cut and doe eyes. A certain *je ne sais quoi*. You're beguiling, yet you don't even realise it. In the past, men may have mistaken you for an ingénue, but that's because you're captivating, and they were not, so they felt the need to diminish you somehow.'

I double blink, taken aback by Geneviève's protestations. Eventually, I manage, '*Merci*.'

'Trust me, Lilou. I'm not the only person on planet earth to notice what a catch you are. Those three men working in close proximity to you are all under your spell. They probably have no idea that they're each vying for your attention. And that makes this exciting, *non*? Do you have romantic feelings for any of them? Better yet, all of them? Who will you choose? Or will you choose them all!'

Laughter bursts out of me. Only Geneviève could get away with keeping three men on the go. She has a soft spot when it comes to me and always talks as if every man will fall at my feet in some sort of frenzy, which just isn't the case. 'It's all fun and games, philosophising about it, but I'm not convinced. So, I cannot answer the question of who.'

She lets out a dramatic sigh. 'Sometimes I want to shake sense into you. What will it take for you to believe it's all three of them trying to romance you?'

I go back to my desk and stash the scroll, mainly to escape a stare-down from Geneviève. 'I – I don't know! Perhaps the modern way. They ask me on a date, that sort of thing?'

She places a hand on her chest and feigns a heart attack. At least I hope she's feigning. 'Lilou Babineaux, have a listen to yourself!'

When she throws my surname into the mix, I know I'm really about to get a talking to. '*Quoi?*'

'You, the keeper of love letters, the reader of diaries, would prefer a man ask you on a date rather than go to the trouble of romancing you the way they so clearly are? The way you read about all the time in love letters you've found from a century ago? They've all heard about the popularity of Paris Cupid, so perhaps that's given them the idea to try something out of the ordinary. What's gotten into you!'

'When you put it like that, no, I would prefer this. It's just I'd have to suspend belief *to* believe it. Be realistic: when does stuff like this ever happen to me? It just doesn't.'

'It clearly does!'

'Well, if so, I'll need some concrete evidence.'

She holds up a hand adorned in so much bling I blink away prisms of light. 'Stop. Stop. Is that your grand plan? To *wait*? You're a fan of slow-burn romance, I get it, but come on, Lilou!'

How is *she* not getting it? 'What else is there I can do? I'm not going to march over to each one of them and ask! How ridiculous would I look if they gave me a blank stare?' Which I suspect they would.

'OK. I'm only giving in because there's no convincing you.'

Geneviève's phone rings, so she holds up a finger to me to wait while she answers it.

I glance outside and view my neighbours as they go about their workday. Could it be real? For one lonely moment, I pretend it is and let myself fantasise about which one is right for me... Felix directly opposite me is concentrating on his printing press. From what I know of him so far, he's more the spontaneous sort, more likely to blurt out how he's feeling. While he tells me every day he loves me and flirts up a storm, I've always thought it was done in jest, just some light-hearted banter. He very well might have sent the Cupid card to make me smile because he's friendly like that.

Next, I move my gaze to Benoit's stall. He's leaning against the counter, a book of stamps open before him as a customer chats away. Even from here, I can see Benoit's eyes glazing over as if the customer has bored him silly, but he's far too polite to make excuses and end the customer's monologue. Could he have written that letter on gossamer-thin tissue-like paper? Then somehow have roped Pierre the bookseller by the Seine into the farce? Pierre's story about the abandoned 4th arrondissement apartment had been believable. Surely he wouldn't have made that whole narrative up? And then there's the beautifully worded calligraphy scroll? I smother a grin as I see Benoit slump that little bit more as his customer gesticulates wildly, not once looking at the book of stamps open before them.

To the left of Benoit is Pascale. Scowl firmly in place as he bashes away on a typewriter, ignoring a customer who flutters around him. Typical. How the man does any trade is beyond me. He must sense my gaze and turns his head towards me. I do the adult thing and spin on my heel out of his line of sight. If I shelve my dubiousness for a moment, could I see myself with any of these men? Really, they're all magnetising in one way or another. Even Pascale. There's something wild about the guy that makes my heart race, not that I'd ever tell him that. Or anyone.

Once she ends her call, Geneviève drums her ruby-red nails on the desktop, the sound like some kind of ticking time bomb, and her scrutiny of me returns.

Didn't I promise myself I'd try love once more? Open my heart again, no matter the cost? 'They're all charming in their own ways, I suppose. Even Pascale can turn it on when he wants to.'

'Especially Pascale.'

'Hmm.' I still find it hard to believe but keep my thoughts to myself rather than suffer another lecture. 'OK. I'm going to risk it and ask Felix on a date. A proper date. It's got to be him. I'm still not one hundred per cent sure how I feel about the guy, but I'm ready to throw myself back into the world of dating.'

'That's the spirit! When will you ask?'

'At the end of the day?'

'Why not now?'

'I'd like some time to obsess over all the ways in which this could go wrong.'

She rolls her eyes dramatically. 'One step forward, twenty-five back. Tell me as soon as you do!'

Once Geneviève takes her leave, I go over my orders and get them ready to post. I finish editing my latest newsletter and send that out to subscribers. On an online auction site, I bid on some special prayer books and pay for orders I've previously won. For the moment I have a healthy range of stock for Ephemera, but that's subject to change. Finding long-lost treasures is the hardest part of the business, and I often worry what I'd do if supply dried up. Paris Cupid is a nice little side biz, and the future of that is looking promising indeed...

* * *

I'm keeping a close eye on Felix and debating whether this is a good idea or not. It doesn't help I sense Pascale out the corner of my eye and wonder why he hasn't complained about anything in weeks. When he leaves, stomping out without an *au revoir*, I take a deep calming breath and approach Felix's stall.

'Nearly done for the day?' I ask as he glances up from his press.

'Lilou! Sorry, I was miles away. I need to get this order finished up. Invitations for an engagement party.' My heart almost stops when I notice they have a Cupid figure in the corner. The exact same as the one on my card, only smaller.

'That's a nice Cupid figure.'

'The god of love. What's not to like?' He grins.

'I think I've seen that same Cupid before actually but on a larger scale.'

'You have? Where?' His usually open face is suddenly blank and hard to read. Is he nervous that I've figured it out? That's he's my secret admirer?

'On a hand-pressed card in a box of goods you took delivery for a while back, remember?'

'*Non*, I don't remember. I'm always taking your deliveries. And for the others too. I guess that's what happens when I'm usually the first to arrive and last to leave.'

Why is he making this so hard? I lose my nerve to ask him on a date and then remind myself it's more of a fact-finding mission. 'Would you like to go on a date, Felix? With me?' Oh boy, this is probably why I'm single. This is *so* awkward and feels all wrong.

'A real date?' He grins.

'Ah, what other kind is there?'

He dusts his hands on his jeans. '*Désolé*, Lilou. I thought you knew? You're not exactly my type.'

Please ground, swallow me up. I want to die of mortification. It's a little shocking that he's so blunt about me not being the one for him. I'd have expected Felix's rejection to be a little more... gentle. But he seems quite certain I am not 'his type'. 'I – ah. Well, sorry to have interrupted you.' I want to run far, far away. This is why I avoid mixing work with pleasure. I spin away but he grabs my wrist.

'Lilou, wait. What I meant was, you're not my *type*. You know?' Who'd have thought sweet, funny Felix really likes putting the boot in when you're down.

'Ah, *oui*, Felix. You've made that abundantly clear.'

He laughs. What on earth is wrong with this guy! I'm never asking another man out ever again!

'I'm gay, Lilou. That's why you're not my type.'

'Ooh!' I slap a hand to my forehead. I did not see that coming. 'That's a relief!'

He cocks his head.

'I mean...'

'I know what you mean.' We both dissolve into giggles. My first attempt at asking a guy out might have ended in a rejection, but this is a rejection I can handle. 'How about that drink then?'

'I'd love to.'

* * *

After a fun-filled evening sharing canapes and drinks with Felix, I text Geneviève.

> One mystery solved – it's not Felix. I'm not his type.

She replies a few minutes later.

> Ah. I see! We'll have to find him a boyfriend…

I shake my head. She knew straight away what 'not his type' meant. He did say he had feelings for someone though. I wonder who it is?

23

After closing up for a few days, I take my usual route wandering through Montmartre, coming to Rue de l'Abreuvoir, one of the most picturesque streets in Paris. It's home of the pretty pink restaurant La Masion Rose. Along the curve of the cobblestoned street, ivy cascades down walled fences, giving the space an almost fairytale feel. It's one of the most photographed places in Paris and it's easy to see why.

I continue down to Place Dalida, the square that holds Buste Dalida; a bronze bust of the famous French–Egyptian singer sits under the shade of a leafy tree. It's believed if you rub the bust and make a wish, it will come true. It's evident many visitors have made wishes as Dalida's chest area is golden from these touches. I've never made a wish on Dalida before, although I've visited her many times. I take a quick look around before I touch the statue, close my eyes and make a wish: *Help me find true love and let go of the past.* There's no guidebook for love. No easy way to trust in the process. A string of failed relationships dented my confidence in men. How can I successfully match for Paris Cupid but not for myself? I step back from Dalida's bust, hoping she'll grant my wish. As I turn, I hear a familiar voice call my name. Colour races up my cheeks. Did he see me touching the bust of Dalida? How will I explain that away? Everyone in Montmartre knows this is a wishing spot usually associated with love.

Benoit jogs down the cobblestones, bag in his hand. By the time he gets to me, his cheeks are flushed and he's out of breath. 'Geneviève told me you walk this way home, but I wasn't sure if I'd catch you in time.'

'Is everything OK?' I ask.

His face is pinched with worry. 'Guillaume needs to speak with you.'

'But he didn't call...' I slap my forehead. 'I must have left my phone at Ephemera.'

'You did but Geneviève had the spare keys to your stall and gave me your phone.' He reaches in his satchel and pulls out my mobile. 'Guillaume called a number of times so I answered it for you.'

'*Merci*. What did Guillaume want?' I ask.

Benoit takes deep inhalation as if he's still trying to catch his breath from running to find me. 'He was quite frantic, something about finding a cat who's been hurt in a presumed cat fight. He's at the vet right now.'

'*Merde!* Minou? Is he all right?' My heart plummets at the thought of him being seriously hurt and missing for all this time.

'As far as I know the cat is being tended to. Guillaume is waiting for your call.'

Where did he find our little friend? I pull up his number and dial. It rings and rings, my heart rate increasing each time as I imagine the worst about the tabby cat. When he finally accepts the call, I blurt, 'Guillaume, it's Lilou. How is he?'

There's a shuffling sound as if he's looking for somewhere private to speak. 'Lilou, how are you without your phone *again*? I'm going to buy some super glue and have it bonded to your hand!'

While his voice is gruff, there's a slight wobble to it. 'Guillaume, I know, I know. How is Minou? Is he going to be OK?'

'A little worse for wear but he will survive. I found him by the cemetery gates in a heap and I tell you, Lilou, my heart almost broke until I saw him move. I've never run so fast in all my life to get a taxi and get him help. After assessing him, the vet is of the opinion that there's been some sort of cat fight for dominance. He's suffered a fair bit, lost a couple of claws, has some deep scratches, is dehydrated and malnourished. The vet has put him on a drip and has tended to the wounds. There's a range of medication that needs to be administered twice a day, but the thing is, Lilou, I'm off to Roeun tomorrow on a buying trip, so I won't be able to give him the medicine.'

I exhale all the angst, all the worry, and focus on the fact that Minou's going to get better. 'Right, right. I understand. But Guillaume, if there's some sort of fight for king of the jungle, won't it happen again once Minou is better? What does the vet say about that?'

He lets out a frustrated sigh. '*Oui*, the vet says for his safety it's best if he finds a permanent home. I'd take him, but I'm often away for work. What can we do, Lilou? I really don't think it's safe for Minou to return to the cemetery, and right now he's going to need a lot of love and attention while he heals.'

There's no question in my mind. 'I'll take him. He can live with me. Unless… you'd like to share him? We can be co-parents.'

He coughs as if clearing his throat, then his voice comes back thick. 'I'd love that, Lilou. I really would. I only hope that Minou is amenable to the idea.'

I laugh. 'Why wouldn't he be? Fresh fish every day and two people who adore him. He can recuperate and I can administer the medication and he'll have plenty of time to rest.'

'The vet believes Minou once had a home because he's been neutered and knows how to use a litter tray.'

'Wow. He must have escaped or got lost at some point?'

'Yes, but he doesn't have a chip implanted so there's no chance of finding former owners.'

'That's OK, he has us now.'

How hard can being a cat parent be? It's not like being a dog owner with all those daily walks. This should be a breeze, especially if the both of us are sharing the care.

Guillaume sniffles down the line. Maybe it'll be good for all of us, not just Minou. 'You're right. He'll live in the lap of luxury for the rest of his life.'

'Where are you? Shall I come and meet you there? How long will he need to stay at the vet?'

'I'm at the *clinique vétérinaire* on Rue Pierre Picard. They have Minou under observation for another couple of hours to rehydrate and then he'll be discharged. There's no point coming now as they've got Minou sedated. Meet here at eight p.m. and you can take him home tonight. Our custody arrangement can commence when I return in a couple of weeks?'

I smile at the thought of us sharing the regal minx. 'Perfect.'

'I'll get him a cat bed and food so you can go straight home with him this evening.'

'Wonderful. And I suppose we'll need to formally adopt him?'

'*Oui*. I'll handle that here.'

We chat for a while about precisely what a cat might need and make a plan to split the costs involved. We say our goodbyes and I pocket my phone and apologise to Benoit for keeping him waiting.

I fill him in on the situation, figuring he only heard one side of the conversation, and am surprised to find my eyes fill with tears when I tell Benoit about Guillaume finding Minou hurt by the cemetery gates.

Benoit gives my arm a rub. 'It's awful to think of an animal being hurt, but he must be a clever cat to have made his way to the cemetery gates so he could be found.'

'*Oui*, and luckily found by Guillaume. I can't wait to see Minou, but I can't pick him up until eight this evening.'

'Then we must have an early dinner. Have you been to La Moulin de le Galette before?'

I find Benoit quietly beautiful, a gentle soul. He radiates a certain calm that's helpful when I'm feeling so worried about Minou. 'I haven't but I'd like to.' Once upon a time, Montmartre was an agricultural area, with many working windmills. Very few remain, and one of those has become the façade for La Moulin de la Galette. Many tourists go in search of the so-called lost windmills of Montmartre having seen them in famous paintings by the likes of Van Gogh and Renoir.

The word 'Moulin' means 'mill'. Most visitors associate that with La Moulin Rouge, the iconic red windmill on the Boulevard de Clichy, home to the famous cabaret show in the red-light district of Pigalle.

'Then it's a date.' His smile fades. 'Uh, I mean, it's a...'

I laugh, enjoying the way he blushes and stumbles when he's nervous. 'It's OK. I know what you mean.' We walk side by side, making our way to the restaurant that's well known for its epicurean delights. We pass through the famous Place de Tertre, the artists' square, where painters and portrait artists are doing a bustling trade. You can commission an artist to draw a likeness or buy their paintings, and it's always awash with tourists who peruse the art or sit in a café sipping wine and admiring the artists as they paint or sketch.

'I take it you don't have any other pets?' Benoit asks as we navigate our way around the busy square.

'Is it that obvious?' I grin.

'Hah. Just that you asked Guillaume what time to put the cat to bed.'

'Right. And now I know Minou will decide his own bedtime.'

Benoit laughs. 'You could always *try* and keep a schedule.'

'Minou might like knowing what his days will consist of,' I joke. I'm going to be responsible for another living creature when I misplace my phone all the time.

'I'm sure he'll love living with you.'

'Minou is my favourite, even though he keeps his distance and is haughty and distrusting. That probably stems from once being domesticated and then having to survive in the wild. Sometimes the cemetery cats are adopted but I've never really agreed with the idea, mostly because they seem so happy there, lazing on the tombstones, soaking up the sun, and who are we to judge which option is better? But with his safety in doubt, the choice is much easier.'

Benoit grabs my elbow to steer me out of the way of a man holding a glass of wine aloft, oblivious to splashing from the sides of the glass as he gesticulates wildly. 'He might prefer the safety of a steady home. I take it from your British-accented French that you haven't always lived in Paris?'

'*Oui*. My dad is British and Maman French, so I spent my formative years going back and forth because they could never agree where to put down roots. I attended university in England and then I moved back to Paris for good. Last year my parents moved back to London because my dad was missing his family. I know it won't be long and they'll come back because Maman will insist.'

'You preferred Paris?' When we're out of the thick crowds of the square, he slows his pace.

'I love both countries, but Paris has my heart. And now I'll have cat responsibilities to keep me occupied. What about you, have you got any pets? Any words of wisdom for me?'

He takes my elbow to steer me around a corner. I'm surprised to find my arm tingles at his touch. 'I have a rather large dog, Hugo, who I inherited from my wayward brother. Like you, I never intended to be a pet owner, but one look into those puppy dog eyes and the choice was made for me. And, as for tips, it's always an adjustment and you just have to roll with the fact they're now in charge.'

I laugh at the idea an elderly grumpy cat will try and take charge. Somehow I can't quite see that being the case. 'You have a wayward brother? Why did he give Hugo to you?'

Benoit looks up to the sky as he lets out a long sigh. 'My brother has always been a handful. He makes these spontaneous decisions and then abruptly changes course. He adopted Hugo and in the next breath announced he'd decided to take a year off to backpack around the world.' He shakes his head at the memory. 'Oh, and could I loan him some money for the trip because it was a now or never thing, and also could I care for Hugo because he didn't want him to go to just anyone?'

I laugh. 'And did you loan him the money?'

'*Oui*. But my brother doesn't understand that loaning means you make repayments. I'll never see that money again.'

'You sound really close, despite your misgivings.'

He nods. 'He gets away with bloody murder but we love him so. He was sick for a long time, and we thought we'd lose him. That sort of scare really changes your perspective on life. How could I say no to this crazy new plan when a few years ago we didn't think he'd make it this far? So, of course, he uses that to his advantage.'

'I'm so glad he made it through.' Benoit is one of the good ones. A man with a big heart.

'*Merci*. We were lucky. And so now I have his ginormous dog who eats more than I do and insists on being walked three times a day. If I don't take him out, he whimpers and wails at the window, driving my neighbours crazy. Really, he's just as needy and conniving as my little brother.'

'How will you feel when it's time to give him back?'

Benoit gives me a wide smile. 'We might have to become co-parents too. But most likely my brother will secede custody and that will be that. I'll have to make sure he doesn't spontaneously buy a horse or a pony or something equally outlandish.'

'Next minute you'll be living on a farm with a menagerie of animals your brother has adopted.'

'While he travels the world and calls me when he needs more spending money.'

We both laugh at his sibling's antics. 'You're a good brother.'

We arrive at the restaurant and I take a snap of the windmill before we go inside. Benoit takes my hand as we're directed by the maître d' to our table. It feels totally natural, as if we've clasped hands so many times before. Like Felix, I feel so comfortable in Benoit's company. Could he be my secret admirer? Those beautiful calligraphy letters certainly point to him. Could he be behind all the mysterious deliveries? I reserve judgement and see how the evening pans out.

Once our orders are taken and wine poured, I take a slice of baguette and add lashings of salty house-made butter. 'Have you heard much about this Paris Cupid scandal?' Benoit asks out of the blue, just as I bite into the bread. It lodges in my throat at an odd angle and I do my best not to die. Death by bread, that would be just my luck. I take an unladylike gulp of wine to help wash it down.

'Sorry, what?' I finally manage.

He blushes as if embarrassed to have to explain such a thing. 'Oh, it's nothing really. I just caught the tail end of some gossip in the market this afternoon as I was tidying up before I closed. There's a Parisian matchmaking site that's got everyone talking. They're trying to uncover who is behind it. It's all hush-hush apparently, leading to a lot of conjecture.'

'Oh, yes, I have heard some whispers about that. I tend to avoid all that gossip. It gets so exaggerated, you never quite know what to believe. Why – are you thinking of joining?'

His blush increases. '*Non, non.* That's not my style at all.'

'So you wouldn't write love letters in an effort to romance a woman?'

The poor man could not blush any harder, but our conversation pauses when the waiter returns with our entrées: two steaming bowls of bouillabaisse – fresh fish and seafood soup with a spicy undertone. Benoit is saved by the soup as he picks up his spoon and dives in... Is he just hungry or is he avoiding the question? Did the question of love letters make him react that way? Suddenly Benoit seems the most likely to have placed the prayer book in Ephemera. Or am I totally off track? He's gorgeous and wise and ticks all the boxes, but is there a spark there?

24

I wake up bleary-eyed and having a sneezing fit. Am I allergic to cats? Or am I coming down with something? Minou lies on the pillow beside me, as if he's a human and not a once-wild cat. 'Oh, now you decide to sleep,' I say, giving him a gentle stroke behind the ears.

Last night didn't quite go the way I thought it would. After a lovely early dinner with Benoit, I met with Guillaume and took my charge home. That's when the chaos began. It seems that Minou has a wild side to his personality. Either that or he really doesn't like glasses, cups, plates, vases, clocks, curtains or sofas. If he can knock it from its perch, he will. The curtains made a fabulous playground for him to run up and down, and my sofa is much more fun as a scratching pole than the actual scratching pole I bought at the vet for an astronomical price.

My phone rings and it takes me a moment to track the sound. I find it under my pillow. The noise doesn't even make the cat stir. Last night he exhausted himself, and me in the process. Woolly-headed, I answer. '*Bonjour.*' A yawn gets the better of me and I fall back against the pillow.

'Are you OK?' Guillaume asks. 'I woke up to your many *many* messages, Lilou. The last one was only a few hours ago! What on earth *happened*?'

I check the time. I've had about two hours of sleep. If you can call it that; it was more that I gave up and fell into a coma. 'How do you feel about changing Minou's name to Destructor Cat?' I explain my wild night with the tabby terror who now sleeps angelically in my bed.

He clucks his tongue. 'Of course there's going to be some issues. He's used to being outdoors and having to fight for everything. This is going to be a period of adjustment, that's all.'

'Uh huh. Said by the man who didn't host a cat party that raged all night long and well into the morning.'

'Perhaps we need to speak to the vet? Minou's supposed to be resting.'

I gaze over at the mound of fur. 'He's quite content now. Maybe he's a night owl?'

He does his usual impatient sigh. 'You panicked, it's to be expected. And his behaviour is probably explained away by an energy burst after being sedated. Today will be better.'

I sneak from the bed so as not to wake the tabby terror and go to the living room, the sight of mass destruction still evident. Cushions lie on the floor, ripped and pulled. My chenille throw rug is a tangled mess. The strap of my leather handbag has tiny bite marks down the length of it. That's not to mention the debris I'd already cleaned up – smashed glass and ceramics. 'All those toys we bought – he didn't touch one of them. Maybe he's never seen a cat toy before, so he has no idea what they're for.' The garish-coloured cat toys lie abandoned and untouched, and the idea that our wild little friend has no idea what to do with them almost makes me well up. Who knew cat ownership would be a roller-coaster ride of emotions?

'Probably. He was once domesticated, so it won't take long for him to learn.'

I let out another long yawn. 'I'd planned to go to the outdoor food market today but I don't think I can leave him. I don't want him to fret.'

'Maybe better to stay in today and see how he goes. Make sure you check his abrasions. The vet said we need to make sure they don't get worse. He's supposed to wear that Elizabethan collar, but as you know he didn't take kindly to that.'

When I arrived at the vet they'd been struggling to get it back on

Minou, who'd awoken from the sedative and slipped straight out of it, despite it being looped around his collar. 'I'll check his injuries when he wakes up. And I'll attempt to put the Elizabethan collar on him again.' I don't like my chances though. That cat is as stubborn as anything.

'You should probably sleep too, Lilou.' His laughter rings out. 'It's like having a baby all over again. Nap when they nap, that's my best advice.' Guillaume has two sons. One lives in Arles and the other in Germany. He sees them regularly when he goes on buying trips.

'Well, unlike you, I haven't raised babies so this is a bit of a culture shock, but I'm sure today will be better. I'll text you later and let you know how our charge is doing.'

I make my way around the apartment looking through a Mon Petit lens. I spy my laptop, a very breakable piece of technology, which I'm sure Minou will relish watching fall and break. I move it to a shelf under the coffee table. I unplug the kettle and stash it in a cupboard. What else is he likely to swat at until it topples over? I remove picture frames, books, the fruit bowl... until the space is virtually empty. I lay out all of his cat toys on the living room rug in the hope he will figure out what to do with them. Even while being destructive, Minou is adorable and I get a pit in my stomach at the thought of leaving him alone. After all, he's had so many feline friends over the years, how will he cope being alone in an unfamiliar place for the entirety of my workday when that comes? Today I can work from home, but I won't have that luxury going forward. We didn't think this scenario through. I'd expected Minou to be relaxed and sleepy just like he is at the cemetery where he drags himself over sedately for some food and puts in the bare minimum of effort to do so.

With the living room now sufficiently empty, I peek in on him. He's still sound asleep, so I take my phone to the kitchen while I make myself breakfast. After I eat, I shoot Guillaume another message.

> Are there such things as cat sitters? We might need to enquire so Minou is not alone too long while he's healing.

I startle when the phone rings as I send the text. I don't recognise the number. '*Bonjour?*'

'*Bonjour*, Lilou. It's Benoit. How did you go with Minou last night?'

I feel a tingle that Benoit has woken up and thought to call and check in. Our evening had been unexpectedly fun and I felt the first stirrings of a connection, or a really good friendship. I'm still not sure which. 'Ah, well…' I go into great detail about the destruction of my apartment. 'Minou is struggling a little with being an inside cat and that's to be expected. If he could break it, he did. I'm not sure where he got all that energy from after what he's been through. I'm most worried about leaving him alone all day. What if he pines for his cat friends, or what if he escapes? He's pretty savvy for a cat and I don't really trust him not to get up to mischief. But mostly, he's supposed to be resting so his cuts and scrapes heal, and he will not entertain the Elizabethan collar. I was thinking of hiring a cat sitter while he's recuperating.'

'That's a great idea.'

I smile. 'Thanks for suggesting dinner last night. I really enjoyed it.' As I lean against the kitchen bench, I feel something brush along my neck, making me jump in fright. I turn to find Minou staring at me through narrowed eyes, paw stuck midway in the air as if he's about to swat me again. 'Argh! He's awake, and by the looks of it, he's not happy.' To prove my point, Minou sweeps my breakfast bowl from the counter. I lunge forward to catch it, but it slips just out of reach and crashes to the floor with a bang. 'The smashing continues,' I say to Benoit. 'But that's my fault. I didn't clean my breakfast things away. How does he sneak around so quietly like that?'

'Cats are stealthy.'

'Right.' From my vantage point above Minou, I can see one of his abrasions is enflamed as if he's been scratching at it. 'Looks like Minou will need the collar back on. God help me, he's going to fight me to the death.'

'When Hugo had a small operation we used an inflatable neck collar. So much easier for them to get around the house in, and he couldn't get it off no matter how hard he tried. Do you want me to stop at the pet shop today and see if they have any for cats? I know you don't want to leave him alone today.'

'If you've got time, that would be great.' I give Minou a cursory look. He's still too thin and his wounds aren't exactly healed enough to call them battle scars as yet. My heart melts staring into his bright brown eyes as I remind myself this is a period of adjustment and I need to be patient. Once he's healed he might prefer the cemetery, but for now this is home.

'Sure, I'll see what they've got and bring it over around lunch time?'

'Really? That would be great, Benoit, thank you. I'll look into finding a cat sitter for the days I'm at the market.'

After I give Benoit my address, I end the call. I gently scoop Minou in my arms and check the rest of his wounds are clean. He wiggles to get out of my grasp, so I place him down on the kitchen floor and get his breakfast ready. He eats with great gusto, a good sign that hopefully it won't take long for him to get back to a healthy weight. While he's eating, I clean up the shattered pieces of my breakfast bowl.

Once he's had his fill of food, I administer his medication with a syringe and thankfully this time he accepts it without fuss. Unlike last night, where we played a game of chase for the better part of an hour. Progress. Soon enough, he slinks back to the bedroom and falls asleep once more. I envy him and have an internal debate as to whether I can get away with a nap too, but I'm already behind and have Benoit visiting too.

I take my laptop and set up at the dining room table. I log in to the Paris Cupid portal, pleased to see how efficient Geneviève has been working. She's matched a range of people and has dealt with a lot of new applications. That just leaves the message box, so I click into that and go through them. They're mainly thanks from members who are enjoying the concept of letter writing. There are two complaints, one from a woman who says she can't read her match's handwriting, the other from a man who says his match claims his handwriting is atrocious and he doesn't like her tone. He explains in his message to Paris Cupid that he has a sprained wrist and is doing the best he can. I reply to them both that perhaps in this special set of circumstances they could type and print their letters until his hand is healed.

There's a message to Paris Cupid from Émilienne with the subject line that reads: *Have I made a mistake?* Oh no! This is my greatest fear. That Emmanuel would revert to his playboy ways and it would all have been for nothing. Not to mention the media would be all over the breakup, and where would that leave the reputation of Paris Cupid? In tatters. Leaving Émilienne – my very first, genuine client – alone once more. I click on the message.

> I'm not sure if this is just cold feet, or if I've genuinely made a mistake giving my heart to Emmanuel. The deeper our connection grows, the starker our differences appear. The man does not stop talking. Ever. He tells everyone he's in love, he's getting married, he's given up his career for me. It's a lot to shoulder. It was his idea to renounce his career, to retire and follow me to India. It seems a big responsibility, and if things don't pan out, I imagine the blame will lie squarely at my feet. We spend every waking moment together; he's always right there beside me, which was sweet at first but is now suffocating. What do you advise? I love him with all my heart, but I need a break from all these protestations of love!

Merde! Émilienne is one of those people who loves company but also loves solitude. They've made this great leap into a new future but haven't accounted for the fact they're together *all* the time. I wish I could email her as myself; instead, I write the same sort of thing I'd tell her face to face.

> I can only give you the type of advice I'd give a friend, so here goes. Those stark differences you mention – would they be as evident if you were both living your regular lives? Is it that you're spending twenty-four hours a day together, living in each other's pockets, so there's no breathing room? No private time where you can take some space and just be. You went from writing letters and slowly building that connection to a very intense journey together. If you stepped

away from it for a moment, what does your heart tell you would happen? Only you will know whether this is worth fixing, worth fighting for, or not. Is your current place of lodging the right kind of environment for this stage of your relationship? Can you confide in your match and explain how you're feeling? Communicating those feelings is the best way forward and his response to what you share with him should make your next steps clearer. Perhaps tell him that time apart is something you need each and every day.

From all at Paris Cupid, we wish you well.

I hit send and hope that Émilienne finds some solace in there. It's hard to know when that niggle of distrust returns and makes me doubt Emmanuel and his motivations.

Back to the message box, I find one from the man himself with the subject line: *What am I doing wrong?*

I adore Émilienne, she's the light of my life, and if I'm honest, this is the first time I've been in love. I'm messing it up but I don't know how. She's pulling away from me, I sense it, so I am trying to be there for her. I tell her at every opportunity how much I love her. I tell everyone! I tell them I gave up my career for her, so she's reminded just how little everything means in comparison to her. Nothing else matters. The more I shout this out, the more it feels I'm speaking into a void. What should I do?

From an outsider's perspective, it seems to me that the issue is she needs space, and he's trying to fill that space because he thinks that's what she wants, when it's the total opposite.

Have you talked to her about how you're feeling? Communication is key in healthy, successful relationships. Oftentimes a partner will need space, but that doesn't mean they feel any different, it just means they need time alone. Time to reflect and centre themselves. Telling everyone you gave up your career for Émilienne could come across in a different way than you intended. Perhaps the next step should be a frank and honest discussion?

From all at Paris Cupid, we wish you well.

Once again, I'm conflicted. Emmanuel really does seem genuinely in love with Émilienne, and maybe he's just as hopeless with love as the rest of us? It makes some sort of illogical sense that when he senses she's backing away, he figures the best recourse is to drown her in protestations of his love so she comes back. When we're in the thick of it, we don't tend to see these glaring mistakes. Only time will tell if they can resolve this, and the romantic in me hopes they do.

25

Benoit arrives with an inflatable collar for Minou and a backpack with a transparent viewing pouch.

'Is that what I think it is?' I ask.

'Yes, a cat pack! You can place Minou inside. It's got air vents and he can see out of all three sides in case he wants a walk and some fresh air. The woman at the pet shop said they're very popular among Parisians. Although, she could have been just after another sale, who knows?'

I laugh imagining Minou trapped inside a see through backpack while I amble along the boulevards of Paris. 'How much do I owe you?'

He hands me a receipt and the amount isn't too bad considering. I find my purse and hand him some euros. 'Thank you for doing this. Should we see if he'll try the backpack?'

'*Oui.*'

But Minou is nowhere to be found. 'He must be here, I haven't left the apartment today.' We hunt high and low and part of me senses he's watching us from some hidden vantage point, laughing at the show we're putting on for him.

'Are you sure he can't have escaped somehow?' Benoit asks, raking a hand through his thick dark hair.

'I'm sure. I haven't opened the balcony door and all the windows are locked. Do you think this is some kind of cat trickery? What if we stop searching for him and pretend we're having a grand old time and see if he appears?'

Benoit's eyes shine with mirth. 'Do you think cats are *that* manipulative? Or is this the lack of sleep talking?'

I slap my forehead. 'I sound like a crazy cat lady already and he hasn't even been in my company for twenty-four hours. Imagine what I'll be saying at the seven-day mark!'

With a laugh he takes a seat on the sofa. 'Ah, I assume the fabric didn't look like this yesterday?' He points to the arm that looks like it had a run in with a cheese grater.

'You assume correctly. I'm not sure how he managed to shred it so viciously when he's only got a few claws left. Maybe it was a way to get his rage out after the cat fight? I tried to be supportive and show him the scratching post, but he turned his nose up at it, and I mean he *literally* put his nose in the air as if the contraption was beneath him.'

'Cats, eh?'

I join Benoit on the sofa. 'Any sign of him?'

He pretends to stretch as he gazes around the room. 'Is that a paw?' he whispers, tilting his head towards an umbrella stand.

Sure enough, behind the oversized ceramic vase I use as an umbrella stand, a tabby paw sticks out. 'We see you, Minou.' At that he sticks his head up over the stand and gives us a wide smile. Can cats smile?

I stand and say, 'I better move that before he breaks – Minou, no!' I dive across the space hoping to catch the oversized vase before it smashes to the floor but I don't quite make the distance. The pot lands safely – upon my head.

'*Aie!*'

The tabby terror sprints from the living room to wherever his next hellscape is.

'Are you OK?' Benoit helps me up from the parquetry floor. I'm slightly dazed as I sit on the sofa once more, rubbing the back of my head with my hand.

Benoit presses his lips tightly together.

'What's that face for?' I ask. Minou has got me on edge. I dart around this way and that looking for his next surprise attack.

'It's... it's...' The dam breaks and Benoit dissolves into laughter.

'This is *funny* to you?' I say, hiding a smile.

'Sorry, sorry, it's not funny. It's only that I've never seen a cat engage in warfare quite like this before and the way you threw your entire body across the room, well, I've never seen any human airborne like that before either.'

Soon we both break into the kind of hysterical laughter that takes forever to get hold of. When we're finally composed I say, 'Was he *smiling*? Or did the bump to the head do some real damage and I'm imagining that?'

'It was a smile, but more of the maniacal kind.'

'OK, that's only slightly alarming,' I say. Minou saunters over, casually as anything, and springs up on my lap, kneading the leg of my jeans as if we're the best of friends. 'Aww, this is the first time he's sat on my lap.'

'These are clearly just teething problems and he's already learning that he's safe here.' Minou accepts a pat from Benoit. 'But I'm not putting him in the backpack and risking him hating me.'

I grin. 'Me neither. We'll leave that contraption for Guillaume. Minou might be a cat but I think he categorises himself more as a human, and I can't quite see him enjoying being bundled up in a cat backpack, and he would not suffer in indignity of such a thing!'

The turncoat moves from my lap to Benoit's, resting his body on his chest and tucking his head into his neck. It's adorable and gives me hope that Minou just might settle in as a house cat.

'While you're getting him off to sleep, shall I make apero?' I ask.

Apero is usually taken in the space after work, the lull before dinner. It comprises a few drinks served with finger food and is a great excuse to catch up with friends without ruining your appetite for dinner. Most Parisians practise this tradition once a week or so. Any time is a good time for apero.

'Apero sounds great. I've got a feeling I might be stuck here for a while.' It's hard not to soften at the sight of Minou sprawled across

Benoit, trusting him implicitly when really he's not the affectionate type, not like Marmalade who loves being rocked like a baby.

I'm still not convinced Minou will acclimatise to a domestic arrangement, but I hope he does.

I go to the kitchen and take some brie, a wedge of Roquefort and some grapes and pile them on to a platter. I realise too late that I don't have a baguette, which is a crime in Paris when you're serving cheese.

'Benoit, I'm just going to the boulangerie on the corner for a baguette. Will you be all right for a few minutes with Minou?' Part of me doesn't trust the tabby terror won't create a ruckus while I'm gone and then pretend nothing happened.

'*Oui*. I'm not going to move a muscle, so he can rest.'

I take my purse and tiptoe out of the apartment, clicking the door softly closed.

At the boulangerie, I grab a baguette and a citron tart. It's only when I'm almost back home that I question the fact I've left a virtual stranger inside my apartment. We've shared a few conversations across the hall and a last-minute dinner, but I don't really know Benoit all that well. Still, what can he do? Not much while the cat has him pinned to the sofa. And he's too sweet to be the type to snoop. It's always at the back of my mind that Paris Cupid is a secret I don't want known. All he'd have to do is lift my laptop lid and he'd see the homepage on the screen. While I trust him, I quicken my steps and tell myself it's my worry about Minou that has me hurrying.

When I return, all my anxiety evaporates. They're in the same spot, only now Benoit is also in the land of nod, his head lolling to the side, his mouth slightly parted. I drop the baguette and tart on the kitchen bench and then tiptoe close to the sleeping beauties and give Minou a gentle pat.

Benoit's eyes spring open and I jump backwards. 'Sorry, I was checking on Minou.'

He laughs. 'That's OK. His purring put me right to sleep and it doesn't look like he's going to move anytime soon.'

'You're stuck here for the foreseeable,' I say. Minou is a totally different cat to the one the night before, but maybe exhaustion from his trauma has finally caught up with him and he can rest now he knows it's safe here.

'He's drooling on me a little bit.'

I laugh. 'And he hardly knows you. How rude.' While Benoit is stuck as Minou sleeps, I pour two glasses of cool crisp Sancerre.

I hand Benoit a glass of wine as he awkwardly slides upright so as not to disturb the furry creature. Minou wrenches one eye open and then promptly closes it again.

'*Merci*,' Benoit says, taking a sip. 'I didn't expect the day to quite pan out like this. But I'm glad it has.'

'Me too. Guillaume has sent me about a hundred texts asking how things are. After my frantic messages last night, I sense he doubts my cat parenting abilities.'

'I'm sure he trusts you. It's probably more that he's in love and not thinking straight.'

What? How does Benoit know such a thing? 'In love? Guillaume?'

He gives me a slow nod. '*Oui*. He joined that site, Paris Cupid.'

'Oh, he might have mentioned that in passing. I wasn't really paying much attention. What did he say about it?'

'He's enjoying it but has reservations about the safety side because of all the conjecture about it being run anonymously. But I assured him his details are safe.'

'Him and technology!' I say with a stiff smile.

'Right, he's a luddite of the finest order. It's not helped by every second person at the market gossiping about Paris Cupid. I suppose it's because of Emmanuel Roux. I don't understand why people care so much about it being run by someone who doesn't want their name involved.'

'I don't get it either. Was Guillaume really worried?' Will that stop him from writing to Clementine? I'd hate to see that happy smile of his snatched away again. All because he's worrying about a data breach or whatever his suspicious mind dreamed up.

'*Oui*. He's worried it might have been some kind of scam, that he'd be cloned, just the usual.'

'Cloned?' I let out a giggle. 'Guillaume says technology has advanced too quickly and we're all going be replaced with robots. The cloning thing is new.'

'I did some investigation into Paris Cupid to put his mind at ease. It looks like a legitimate site to me.'

I try my best to keep my expression neutral but to hear even Benoit is digging around Paris Cupid is alarming. 'So you said Guillaume is in love?' He's been writing for well over a month, so I suppose they could have agreed to meet, but I just don't see Guillaume going that fast with this, and to call it love, well, that's a whole leap I didn't expect he'd take, not for a very long time at any rate.

Benoit makes a face. 'I hope I'm not speaking out of turn, but he asked me to write one of his love letters in calligraphy.'

'Oh…?'

'He wanted to meet. He wasn't sure if he was being too forward, rushing into things, hence he wanted me to use an elegant script to show her his romantic side and that he was taking their relationship seriously. After she read that letter they arranged to meet. As far as I know things progressed fast because he told me she was joining him for a few days on his buying trip to Roeun.'

'I'm…' Lost for words. So much for taking it slow! It hasn't been very long and they're going away together already? 'I'm a little taken aback. Guillaume confided in me about Paris Cupid and I figured he was searching for a friendship more than anything else.' First Emmanuel and Émilienne and now this. None of my matches are panning out the way I expected.

'Apparently sparks flew. They're both smitten.'

It's like my brain is on overload and can't compute the information. None of this came up when I met him at the vet but I suppose our focus had been on Minou. I consider Benoit's job, penning the private innermost thoughts of his customers, writing their secrets, their sweet nothings onto delicate parchment, taking a love letter and making it into art with his beautiful calligraphy. It's just like Guillaume to elevate his humble letter-writing, using Benoit to make it even more special. 'I guess it was love at first sight for Guillaume and Clementine.'

'Looks that way.'

Mortifyingly happy tears spring to my eyes and I hurriedly wipe them away. 'Ignore me.'

'You really care for him, don't you?' For a moment I get lost in Benoit's deep intelligent gaze. He manages to pick up on just what I'm feeling without me having to voice it.

'I do. I've been so worried about him since Mathilde passed away. Each year he gets thinner, wasting away before my very eyes, and nothing I could say or do would help. Mathilde had been adamant he should find love again, but he was dead against it. To hear this news, well, it's a real privilege to have been...' I stop short, catching myself before saying too much. Blame the emotions of the moment. 'To hear this wonderful news.'

Benoit gives me a strange look. Or am I reading too much into it after my gaffe?

'Cheese?' I say brightly, holding the plate up.

'Sure.' He takes a slice of baguette and cuts a wedge of brie to place on the top.

'It seems like everyone in Paris is falling in love...' I muse almost to myself as we lock eyes.

'There was something I wanted to ask you...' Benoit says, but the thread is lost when Minou jumps up and steals the brie from Benoit's fingers and dashes to my bedroom.

'That cat!'

26

Minou is safely ensconced at my apartment with a cat sitter. A no-nonsense teenager who promises me she's seen it all before and whatever the cat throws at her she'll be able to handle. She'll administer his medications and make sure he doesn't escape his inflatable collar. I've come to learn Minou has about six different personalities and with no warning he will turn from sleepy cuddler to acrobat. Eventually his energy wanes, and I clean up the debris as if a hurricane blew through and left only destruction in its wake.

As I come to the market square, I stop at Coraline's stall to buy flowers in the hopes she'll share any news about her Paris Cupid match.

'*Bonjour*, Lilou,' she says, giving me a wide grin.

'*Bonjour*. How are you?' I peruse the flowers on offer, picking up a bouquet of bright yellow daffodils.

'Daffodils mean new beginnings, Lilou. Is that what you're after?'

I smile. Has the old Coraline returned so quickly? 'Hmm.' I pretend to consider it. 'New beginnings are exactly what I'm after. Leaving the past behind and moving on is what I'm aiming for.'

'Let me wrap them for you.' Coraline hasn't wrapped my flowers in years. It's sweet to see her take pride in her work once more.

'*Merci*. There's something different about you today? Your cheeks are aflame, your eyes are shining; if I didn't know better I'd say you're in love.'

She lets out a girlish giggle. Love really is the tonic. It's as though Coraline has been transformed. Even her hair is shiny and sleek. It's such a marked change, seeing the smile reach her eyes and every part of her radiating. 'I got matched on Paris Cupid.'

'Ooh! Right, I almost forgot about that. I take it that it's going rather well.'

She nods as she hands me the beautifully wrapped bouquet of bright yellow daffodils. 'It's been lifechanging. I know that sounds dramatic considering we haven't met in person yet, but I'm taking it slow this time.'

'And your match, what makes him so great?'

'He's a bookseller and he writes the most romantic prose. Like me, he's been lonely but unsure of where to look for love. I don't know where this will lead, so I'm enjoying it for what it is – a pen pal relationship that has the potential to become more. If it doesn't develop into love, we've promised each other to remain friends and catch up eventually anyway.'

I love this for Coraline. It appears she's figured out that rushing into relationships, and having a sort of saviour complex with men who were poised to take advantage, was not the best way forward even though she did nothing wrong and her intentions were pure. How many other Parisians make just the same mistakes when it comes to love? We all want to believe in the person beside us in bed.

'I really hope it works out for you both.'

'It will. Because even if I don't find love, I know I've found a friend and that's enough for me.'

It's hard to know which way the wind will blow, but I send up a prayer to the love gods and will it to be so. 'I'm glad you tried Paris Cupid. It seems like everyone is talking about it these days.' I really shouldn't pry but Coraline is the go-to for gossip so she'll know if there's anything new in the rumour mill.

'Thank you for suggesting it. Without you, I wouldn't have taken that leap. Are you sure *you're* not Paris Cupid? You do have a penchant for love letters!' She laughs at her own joke while I use every effort to keep myself from fainting at her feet.

'Ha! It's not me.'

'Well, I didn't think so. Not with your disaster of a dating life. Didn't you date a cryptomancer once?'

As always I come so far with Coraline and then jump two steps back. 'We didn't exactly get to the dating stage; we were chatting for a bit and then he tried to get me to invest in crypto. Men, eh?' More fool me for sharing these titbits with Coraline.

'And then there was that married guy...'

I reel back as if slapped. 'That wasn't my fault.'

'Still. It doesn't look good, does it? Everyone always says they don't know, when they actually do.'

I cock my head. 'Why are you bringing all of this up?'

'I want to solve the Paris Cupid mystery! I'm intrigued. I joined an online sleuth group and their main focus is finding Cupid. There hasn't been gossip this juicy for an age. The current theory is it's someone from Saint-Ouen Flea Market. Your name was mentioned because of the love letter link.'

It takes a lot to remain calm. 'My name? How ridiculous. Why do they think it's linked to the market?'

She gives me a lazy shrug. 'Lately there've been a lot of matches with market vendors. Almost as if someone around here is orchestrating it.'

Geneviève and I *have* focused on those we knew from around here because we knew bits and pieces about their dating histories and felt they deserved a happy ever after.

'I can't believe there's another group digging into it. Don't you feel bad considering how Paris Cupid has helped you?'

Coraline squares her jaw. 'Why should I?'

Seriously! 'If the people who run Paris Cupid wish to remain anonymous why would you not respect that after what they've done for you? You've just spent ten minutes telling me how much you're enjoying a burgeoning new friendship with P...' I stop short, his name dying on my tongue. Did she pick it up? I scramble to cover my folly. '...with a Parisian bookseller, and now you're ready to throw that back in their face. It's not nice, Coraline.'

She narrows her eyes. Why am I even having this conversation? The longer I talk to her the more likely I'm going to speak out of turn and then the jig will really be up.

'Our sleuth group doesn't agree with all the secrecy. Transparency is good business practice. We have every right to know about the face behind the site. After all, members have shared personal information with Paris Cupid and I for one would rather know that *my* privacy is going to be guaranteed.'

All of the confidentiality guarantees are written into the terms and conditions that each member signs, but I can't exactly bring that up without exposing myself. 'That's hypocritical! You'll expose their anonymity to make sure yours is safe?'

She grunts as if I'm too dense to understand the complexities of such a thing. 'I'm not the one making millions of dollars here.'

Millions of dollars! It's nothing of the sort. Sure, there is a cost involved, but my time is worth it. 'Oh be real, Coraline, you just enjoy the drama.'

'Maybe. My theory is it's got to be someone with a connection to love letters, so if it's not you then it has to be Benoit, who writes those calligraphy letters, or Pascale maybe. Although Pascale doesn't seem like the romantic sort but he could be hiding in plain sight. Then there's Felix with all those hand-pressed greeting cards?'

Mon Dieu! This has escalated fast. I'd been of the opinion speculation had died down, when it's actually been building up in the background. 'It's a shame you can't be happy to be matched and leave it at that.'

She makes a show of rolling her eyes with dramatic flair. 'If you don't get your daffodils in water soon, they'll droop.' With a flick of her hair, she flounces behind her display of flowers.

There's nothing else I can do except stomp into the Marché Dauphine, muttering and mumbling under my breath. I manage to catch Pascale's attention. He frowns as we exchange a glance but I don't have the energy to worry about him. I open my stall and deposit the daffodils in a crystal vase. Their beauty has been marred by Coraline, but I try not to hold it against the yellow flowers.

I move my display tables out front with a loud grunt – did they get heavier? I'm so mad I'm sure steam is coming out of my ears. It's not only that Coraline is hell-bent on digging into the face behind Paris Cupid, it's that she has no compunction about doing such a thing even after finding a successful match herself because of *our* help! Geneviève spent hours upon hours trying to figure out what made Coraline tick so she would find her the perfect correspondent in the hopes she could build a real relationship with a person who wouldn't take advantage of her like so many men have in the past.

I don't bother putting my pot plants out; instead, I launch myself on the chaise and replay the conversation with Coraline. Will it all go away if I ignore it? Hard to tell with Coraline, who embellishes the truth for sport. When I consider it, she doesn't have any concrete details.

I close my eyes and take a deep breath and then exhale all the angst.

'Rough morning?'

Can this day get any worse? I open my eyes to find Pascale leaning against the door jamb, smiling like a loon. What's that all about?

I grimace. The morning has been a nightmare but I'm sure he doesn't really care. 'You could say that.'

He lifts a brow. 'What's up? You're usually so happy in the mornings. This is the first time I've seen you banging and crashing around the place like you've got something big on your mind.'

'Well, if you've come to complain, now is not the time.'

He grins. Why is he grinning! Can't he see I'm absolutely furious?

'I've come to see if I can help. Who should I hunt down? Point to them and it will be done.'

My eyes widen. 'You think *violence* is the answer?'

'Depends on the question.' That provokes a slight smile that I try my best to extinguish. Pascale might not be so laissez-faire when he finds out he's part of the plot.

'Coraline is in an online sleuth group who are set on exposing the person behind Paris Cupid and is suspicious of me, but then she discounted it because of my woeful dating history. It upset me. She always manages to annoy me, so I don't know why I keep trying with her.' Why do I? Time and again she shows me her true colours.

His eyebrows shoot up. 'Why did she think *you* were Cupid?' He says it with so much disdain, like I couldn't possibly be that person. I'm almost tempted to tell him the truth just to throw it back in his face.

'Why couldn't I be Cupid? Are you saying I'm not capable?' Why does this man bring out the worst in me?

'What? No, you're misunderstanding me. I'm on your side. It's just this Paris Cupid avalanche of speculation is taking its toll. It's all anyone around here ever talks about.'

Thanks to Coraline, I bet. I should have trusted my first instinct and kept my mouth shut, but no, stupid me had to help her.

'Why are they invested in such a silly thing anyway? Who cares who Paris Cupid is? What does it matter to any of us?'

'I've only heard small bits of gossip about Paris Cupid here and there. I didn't know it had gathered so much momentum.'

With a sigh, he lifts his palms in the air. 'Who knows, but if the rumours are anything to go by, it's someone who works in the market.'

My heart beats hard against my ribs. 'You've heard that too?'

'Yeah, apparently it's Geneviève because she's been encouraging people to join for months.' I rub my temples as a headache takes hold. 'Are you OK?' Pascale asks, his eyebrows pulling together.

'No... not really.' I'm close to confessing to him. And where would that get me? Not far, I'd imagine. 'It's just... it feels intrusive. Like they're trying to ruin a site that's helped many who struggled to find love the usual way.'

'It's a shame but that's how it always is around here. When there's a lull between customers the gossip starts. Don't worry about it. It's got nothing to do with you anyway.'

Little does he know. 'I like this version of you.'

'This *version*?'

'*Oui*. Who knew there was a practical comforting side to you? Usually you're glowering and grunting and shooting me glares.'

He folds his arms across the wide expanse of his chest. 'Is that so?'

'Here we go. Tell me I'm wrong.'

'You're wrong.'

I arch a brow.

'I might be a little testy occasionally but that's because I'm constantly being interrupted when I'm trying to write.'

'Not this again!'

'It's true. I'm writing a novel and I'm easily distracted, and then I lose the thread and it all feels so hopeless.'

'What's your book about?'

'An anonymous matchmaker in Paris.'

I grin. 'It is not.'

'*Non*. It's a coming-of-age story, but I'm doubting my ability to finish it. I can't seem to concentrate since I moved here.'

'All those scented candles and my obnoxious laughter?'

'Exactly.'

We lapse into a comfortable silence. Who knew that Pascale had literary ambitions?

'So the big move disrupted your writing mojo?' And that's why he's stomped around like a tyrant?

'*Oui*. I've been... distracted by other things and now I can't connect to the book. It's frustrating.'

'Have you always wanted to write?' Is it Pascale who has the soul of a poet, and not Benoit, like I presumed just from the way they looked? Have I judged him too harshly?

'I've been bashing out words ever since I was a teenager. I've got lots of half-finished drafts, many abandoned projects. This time I promised myself I'd get to the end. And yet here I am stuck in the middle again.'

'What's stopping you though?'

'Writer's block? Stubbornness. Fear of failure. Imposter syndrome.'

I can't help but scoff. 'I just can't see you being plagued with doubt. You exude confidence. You're like a superhero stomping around all over the place, bellowing down your phone or ignoring customers.'

He tilts his head. 'Me?'

Is he serious? 'Yes, you!'

'Well, I guess I don't see myself that way.'

'How do you see yourself?'

'Usually through a lens of crippling self-doubt.'

'*Oui*, you *are* a writer!'

We break into laughter. This conversation is so refreshing and paints Pascale in a whole new light.

'I'm hoping to get this book published. But first I need to finish it.'

'So stop making excuses and get it done.'

'Yes, boss!' He salutes.

I grin. 'I know you can do it if you set your mind to the end goal.'

'How do you know?'

'I just do. You fit the stereotype of frustrated writer.'

Benoit appears in the hall outside, waves and strides over to my stall. 'I better go,' Pascale says as Benoit approaches. 'I've got customers to ignore. Hope your day gets better.'

'*Merci*, you too.'

Benoit takes Pascale's spot and leans against the door jamb.

'*Bonjour*, Benoit. How are you?' I feel lighter after talking to Pascale, a feat I'd never have imagined before. Electric, even. Is it that he's not the grumpy brutish guy I'd pegged him for? My bad mood has evaporated and I feel fully charged.

Benoit is fidgety, distracted, as if he's got something on his mind. 'Good, good. How is Minou?'

'The same – happy one moment, crazy the next. I used the cat backpack! Let me get my phone and show you the photo of his face. Minou is definitely going to be in contention for the next grumpy cat meme.'

I leave Benoit and search for my handbag and locate my phone. I flick through until I find the photo. Even now it provokes laughter. 'Minou despised the indignity of having his photo taken at home in the carrier before we enjoyed a stroll around the neighbourhood. He was more settled that evening.'

Benoit's face breaks into a wide smile. 'I see what you mean about the meme potential. Hilarious. How did the inflatable collar go?'

'So far so good. He hasn't managed to pull it off and his abrasions are healing nicely because he can't get near them.'

Felix arrives holding a café crème and joins us at the door. '*Mademoiselle.* Caffeine to start your day?'

Benoit drops his gaze as if suddenly shy. 'Enjoy your coffee. And keep the cat memes coming.'

I laugh. 'Sure. *Au revoir.*' I take the proffered cup from Felix. 'How's your week been?' I ask.

'Busy! Yours? You're a cat parent now?'

'*Oui*, a part time co-parent. And better yet, I've lived to tell the tale. Secretly I love the tiny terror, but I'm also looking forward to a decent night's sleep once Guillaume takes his charge. Minou loves zooming around the house at nighttime, specifically using my face as his launch pad. This can go on for hours, and if I shut my bedroom door he meows from the other side until I give in and open it and the whole exercise starts again. I suppose he spent his days at the cemetery snoozing in the sunshine and nighttime is where he got up to mischief.'

Felix grins. 'How will Guillaume go handling such a wily beast?'

I sense how things are going to go for Guillaume because the clever cat knows exactly what he can get away with. 'I bet Minou will be on this best behaviour around him. Guillaume will tell me the nocturnal behaviour is all in my mind, that his darling cat would never do such a thing. I've hired a cat sitter for Minou when I'm working at the market, to keep an eye on him during his recovery.'

'Ah! I'd planned to invite you on a ghost tour tonight. Perhaps we'll have to leave it until your fur baby is with his other parent?'

'A ghost tour?' It's such a Felix thing to do, something wacky and fun.

'It's a walking tour visiting a range of spooky places around Paris. While it's a little macabre, it's also got a historical element to it.'

'Another time, for sure, once Minou is better. Ooh, I almost forgot. A customer came looking for you yesterday but you'd already locked up, so she left a package for you. One moment and I'll find it in my desk.'

I go and find the envelope in my desk. 'Here you go. She said it's full of design ideas for her wedding invitations.'

He groans. '*Merci.* She only wants one hundred of them, and by next week. No rest for the wicked, eh?'

'Get to it. My turn tomorrow.' I waggle my keep cup. When he leaves,

I take a feather duster and make my rounds. When I get to the bookshelf near the front door, I find a diary that isn't one of mine. Did Benoit or Pascale plant it? They each had time to when I had been distracted. I lean against the door jamb and survey them. Neither of them is paying any attention to me; they're all busy working. Perhaps the diary will give me more clues.

27

When I lock up late, all my neighbours have shuttered their shops. Geneviève didn't turn up today so I send her a text:

> Want to meet tonight? Catch up on some Paris Cupid work?

I have to tell her about the exchange I had with Coraline.

When I get to my apartment, I kick off my shoes and call out for Minou. The apartment is in reasonable shape; there's some shredded paper on the parquetry and the corpse of a banana by the fridge. When there's no answer to me calling his name, I add some biscuits to his bowl. The tabby cat then launches onto my shoulder and frightens the life out of me. Why can't he just say hello the normal way? Maybe I'll get used to these jump scares eventually.

I give his fur a pat as he balances on my left shoulder as if he's a bird. 'Did you have a good day?' There's a note from the cat sitter telling me she's administered his medications and that he spent most of the day sleeping in her lap.

Minou jumps to the ground for his dinner, so I leave him to it and go and investigate the bedroom. Sure enough, he's had a fight with the pillow and the pillow has come off worse.

The vet is scheduled for tomorrow morning so I'll ask what might be causing such behaviours. Is it boredom? Maybe Minou needs a feline friend? Would two cats create even more mess and angst? Whatever the solution is, I'm willing to give it a shot. Coming home to him is a joy despite him having a burning hatred for décor. I clean up the mess of pillow before administering Minou's meds when there's a knock on the door.

'Now, pretend you're a well-behaved cat, Minou.'

He lets out a long meow and licks his paw and appears angelic as anything. It's such a lie.

'Geneviève! I was just about to pour a wine. Would you like one?'

'What a silly question!'

'I take it that's a yes.'

She passes me her light coat and handbag as if I'm some sort of concierge. I would usually put them on the coat rack, but I'm one step ahead of Minou this time and go through to my bedroom and place them out of harm's way in my cupboard.

When I reappear, Geneviève's sitting at the dining table, bottle of wine opened and two glasses poured. She takes a long sip and smacks her lips together.

'I needed that,' she says. 'Now to business. I've had a number of texts asking if you're Cupid.'

'I know. Pascale told me that there are rumours *you're* Paris Cupid because you were encouraging people to join.'

Geneviève gives me a wide smile. 'I love being the centre of gossip.'

'I don't. But they can't prove anything, can they?'

'Not unless we make a misstep.'

Geneviève goes to the kitchen to retrieve the wine bottle and returns to fill our glasses. 'Do we care if the truth comes out? I know you're worried about your dating history coming to light but, in the grand scheme of things, does that really matter any more?' She softens her words with a warm smile, but just the thought of the truth coming out is enough to make my toes curl.

'I'd hate it Geneviève, I really would. The married man saga will be dredged up again. And Coraline has joined some amateur sleuth group who want to find the identity of Cupid because they feel everything should be transparent.'

'Coraline said all of *that*, after what we've done for her, what Paris Cupid has done for her?' Geneviève says, aghast. 'That's really upsetting, Lilou. She was the one I was most excited would have a beautiful romance and a sort of... transformation. Are you telling me she's just the same as she always was?'

I nod. 'It's disappointing to see she hasn't changed. I guess she doesn't know it's us behind Paris Cupid, but she's suspicious because of the links I have with love letters and Benoit, Felix and Pascale with their businesses.'

'All that aside, she *does* know Paris Cupid helped her when she most needed it.'

'We should have known better. *I* should have known better when it comes to Coraline.'

'If they get close to the truth, why don't I say I'm Cupid?'

'But... what if they bring up your past? Won't that bother you?'

She scoffs. 'Hardly! I wouldn't care a jot. I've loved and lost and I've picked myself up and tried again. Nothing to be ashamed of. But full transparency – if they want to be sensational about it, there's plenty to work with. Just like everyone, I've made plenty of mistakes with men. But that's just the thing, Lilou. We live and learn! And that's what I want you to take from this, *ma Cherie*. They can sky write my dating disasters for all I care. They can splash each sorry past affair of mine online and make an example out of me. I'll celebrate! I'd take that risk time and again because love is always worth it. Even if it's not always easy to find.'

Minou takes that moment to jump on the table and swat at my glass, but my cat mummy senses must be improving because I catch it before it falls. 'Hah!' I turn to Minou. 'Too slow this time!'

'Are you goading that cat?'

'*Oui*. But trust me, I'll pay for that later when I'm asleep and he springboards off my nose.'

Minou regally assesses Geneviève. 'So what are your thoughts?' Geneviève asks. I take a sip of wine and consider it from both sides.

'It's really not fair to make you the focus of their scrutiny in whatever way that plays out. I couldn't do that to you, no matter how much I'd hate the scrutiny on myself.' Geneviève would probably kill for me, but it doesn't mean I'd ask her to.

'OK, option two: we acknowledge that people are curious to the identity of Paris Cupid but we're not sharing that information because the person in question wants to maintain a level of privacy in their everyday life.'

'I'm wondering if that will flame the fire.'

'Sleep on it tonight and we can chat tomorrow. Now, to happier subjects. How are you going with finding out who your secret admirer is?' She waggles her brow suggestively and says 'Could it be Benoit, or could it be Pascale?' I laugh at her theatrics as I think about the two men. I realise that only a few weeks ago, I'd been annoyed with Pascale and his tense behaviour, but perhaps with everything going on with Paris Cupid, that has somehow evaporated. He's more of a friend than foe now, or at least we're heading in that direction.

'Honestly, Geneviève, they're both wonderful. They really are. Even Pascale is slowly opening up, or at least he isn't just using grunts to communicate.'

She inhales deeply, which I know means a monologue about love is coming.

I put a finger to her lips to stem the tide and say, 'Also... another diary appeared this morning. Another item that I didn't purchase. It was just sitting on a shelf in Ephemera.'

'And clearly you didn't see who put it there?'

'That's just the thing. Pascale and Benoit both stopped by this morning, in a short space of time. It could have been either one of them.'

She taps a finger to her chin. 'Or... both of them! Maybe they both wrote in it! Have you looked? The plot thickens!'

I frown. 'Wouldn't that be a stretch? I haven't looked inside yet. Let me find it.' I go to my room and take the diary from my handbag. When I return, Minou is sitting in Geneviève's lap, kneading her dress, what's left of his claws hooking the material. 'Ah, Geneviève, isn't that raw silk?' Geneviève is one to wear designer labels, always promoting the fact I should invest in quality that will last a lifetime, not fast fashion.

'It is, but look at his little battle-scarred face. I don't have the heart to stop him.'

It appears that Minou's charms are endless. I find one of his rugs and place it on Geneviève's lap to help save her dress. 'Here's the diary.' I hand over the notebook, which has the most beautiful floral-embossed cover.

'OK, so if you don't think it's both of them conspiring, best guess who penned this one?' she asks as she dons her diamante specs.

I go to the fridge and take a range of cheeses and some fruit and assemble them on a platter. 'I'm really not sure. Benoit came over the other day and said he wanted to ask me something, but then Minou jumped up and the moment was lost. Do you think he was going to confess it's him?' I bring the platter back to the table and have to wrestle Minou away from the brie.

'Could be. Why don't you ask him out? You've got extra time now that I'm helping with Paris Cupid. I'm having far too much fun helping with that, but what's more important to me is that you *continue* to date and mingle and put yourself back into the path of love. And don't think I didn't pick up on the fact you avoided answering my question – who wrote this one?' Geneviève waggles the diary in the air as Minou tries to paw at it.

I don my own thinking pose. Pascale is still an enigma, but today's visit chipped away at my former opinion of him. He could see I was struggling, and he dropped his usual peeved act and checked in on me. Can I really trust in that? For all I know, he could be in cahoots with those who chitter chatter around the market and has noted the change in demeanour and pounced. I'm not usually one to catastrophise like this, but it's an unnerving feeling not knowing who to trust.

The impatient tap of Geneviève's fingernails on the table reminds me I haven't answered. '*Forced* to guess, I'd say Benoit. His job is romantic; he writes other people's love letters all day every day.'

'Right. But this kind of diary, this is the sort of thing Felix prints, isn't it?'

Is it? I hadn't thought of Felix hand-pressing diaries before. 'Can he do work like that? I've only seen him print cards, posters, wedding invitations, that sort of thing.'

Geneviève sneaks Minou a slice of Comte. I'm about to rebuke her when she says, 'I've known Felix has bound handmade diaries before. He made a range for the teachers at École de Musique in Paris.'

'When was that?'

'A year ago, two? When he was on the other side of the market. I only know because I'm friends with the principal and he asked me to help him with the design.'

'We know it's not Felix, though. But are you suggesting that Felix must know who it is?'

'Yes, he must. You don't think it's Pascale?'

I shrug. 'He doesn't seem the type.'

'I can't handle the suspense any longer.' She opens the diary and gasps.

'What!' I ask. 'What is it?'

'Well, one mystery is over. You cannot doubt this is about you any more! Take a look.' She points to the top of the page. '"Dearest Lilou".'

'It really is for me.'

Geneviève reads the first entry. 'It's a poem about unrequited love!'

'Let me read it!' I take the diary from her hands and scan the loopy handwriting. A warmth spreads through me at the sight of my name at the top of the page. The poem is evocative and sweet, an ode to a woman he loves but to whom he doesn't have the courage to admit how he feels, for fear of rejection. 'It's got to be Benoit. He's the shy one.' When he speaks, he often says startlingly beautiful sentiments before freezing up. When we discuss anything domestic, like solutions for Minou, he's practical and confident, as long as we don't veer far off those sorts of conversations into anything personal. I'd thought that could be politeness. But what if it is that he's unsure in my presence, like I so often am around men these days?

'I don't know,' Geneviève says. 'It could be Pascale. His gruff exterior might be a front.'

'What about the handwriting? Won't that give us a clue?'

'Ooh, *oui*, of course!'

'We need to compare the handwriting of all the correspondence that have arrived, but they're in my desk at the market.'

She clucks her tongue, frustrated at the wait. 'How about tomorrow I go on a little fact-finding mission? I'll get Pascale and Benoit to do a writing sample for me and we can compare.'

'How will you manage that?'

With a smirk, she says 'I have my ways.'

I laugh and take a sip of my wine. My mind spins with scenarios and lands on another issue. 'If whoever it is finds out I'm Cupid, will it change their mind about me?'

'*Ma Cherie*, how could it? If they love you, then they love all of you.'

'*Love*? Really, Geneviève?'

'*Oui*. It's love they've written about here.'

'But which one is it?'

'We'll see.'

Minou lets out a plaintive meow. 'What is it, my little friend?' I tickle his ears as he gazes mournfully outside. 'Are you missing the cemetery?'

As his wounds heal and he recuperates, I get the feeling my shoebox size apartment isn't going to be enough for my tabby friend. 'Would you like go for a walk, Geneviève? Minou needs a bit of air.'

'And how do you suggest we walk a cat?'

I smother a grin. 'We've got a cat pack. I've drawn the line at buying a pram, that's possibly one step too far.'

'A pram?' She shakes her head. Minou meows again as if trying to tell us something. 'Let's take him for a stroll, Lilou. He does seem to want to go out.'

28

I'm at the vet bright and early with Minou for his check-up. The temperamental beast rolls on his back, making it easy for her to examine him. 'He's healing remarkably well,' the vet says. 'Administer the remaining meds and keep an eye on his water and food intake, but I'd say he's almost back to normal, albeit with a few more scars to tell the tale. Without you looking after him it would have been a different outcome for Minou.'

'*Merci.* I've loved having him as a house guest, although I'm not convinced he's enjoyed it as much.' I fill her in on his nighttime shenanigans and the destruction around the apartment. The times he goes quiet or the evenings where he lets out haunting meows as if he's calling for someone, or something.

'He's used to hunting, catching his prey at night when the cemetery is empty of people and filled with rodents, so it will take some time for him to adjust to apartment living. You've done everything right buying all those stimulating cat toys and taking him out in the cat pack. You could always adopt another cat, although you'd have to allow them to meet and see if they get along first. There's also the option of fostering. That way, if there *are* any dominance problems, the foster cat can go back into the shelter. But it'd give both cats a chance to be social and live in a much better environment than the shelter can provide. Fostering is a great way to help strays get the warmth and love they need before they're officially adopted.'

'I'll speak to Guillaume about it. We're co-parenting and I'm not sure what his thoughts on the matter will be.' Going from one cat to two before he's even had his new house guest stay might be pushing the limits, but already the idea appeals to me.

She grins. 'I love the co-parent idea. Actually, another stray was handed in yesterday. She was found wandering the streets, apparently. We've looked her over and are waiting for the cat shelter to pick her up. Would you like to see her? Aside from being dehydrated and covered in fleas, she's in good shape. We've given her flea treatment and she's been on a drip to rehydrate. She's already been sterilised at some point, so there's no need to worry about any of that. Why not meet her while we've got Minou here? He could too – to assess if they're a good fit? No pressure of course, but it will be beneficial to monitor the cats' behaviour towards one another if you do consider fostering her.'

'Sure, let's meet her. What do you say, Minou?' He covers his eyes with a paw. 'He can be quite a diva.'

The vet laughs and scoops Minou into her arms. 'Follow me. She's in one of the observation rooms.'

We follow her into a small room with a big cage with bedding inside. I bend down to get a look at the stray who has been rescued and brought in for medical attention. What will Guillaume think if he comes back to find the number of cats has doubled? What am I even thinking? I won't act until I have his permission as this is a co-parent situation.

The cage is dark, so it's hard to make out the face of the little orange cat who slinks slowly over as the vet coos to her. 'Is that...?' I squint at the cat who, like Minou, looks like she's been starved of her food source for a while. The waif-like cat drags herself to the front of the cage, into the light of the room. I gasp when I see her face. She's thinner, dirtier, but instantly recognisable. 'That's Marmalade!'

'Marmalade?' the vet asks quizzically, and at the sound of her name she meows. Minou wiggles to be put down and the vet complies. He pushes his nose to the crate to meet Marmalade's. It's the most beautiful thing I've ever seen. A homecoming of two lost souls. They purr and paw as if communicating in their own special language. 'You know this cat?'

'*Oui*. Marmalade is Minou's best friend from the cemetery.'

'*Ooh la la*. That might be why Minou hasn't settled in if he's been missing her.'

I slap a hand to my forehead. '*Mon Dieu*. I bet Marmalade left the cemetery and got lost because she was looking for Minou!'

'How sweet they're reunited.'

The vet gives me decisive nod and a watery smile. It must be hard doing what they do, in their attempts to save every animal that comes their way. 'So, what you do say? Is fostering in the realms of possibility? I understand we'd need to wait for confirmation from Guillaume, but someone from the shelter will be here soon for Marmalade, and honestly, while the shelters are wonderful and prolong the life of many an animal, they're not the best environments long term for any of them.'

My mind ticks with possibilities. 'Fostering means someone could fully adopt Marmalade at any time, doesn't it?'

'Yes, fostering would be a temporary arrangement, but full disclosure – sometimes cats of this vintage don't get adopted very fast. You could be committing to a lengthy foster process.'

'I think... I'll adopt Marmalade.' I look at the two cats delightedly purring at each other and make a firm decision. 'They clearly can't be apart, and I can't take the risk that someone might fall in love with her sweet little face and take her from us. I'm sure Guillaume will be amenable.' I cover Minou's ears so he doesn't hear and whisper, 'Marmalade is Guillaume's favourite, so I'm almost positive he will agree anyway.'

The vet's eyes shine with happiness. 'Perfect! I'll let the shelter know you're going to go ahead with the adoption. Do you want to take Marmalade home with you now and I can forward the adoption paperwork on to you later?'

'If she's ready, why not?' Will this reunion help Minou to settle down or have I just doubled my problems? Either way, I'm sure I've made the right decision by the way the two mangy felines stare into each other's eyes as if they've found... *home.*

29

The morning speeds by after taking the cats home and leaving them in the care of the pet sitter, who graciously informs me two cats will cost double to cat sit. While Minou is almost back to full health, Marmalade is not. She's far too thin and weak from her time on the streets. There's no time to negotiate with the cat sitter so I agree and set off for work. I shoot Guillaume a text to let him know his co-parent responsibilities have doubled.

He responds quickly:

> What! You can't just go around adopting every stray, Lilou!

I consider drawing it out and teasing him but I'm already far too late for work so I reply:

> Ooh? So shall I cancel the adoption of Marmalade who went on an adventure searching for Minou and came off a little worse for wear in her efforts?

I hit send and wait for the inevitable lecture.

> You could have led with that, Lilou. Of course we'll co-parent Marmalade! How is she? If she's seriously hurt, my heart will surely break.

He's a softie underneath all that bluster.

> She's going to be fine. Nothing a little TLC won't fix.

Geneviève's shop Palais is open when I arrive, so I head straight in to see her, hoping to share with her the outcome of my morning. '*Bonjour*, Lilou. Why do you look so happy? Was it the diary? Did you read the rest of it?'

I'd almost forgotten about the diary after the excitement of the morning. 'I did. There were only a few more poems! But I still have no clear idea who it is.' What I don't say is I fell in love with the words, the sweeping statements of adoration and expectations on what love between us could be. But how can such a thing be possible when I don't know who the author is? The thing is, my heart knows what it wants, but I'm just not sure the person I've fallen for feels the same way so I can't voice it to anyone, not even Geneviève. 'My main news is that I adopted another cat. Marmalade from Montmartre cemetery.'

Her eyebrows shoot up. 'What? How can that be?'

I explain about Minou's check-up and finding Marmalade had been handed in, after presumably going on an adventure to find her feline best friend.

'Wow, I can see this cat adoption thing getting out of hand. Are you going to swap real love for the love of pets?'

'It would be easier,' I admit. 'It's not that I'm becoming a crazy cat lady, but who wants to be the person who splits relationships up, cat or otherwise?' And really, what's the difference between facilitating love between two furry felines, or two humans, myself included?

'Next we'll have Paris Cupid for Cats.' She laughs. 'Mimosa?'

'Geneviève! If I have a mimosa at this hour, I'll be asleep at my desk. Minou prefers to sleep during the day, so I'm already running on empty with all his nighttime high jinks.'

'Pah!'

'OK?'

'Sit, sit while I pour you an orange juice then.' She saunters to the bar fridge and comes back with our drinks. Honestly, how the woman has the energy to get through long market days when she has a mimosa for breakfast and wine at lunch most days is beyond me. 'What did you decide to do about Paris Cupid?'

I blow out a breath. 'I decided to face it head on myself. If it happens, it happens.' I shrug. 'I might be a laughingstock for a while and people will judge me for the married man thing, if they find it out, but I know the truth so…'

'Lilou, if they judge you, that says more about them than you. Though the offer is still there if you'd like me to take ownership.'

'It's fine. And anyway, I'm still hoping it might all go away.' I would much prefer sinking my energy into finding love for people than worrying about being outed as the face of Paris Cupid.

'Oh *ma Chérie*, this is why we drink champagne for breakfast. It won't go away, but the bubbles make it easier to digest.'

I laugh. 'That's terrible advice, Geneviève, but thanks for the sentiment.'

'You're welcome. Now, I need breakfast, would you like a *croissant aux amandes* from Lumière Boulangerie?'

I'm about to agree when I see a customer waiting at my stall. 'No, thanks. I'd better go, but let's meet for lunch?'

'*Oui*. We've got a lot to discuss.' She drops her voice. 'I'll get those handwriting samples today.'

I nod, wondering just what scheme she'll use. I say goodbye and dash back to my stall. '*Bonjour, bonjour.*' I take my keys from my handbag and unlock the door. 'Come in. Sorry I'm late, I was chatting to my neighbour and didn't see you waiting.'

There's something cagey in the man's eyes. It's the way he's squinting at me like he's trying to get a read or something. 'Are you Lilou Babineaux?'

'*Oui*,' I say slowly. 'And you are?'

'Jorges from *Paris Scandale*. I'd like to ask you about your part in Paris Cupid. Can you confirm you're the owner of the site?'

The ground beneath me tilts. I freeze, unbalanced and unsure of how to answer. Why are *Paris Scandale* involved!

'Well?' Jorges prompts. 'I'd love an exclusive with you. You can get your side of the story out first.'

Eventually my brain catches up. 'What do you mean "*my* side of the story"?' Is there any point denying it at this stage? All I can do is try and minimise the damage.

Jorges gives me a sly smile that makes my skin crawl. 'Well, it's not going to look good, is it? A matchmaker with a rocky love life according to your social media posts going back the last few years. There was the married man and seven children. The catfish from America. The engagement that lasted all of three weeks before he stole your bicycle and ghosted you. The list goes on. You really should have used your privacy settings if you didn't want that sort of thing found.' He glances at a notebook in his hand and flips a page. 'With that sort of history, what makes you think you're capable of finding love for other people?'

I want to slap my own forehead. Why didn't I delete all those old posts? But he's not simply going back a few years, he's also going back to my early twenties, a decade ago. When I shared online in detail all about those silly heartbreaks just like everyone else did.

My dithering is replaced with white-hot fury as anger roils up inside of me. 'Dating mistakes aren't a crime, last time I checked! Yet here you are making it seem like it's my fault for believing in what a man tells me on face value. Shouldn't you be doing an exposé on men who date and dash? Men who lie about their identity, their marriages? Isn't that a much more *important* story?'

He lets out an impatient sigh as if the truth is boring him. Pen poised, he says, 'So you admit you're Cupid?'

I'm so taken aback, my mind a scramble as I desperately try to think. 'I admit no such thing.'

He slips his pen into his jean pocket. 'OK, then we'll run the angle we want and you won't get a say how this plays out.'

'You're threatening me?' How dare he! 'You're a scourge on society, you know that? You're the reason people stop believing in love, when you write shallow exposés about innocent women trying to find the one.' I'm surprised to find my eyes fill with tears. If Jorges from *Paris Scandale* is this brutal, how is everyone else going to react when the news gets out? Jorges stands there as if rooted to the spot. 'I want you to leave. Get out of my stall!'

There's a thunder of footsteps and I turn to find Pascale stomping towards us, glower at the ready. 'Is everything OK, Lilou?' he asks me, shooting daggers at Jorges, who is suddenly looking a lot less confident with Pascale breathing down his neck.

I swipe at my eyes, hoping Pascale doesn't notice my tears. 'Not exactly. I've asked this man to leave, but he's not listening.'

'It's not that,' Jorges says jovially as if he wasn't just threatening me. 'I was giving you one last chance to tell your side of the story, that's all.'

'Never in a million years,' I say through gritted teeth.

Jorges shrugs. 'Don't say I didn't warn you.'

'Do *not* speak to her like that.' Pascale's practically breathing fire. 'It's best if you leave now or I'll *make* you leave.'

Jorges lets out a pig-like squeal and jogs away, looking over his shoulder as if he's worried Pascale is going to change his mind and chase him out. From the murderous expression on Pascale's face, Jorges is right to be worried. And it's really rather upsetting to me that a man will only comply when another man arrives, all guns blazing. This is exactly what women are up against.

'Didn't I tell you already violence is never the answer?' I say, my weak joke falling away as I glance at Pascale, who has his hands fisted at his sides.

'What was all that about, Lilou?' A muscle works in his jaw and it's all I can do not to confide in him.

How to answer? Do I even need to? 'You'll soon find out. I've got to speak to Geneviève.'

'Lilou.' He places his hands on my shoulders. Big strong man hands that make me feel safe. I roil against the feeling of being the meeker sex. The woman who needs a knight in shining armour. I want to be able to take charge myself. Not rely on a man to scare away other men.

'Take a moment to breathe. *Breathe,*' he says. 'Your whole body is trembling.'

I'm practically vibrating from the adrenaline that's coursing through me. My hands shake so hard, I clasp them together and focus only on my breaths. I close my eyes and will myself to relax. I can't make any decisions when I'm wound up like this.

'Good, that's better. Give it a couple of minutes. Do you want me to find Geneviève? Sit down for a minute, I'm worried you're going to faint.'

It *feels* as dramatic as all that. The barely disguised threats Jorges gave me about what he was going to write to make me look inept as a matchmaker. '*Oui*, find Geneviève.' She's the only person who will understand and will tell me straight.

Worry gnaws at me. How am I going to face public scrutiny if I can't face one reporter? Pascale takes me into his arms and gives me a hug. The gesture grounds me, brings me back to the now. Once again, there's a real sense of being safe with him. As though he's a life raft in stormy seas. I don't overthink it; I don't have the energy right now.

When he releases me, I miss the warmth of his embrace. 'I'm going to find Geneviève, OK? Sit on the chaise and sit tight.'

I fall back on the chaise longue, holding my head in my hands, wondering how to salvage the situation.

A few moments later, Geneviève appears, clutching a paper bag of croissants, worry lining her face. 'Lilou, what happened? Pascale said you needed me urgently. Are you OK?'

'Ah – well...' Pascale is still hovering, hands on hips, eyes wild as if he's hoping Jorges will return for round two so he can have a piece of him. I furtively motion to Pascale, and Geneviève gives me a nod as if she understands the message loud and clear.

'*Merci*, Pascale. Lilou is fine with me now. Is that a customer at your shop?'

'They can wait.'

'Ooh, aren't you lovely? But I can take it from here. Lilou's had a bit of a morning, you see. She's probably got a cracking headache. Though it's nothing a mimosa won't fix.' Her voice is high and giggly, and it sounds false even to me.

'Are you sure? That man gave her a fright and I'd like to know why. I didn't like the weaselly look about him.' Pascale's face is pinched with worry. I've never had a man stand up for me like that before. Part of me likes it, but the other part wants to tell him I don't need anyone to do my shouting for me.

'I'm fine,' I say. 'Geneviève is right, it's just a slight headache.' I run with her excuse. 'And an obnoxious visit from some random gutter journalist to contend with.'

Pascale surveys me so hard I blush. 'He said he was giving you a chance to tell your side of the story. What did he mean? What story?'

The truth sits on my tongue. 'I'm...'

'She's being investigated about a cat smuggling ring. Lilou is perfectly innocent, of course.'

Whaat! A cat smuggling ring? Has Geneviève lost her mind?

Pascale lifts an eyebrow. 'A... what?'

If we dig ourselves into a hole any further, we'll be buried.

'She has adopted both her cats, and we can prove it!' The situation has an unreal air to it and I have to bite back on sudden laughter. Although, on reflection, maybe it's best if we discuss the way forward before I confide in anyone, especially Pascale, that I'm Cupid.

'I did. I adopted them from the vet, and yes, they were cemetery cats, but they needed care. There was absolutely no smuggling involved.'

He gives us a long look that implies he believes not one word but can't prove it. 'So that guy was after some kind of admission about a... cat smuggling ring?'

Geneviève nods so fast I'm sure her head is going to come clean off. 'Aha. It's rife around Paris, allegedly. If you wouldn't mind keeping this between us for now, we'd appreciate it.'

'O... K.' Pascale's posture softens as if he can't quite believe he nearly launched Jorges from the market over an accusation of smuggling felines. 'While I've got you' – Geneviève takes a piece of paper from her handbag – 'would you mind filling in this quick survey for me?'

He takes the proffered paper. 'A survey about my favourite haunts around Paris? Why?'

'Why not? We get plenty of tourists in the market, and I thought it would be nice to give them a guide to our beautiful city. Just fill it in at your leisure and have it back to me by no later than' – she glances at her watch – 'lunchtime.'

He frowns, as if trying to work out what's really going on but comes up blank.

'I've filled in mine,' I say as if in solidarity. 'We're lucky to live in Paris, are we not?'

'Ah – *oui*.' Confusion is evident across his features. Geneviève has managed to waylay his suspicions about reporter Jorges with the supposed cat smuggling ring. At least that's something. For now. 'Lunchtime. Got it.' He gives me one lingering look before he turns and heads back to his stall.

I exhale a pent-up breath. 'Geneviève, what the hell?'

She dons the wide-eyed Bambi look. 'What?'

'A *cat smuggling ring*?'

With a loose shrug she says, 'You were about to admit to him you're Cupid. I could see it written all over your face. And while I adore Pascale, I think it's best if we make a solid plan before you go blurting it out to all and sundry.'

'*Oui*, you're right. It's just he was so... nice. So comforting. I briefly lost my mind.'

Her eyes light up which can only mean one thing. I stop her before she can voice it.

'No, Geneviève, it doesn't mean anything. That horrid journalist caught me unawares is all, and then Pascale playing the superhero only added to my confusion.'

'*Oui, oui*. I wasn't about to suggest anything. Except...' She toys with a strand of her hair. 'Who doesn't like a man who defends a woman's honour in such a way? Call me old fashioned but men like that don't really exist these days, do they?'

I scoff. 'Shouldn't we be more concerned that Jorges only left me alone when Pascale came to my rescue? When I asked him to leave, he blithely ignored me. That's the bigger issue here.'

'Of course, you're right, you're right. But...' She gazes wistfully across the hallway to Pascale's typewriter stall. 'Isn't it remarkable that Pascale was on your side without knowing a thing about what the conflict between you and Jorges was? It means no matter what, he's there for you.'

Does it though? Or is it just some macho thing? A flex. A show of dominance? 'Hmm.'

'Oh, you and your hmms,' Geneviève says. 'I'm going to give Benoit his survey.'

'But shouldn't we discuss Paris Cupid first?'

'*Oui*, I'll be right back for that.'

'Don't you think this is more important right now? What if Jorges comes back?'

'Call out for Pascale! Although, by the looks of it, he's already standing sentry.'

Instead of sitting bashing at his typewriter temperamentally the way he usually does, he is leaning against the door of his stall, shooting daggers to all who cross his path. Really, if the man continues like this he'll be out of business by the end of summer.

'OK, Geneviève. Hand out the survey to Benoit and then we'll convene a Paris Cupid meeting.'

'Done.' She flounces off in Benoit's direction as I spot Guillaume coming up the stairs. He makes his way to me, a box in hand.

'*Bonjour*, Lilou.' We exchange *la bise*. 'I've just got back from Rouen and have some stock for you to look at.'

'Why aren't we meeting at Montmartre cemetery?' I love our meetings there in the sunshine surrounded by cats and ghosts.

'I'm pressed for time, so I figured I'd just pop in. I'm trying to get everything done as quickly as possible so I can pick up the cats this evening. I hope that's amenable to you?'

I search his features. His complexion is pink, his eyes darting around as if his mind is elsewhere. '*Oui*.' What else can I say? I don't want to discourage him while he has stock on hand, but I really want to discuss the Paris Cupid disaster with Geneviève. 'We can chat now, Guillaume, but I don't have much time.'

'*Oui, oui*. Always rushing, is Lilou.'

'*Moi*?'

He rocks on the balls of his feet. 'Let me show you what I found.'

At my desk, he opens the box to reveal a stunning gold embossed prayer book. It almost glows, the gilded cover is so bright. 'It's very rare, Lilou. Very delicate. You might search further than Paris for its next owner. Maybe you could list with a prestigious antique auction?' From his pocket he takes white cotton gloves and puts them on before lifting the prayer book from the box. 'It's circa 1800, and as you can see it's more a piece of art than a book to be read and thumbed through.'

I agree that the artefact deserves a unique approach and recognise Guillaume is being very generous sharing this prayer book with me when he could have easily resold it himself for a hefty profit. 'It should be in a museum.' We discuss the book and its possible provenance. It's decided I'll ask contacts in the museum world first about a possible sale. We haggle over price but I know I've got myself a bargain and the profit margin will be a healthy one. Once our business is concluded I bring the conversation around to the cats. 'What time are you picking up Minou and Marmalade this evening?'

His face softens. 'I have a full day of client visits but I plan to finish around six pm if that suits you?'

'Sure, I can be home by then. How are things with you and Clementine?'

He blushes and fumbles with his key chain. 'Wonderful, wonderful. Clementine took it upon herself to visit Rouen for a few days while I was there. It was lovely to do some sightseeing with her in the medieval town.'

I give him a wide smile and pretend I don't already know. 'Things have moved swiftly, I take it?'

He clears his throat and holds his head high. 'My private life is just that, Lilou. Private.'

'I understand, Guillaume, but you may remember I suggested you try Paris Love Letters, and now I'm really rather invested in your private life.'

His shoulders rise as he takes a deep breath and exhales theatrically. 'It's Paris Cupid, you infernal busybody, and if you insist on being meddlesome, I suppose the only solution is to give you some breadcrumbs, otherwise I'll never hear the end of it.'

'That's true. I can only escalate from here.'

The obligatory head shake returns but his face is full of colour, as if he's been renewed by his time away with a visit from Clementine. 'Fine. Our correspondence went remarkably well. In fact, we were writing back and forth every day, our letters arriving out of sync, which I didn't even mind since we were simply enthusiastic about getting to know one another.'

'Them arriving out of sync bothered you a *little*, didn't it?' I grin and fold my arms, ready to battle him on this point. My friend is pedantic in the purest sense of the word.

'*Oui, oui.* It bothered me greatly but I was a willing accomplice so I let it go, despite them being out of order and making no sense. After six weeks of back and forth, just like Mathilde foretold, I felt a level of... *certainty*. She said I'd know when the time was right and that seemed to be the case.' He flushes scarlet and his chin dips down, as if he's embarrassed to share this so openly with me. 'I had the Rouen trip coming up and I felt like it might be time for us to take things to the next level.'

'So then what happened?' I lean against the counter.

'I asked Benoit to pen my next letter in formal calligraphy as it seemed fitting for what I was about to suggest.'

'To meet up?'

'I wrote about how my feelings were true, and that I only had good intentions. And if she felt the same and was amenable, would she care to accompany me to the ballet at the *Opéra National de Paris.*'

My eyebrows shoot up. 'The ballet?'

He lets out a giggle. An actual giggle! 'I have no idea about romance, Lilou. I asked the *bibliothécaire* to help me use those hellish machines at the library and I googled what women like when being courted.'

I press my lips together. Could he *be* any more adorable? 'Great idea.'

His faux-grumpy expression returns, as if he wants to disguise his efforts in the art of wooing a woman. '*Oui, oui,* all very silly really. Advice such as deliver chocolate-covered strawberries to their place of work, or a dozen long-stemmed roses. The *bibliothécaire* pointed out some of the advice was out of date, and I was best to go with the ballet invitation.'

'How was the ballet?'

'I fell asleep, but that's not exactly my fault. We shared a bottle of Beaujolais at dinner before and the event started rather late. I caught the end. There was a lot of pliéing and whatnot.'

'Did Clementine enjoy it?'

He gives me a decisive nod. 'Then it was she who suggested she visit Rouen for a few days during my jaunt there. At first, I was rather taken aback. Is that the done thing these days, women asking men? It was very forward, in my opinion, so I asked the advice of the *bibliothécaire* once again and she gave me a stern lecture about the progression of women's rights and how I was acting like a dinosaur. Sufficiently reprimanded and more than a little regretful that I'd judged Clementine, I accepted her offer and gave her details of the hotel I'd be lodging at.'

I can't help but grin as Guillaume learns the ropes to modern day dating. 'And just like that you spent a few days together?'

'What's that ridiculous thing you're doing with your face? For your information, we had separate hotel rooms, not that it's any of your business. While our relationship has progressed, we're still in the very early stages.'

'Hand holding?'

He reels back. 'This is private, Lilou! I'm a gentleman!'

'*Désolé*, of course. As it should be. And how about the matchmaking site itself? Were you happy with it?'

He grumbles under his breath. 'Mostly. Benoit said it was legitimate but with all this talk about who is running it, it does make a man worry.'

'Oh? What talk is that?'

'Allegedly the person behind it won't reveal themselves, so the general consensus is that they're obviously hiding something. I just hope my bank accounts are safe.'

'Why wouldn't they be?'

'The *internet*, Lilou, that's why! There's probably another Guillaume wandering around Paris right now, taking out mortgages in my name, living a life of luxury.'

'That's not quite—'

'I've heard all about it. Identity theft. Cloning. The list goes on.'

I shake my head. 'Well, at least you've found a match.'

'*Oui*.'

'And Clementine, what does she think of Paris Cupid?'

'She thinks all the speculation about who is running it is a waste of time and that we should all be happy such a service exists, but this is coming from a woman who enthusiastically shops on the internet when there are brick and mortar shops all around as far as the eye can see. It befuddles me, but the *bibliothécaire* told me to keep my trap shut when it comes to a woman's proclivities for retail therapy, online *or* off.'

'I like this *bibliothécaire*.'

'Bossy, she is, unrelenting, like someone else we won't name. *Lilou*. Anyway, I'll pick up the cats this evening, and they can stay with me for the week. Clementine is excited to meet them too. She's coming over for apero tomorrow.'

'She's going to fall in love with them like we have.'

I wonder what he'll think when the news breaks that I'm Cupid. I only hope it doesn't change anything between us.

30

My head pounds as the interminable day continues. The gossip around the market is on overdrive and I'm sick to death of hearing about Paris Cupid rumours. Many a time I almost screamed the truth from the top of the stairs but stopped myself from being hasty. What if the reporter was all bluster? Although, deep down, I guess investigative reporters have ways and means to find out faster than online sleuths.

I'm about to close when Geneviève comes rushing in, brandishing paperwork in her hands. 'Lilou,' she whispers. 'I have the handwriting samples!'

That gets my attention. I guess I have been more invested in finding out who my so-called secret admirer is than I've let on.

'Have you got the other correspondence they sent?' she asks.

'*Oui*, in my desk. Shall I close up? What if one of them walks in?'

Geneviève shakes her head. '*Non*, if they happen along, we can gauge their reaction. Get the letters, Lilou.'

I find the previous deliveries and open my phone to the picture of the delicate parchment with calligraphy from the copy of *Madame Bovary* that's framed and by my bedside in my apartment. We study them all one-by-one. My posture stoops. 'Not a match. Not even close to a match,' I say.

Geneviève blows out a breath. 'How can that be?'

'It's not one of them, I guess.' Why then do I feel so deflated? I take a moment to piece it together. Is it because there is a man across the hall who makes my heart beat double time? Though apparently I can't admit it, even to myself? Why *is* that? This is proof that making a wish for love on Buste Dalida is another Parisian myth. I've always admired Dalida and, even though it seems so childish, I really did hope my wish would be granted. Clearly desperation. Not only am I unlucky and hopeless in love, but my alter ego is about to suffer a mortifying public execution.

'I'm sorry, Lilou. I was *so* certain.'

'It's OK. It's probably a practical joke, and there is no secret admirer. That would be just my luck to start falling for the words of a ghost, a fake. I can add that to my repertoire.'

'Absolutely not! But who else could it be? Another man from the market?'

'It's been a long day, Geneviève. I'm going to shut early and head home. Play with the cats before Guillaume comes to collect them. Consider adopting a third one. Maybe a fourth.'

She laughs. 'Don't let it get you down, Lilou. We'll figure it out.'

I'm glum and ready to eat my feelings because I know soon enough the Paris Cupid news is going to break and then my secret admirer will probably run away screaming too. '*Au revoir*, Geneviève.'

* * *

I stop past Maison du Croquembouche and buy far too many sweet treats before continuing on foot to home. I head to Place Marcel Aymé, walking by the statue of Le Passe-Muraille, the sculpture of a man who can walk through walls. I love the quirkiness of the street art. He really is situated halfway between the wall, and his hand is golden from all the visitors who have tried to pull him out. Next I stop at Rêves de Champagne to buy a bottle of wine. A few months ago I matched the owner with a woman who works at the Louvre and I'm thrilled to see her hovering by the door to say hello to him as I leave. I recognise her by her bio picture, but in real life she's even prettier and has love hearts for eyes when she chats to him.

Once home, the cats circle my feet as the cat sitter jumps from the sofa, eager to escape the confines of my tiny apartment. 'They've been good today. Minou is a different cat with Marmalade here. I don't want to put myself out of a job or anything, but I don't think I'll be needed here any more.' Marmalade's injuries aren't as severe as Minou's, it's really only that she was dehydrated.

'That's great to hear. They are settling in much better now they're together again.'

Her phone beeps. 'Sorry, it's my sister and if I don't reply she'll bombard me with messages until I do.'

'Is everything all right?' It strikes me I know virtually nothing about the cat sitter, having trusted the pet sitting site because I didn't have much choice at the time.

'*Oui*. She says she's figured out who this Paris Cupid person is. Honestly, it's all she ever talks about.'

Seriously! I double blink. 'Who does she think it is?'

'All she said is it's someone who works close to her. A guy.'

A guy? 'Where does your sister work?' Have they turned their attention in the complete wrong direction? 'Saint Ouen Flea Market. She's a florist.'

Mon Dieu, what are the chances? I've only got Coraline's younger sister pet sitting for me! We've never shared personal details. She usually dashes out as soon as I get home, off to do whatever it is teenagers do over the summer holidays. Other times, she leaves an hour or so before I get home because she has another long-term cat-sitting job to get to.

'A florist. How nice. Did you reply to her?'

'*Oui*. She'll dangle that carrot now and won't give me any details until I beg her for them. And really, who cares about Paris Cupid? It's a matchmaking site for old people. Like, really old people. Who'd want to write love letters when you could easily text? It makes zero sense.'

I can only laugh at such a teenager statement. 'Ah-huh. Texting would be a lot more efficient. So did she have a name for the guy?' Who have they pinned this on?

'No she didn't say. Anyway, here's your key. If you need me back let me know.'

'*Merci*, I will.' She gives the cats one last cuddle and leaves. 'Now, where's that wine?' I say to my charges before I pour myself a large glass and tell the cats all about my day and the relevant drama in my life. Minou stalks off, as ever not the best listener, but Marmalade stands riveted to the spot as if fascinated by human life.

31

I get to the market bright and early and am relieved to find Geneviève inside Palais. I rush inside and greet her. '*Bonjour*, Geneviève. Have you seen *Paris Scandale*'s socials today?'

'*Oui,* why do you think I'm here so early? What do you make of it?'

She pours two mimosas and today I don't bother arguing. I take the proffered glass and big gulp. 'I'm not sure. How could they get it so wrong?' *Paris Scandale*'s article this morning announced:

> The face behind Paris Cupid exposed! We can report the face behind the popular matchmaking site Paris Cupid is a thirty-three-year-old man who, despite his claims to help others in their quest for love, remains resolutely single. Scandale! Stay tuned for an exclusive interview with Cupid himself as he says, 'I'll tell you everything, if you then leave well enough alone.' What we know so far is, he set up the company in a friend's name, in the hopes to keep his own identity secret. When our reporters tracked this "friend" down and confronted her, he then contacted us and admitted he was Cupid. Stay tuned. Exclusive coming tomorrow!

'Who is this man? Someone chasing clout?'

I shake my head. 'Surely they'd do some sort of due diligence and check? They can't just believe anyone who walks off the street and announces something like that.'

Geneviève refills her mimosa with champagne. 'So he's managed to convince them somehow, but who could it be? Who would know enough to be able to pull that off? There's no one. Is there?'

It hits me. The question in his eyes, the way he surveyed me looking for an answer. 'It's Pascale!'

Geneviève's eyes widen. 'How would he know for sure?'

'Yesterday Pascale wanted to eject that reporter by his ears. You told him I was being accused of cat smuggling!' The idea is so preposterous I laugh. 'It wouldn't take a genius to figure out we were lying. Plus, he comforted me the day Coraline riled me up about digging into the identity of Paris Cupid, even though the site had matched her. He knew those online groups had a strong theory that it was someone from the market, and their focus narrowed in on us. It's not hard to join those dots when it's clear I sell love letters, and Paris Cupid's ethos is all about keeping them alive in a modern day world.'

She smacks her forehead. '*Oui*. He figured it out. So why then would *he* claim to be Paris Cupid?'

My mind spins. 'To protect me.'

Outside, Felix arrives and wiggles his hand as if he's carrying a coffee cup. I hold my champagne glass aloft to let him know Geneviève is a very bad influence and coffee is not on the agenda today. He waves a finger as if telling me off and I laugh.

'So what will you do? Ask Pascale outright?'

'I guess. Do you think he's done the exclusive interview already?'

With a shrug, she says, 'I doubt it, or they'd have rushed to get that released, to break the news first.'

'I'd really hate that smarmy reporter to get the exclusive, even if it *is* all a lie.'

'Ask Pascale. It seems odd that he'd give that smarmy reporter the exclusive if he wanted to throw him out by his ears.'

'It's to save me from being exposed.'

Benoit arrives and gives us a friendly wave, before opening his shop. He pokes his head into Felix's shop and soon their laughter floats over.

Geneviève takes a seat behind her desk and holds her chin in her hand. 'That's the mark of a great man. Pascale doesn't seem to be the type that would like public scrutiny any more than you do. In fact, he'd like it even less and that's saying a lot. Makes you wonder why he'd go to such lengths…'

'You offered to do the same thing.'

'We've been best friends for years, and I love a good scandal, as you well know.'

'Just say it, Geneviève.'

'The man loves you. Pure and simple.'

'But we've already ruled him out. The handwriting didn't match.'

'*Oui*, that one bothersome fact.'

Pascale arrives and opens up his shop. Geneviève elbows me so hard I'm sure it's going to leave a bruise.

'I can see him, Geneviève, there is no need to physically assault me.'

He doesn't wave. Doesn't even look in our direction. Have we got it so wrong? If it was him wouldn't he be even the slightest bit curious to glance over and see how I am?

'Go, go ask him!'

'I'll go later.'

'It's *always* later with you! And that won't do! The time is now, Lilou, and if you don't go I'll march you over there myself.'

'Ooh,' I say, glancing to Ephemera. 'There's Pierre, the bookseller. Better run.' It's unusual for Pierre to visit, he rarely leaves his bookshop by the bank of the Seine during the day but at least he's saved me from another Geneviève lecture while I process what to do. What to *think* about Pascale.

'OK,' Geneviève says. 'Come back when Pierre leaves.'

'*Oui*.' I kiss her cheek and go to Ephemera. '*Bonjour*, Pierre. To what do I owe this honour?'

'I know.'

'You know what?'

'Everything. And I want to thank you. Coraline is going to be a great friend, something I desperately needed.'

How does he know I'm Cupid? Does that mean everyone knows?

'Ah...?' My mind spins what to say. Do I outright deny it, or admit the truth?

He gives me his lopsided grin. 'It's OK. Your secret is safe with me. I just wanted to pass on my personal thanks.'

'So it's just friendship between you and Coraline, nothing more?'

'Nothing more. But that's enough for now.'

'How do you know it's me?'

'A friend.'

'Who?'

'You'll see.'

'Why all the mystery?'

'Why not?'

'OK. While I've got you, that calligraphy letter you gave me, was that story about the apartment in the 4th all a lie?'

He frowns. 'No, the abandoned apartment was real.'

'But the letter inside *Madame Bovary*?'

He has the grace to blush. 'Another gift from your secret admirer.'

'Who is...?'

'Enraptured with you and got a bunch of us to help, because he wanted to romance you the way you would enjoy. He's a great guy. Speaking of, here's one last letter from him.'

I narrow my eyes. What is going on? I open the letter and all it says is:

Meet me at the Jean Rictus garden square

'Give love a chance, Lilou. You've helped so many others. Now it's your turn.'

Geneviève sashays back in and reads the letter over my shoulder. 'Ooh, the love interest! Well, what are you waiting for, Lilou? Go! I'll watch Ephemera for you.'

'What if it's someone I don't know? Or worse, don't like? What if he's a cat smuggler, a serial killer?'

Geneviève turns to Pierre. 'See what I'm working with here?'

He smirks. 'Go, Lilou. What have you got to lose but a bit of time?'

'Think of what you've got to gain! You tell people all the time to trust in the process. It's time for you to trust in this.'

'But...' But they're right. What if this is the man of my dreams? There is a man I've come to adore, but I can't even admit it to myself most days. 'Fine, I'll go. But I just need to do one thing first.' I log on to the Paris Cupid website and type. I'm not going to hide any more. I have nothing to be ashamed of.

> I'm writing today to demystify the truth about who I am and why I built Paris Cupid. My name is Lilou Babineaux and I'm Cupid. I wanted to remain anonymous because I didn't think matches would trust in a matchmaker who couldn't find love herself, and because some of my past relationships were a disaster. But what I've learned along the way is that those disasters are part of the journey to finding real and everlasting love. We've all had relationships that didn't work, betrayals of trust – I am just the same as my matches who only want to believe that love is out there for them, it's just a matter of finding it. I wanted to bring the lost art of love-letter writing back so we'd have these keepsakes in the future and we could look back to the past and remember how it felt in that first bloom of love by sharing all of our hopes and dreams on paper. I'm incredibly proud of Paris Cupid and the commitment each match has made to try this new way of finding love, friendship or a pen pal. That's all I hoped for. After all, isn't life so much better when you've got someone to correspond with? I hope by sharing who I am, you'll understand my motivations were pure. All I ever wanted was to help ease the lost, the lonely and the heartbroken, but it's developed into so much more than that. I might not be the matchmaker you imagined, but I promise you, I'm good at what I do. And I did it all for you.

I post it on the site and on my personal social media accounts. 'OK, I'm ready.' From behind the desk I grab my personal diary and shove it in my handbag and dash out the shop, but not before I see my neighbours' eyes trained on me. Does that mean it's not one of them?

32

I thank the taxi driver and jump out at Jean Rictus garden square. I smother a smile when I see where I am. The famous Wall of I Love You. Where the sentiment 'I love you' is written in over two hundred and fifty languages. That's a lot of love languages. I gaze around, trying to spot who my secret admirer is, but can't see anyone. Then I spot a familiar face. Coraline.

She walks over and hands me a bunch of long-stemmed red roses. 'Red roses symbolise passion, desire and romance. These are from your secret admirer, and he'll be along shortly.'

I take the perfumed bouquet from her hands.

'Also, for what it's worth. I'm sorry for the way I've acted. The things I've done. I'm a work in progress and I still mess up more often than not. I've got a lot to learn and I hope you'll forgive me.'

'Okayyy... What's brought all this on?'

'A little birdie had a chat with me, made me see your side of things. *Au revoir!*' She dashes off, before Guillaume takes her place.

'Guillaume, what are *you* doing here?'

He hands me a pretty box full of chocolate-covered strawberries. 'A delivery from your secret admirer, who is not me before you get your hopes up. I'm sorry, Lilou, but I'm already accounted for.'

I try my best not to laugh. 'So why are you here?'

'A friend had a quiet word. Explained things are not always as they seem. Mostly because of the internet and mainstream media, but I already knew that. What I didn't know, Lilou, is that you are responsible for Paris Cupid. Thank you for making an old man happy in his twilight years. I hope you find love. You deserve it.'

Clementine stands beside him holding a picnic basket. 'Dear Lilou, I always knew it would be someone charming and whimsical behind the matchmaking site. And I wasn't wrong. Your secret admirer arranged this basket of fromage for you to enjoy together. Thank you for matching me with Guillaume. You have a gift and I only hope your efforts return tenfold.'

I'm almost in tears with the outpouring of love and support from my friends and matches. Just when I think the show is over, I'm blown away when Émilienne steps up. I hold my breath, wondering what's happened between her and Emmanuel.

'Darling, what a surprise this was!'

'You were the first match, Em.'

'You did it for me?'

I lift a shoulder. 'For you and others just like you.'

Émilienne gives me a tight hug. 'Well, I'm pleased to say you've changed my life for the better. Without you, I'd have given up on love completely, and I really mean that. I was so sick of being too much or not enough.'

I'm about to ask Émilienne where she stands with Emmanuel when he taps me on the shoulder.

'Thank you for connecting me with Émilienne. I'm learning how to give her space, and learning how to enjoy time alone too. Without you, I'd have been lonely for the rest of my life. I didn't know the true meaning of love until I had to earn it. Writing love letters opened up a romantic side to me I didn't even know I had. When I shouted to the world about Paris Cupid, I meant you no harm. I'm sorry if it threatened your anonymity and your ability to cope with the site.'

'*Merci*, Emmanuel. I know your heart was in the right place.'

Who organised all these people? Who knew enough to do so?

Really, only Geneviève is privy to behind the scenes. Unless… And there he is. My heart pounds in my chest. He's changed into a white linen shirt and jeans. He walks towards me with all the confidence in the world, but I know that's just for show. Really, he's just like me, unsure and wary in the pursuit of love, while outwardly scowling to keep people at bay. We clashed since we first met because of that frisson between us, a spark, fireworks, the *coup de foudre,* the thunderbolt that rocked my world and showed me he was the one I've been searching for.

'Li.'

I grin at the shortening of my name that used to irk me so. 'Pascale.'

He takes my hand and kisses the top of it. 'I'm not one for grand gestures…'

'You're not?'

He grins. 'I'm not. And then you came along.' The crowd grows silent. Everyone's gazes are riveted to us but I only have eyes for him.

'And then what happened?' I ask.

'I couldn't focus, I couldn't sleep. If I did, my dreams were full of you. The only slight hiccup I had was… I couldn't form coherent sentences in front of you. I'd freeze up, lose my train of thought, say the opposite to what I was thinking. It was love, love at first sight, a notion I'd laughed at before, so many times. I had to act, and I wanted it to be special. I asked Benoit to write a love letter in calligraphy, Pierre to hide it, Felix to make a hand-pressed card.'

I turn to the group and see Felix and Benoit who give me a wave, then hold hands. Ah! Now all those long looks across at each other make sense! All those times Benoit blushed in front of Felix. And the question Benoit wanted to ask me… Was it some advice about his feelings for the ginger-haired printer?

I smile at them before I turn back to Pascale and say, 'You went to such great lengths. For me.' I still can't believe it. As I gaze at him, I find myself woozy, weak. He's everything I ever wanted in a man. Sweet, passionate, with that intensity that stops me in my tracks. A fierce protector who is really a teddy bear underneath but will rise in my defence if ever I need him to. The heart and soul of a poet with a romantic streak that is worthy of all those love letters from the past combined.

He smiles and it lights up his whole face. 'I wanted to show you – via every medium you love – what I felt for you since I couldn't do it in person.'

'But... your handwriting sample didn't match.'

He lifts a shoulder, 'I wanted to keep my identity a secret until I knew better how you felt.'

'You really thought of everything.'

'I tried.'

'And you got everyone here today? You told them I'm Cupid?'

He nods. 'I hope that's OK? When that slimy reporter came after you, I needed more time to figure out what to do. With Geneviève's help, I got everyone here together and explained the mission behind Paris Cupid. The reason why it needs to be protected. We've got a plan for that.'

'It's OK. I've admitted I'm Paris Cupid. I'm proud of it and I'm not going to hide any more.'

Geneviève appears and waves a bottle of champagne and I shoot her a wide smile.

I turn my attention back to Pascale. 'I can't believe you did all this for me.'

'I wanted it to be memorable.'

I grin. 'Here's the thing. I've been writing my own diary for the past little while...' I take it from my handbag and hand it to Pascale.

He opens it up and reads, *'Dear Pascale...'* His face breaks into a smile.

I take his hand and summon the courage to tell him what's in my heart, 'From the first moment I locked eyes with you in the market square that day, it was as if I'd been shocked awake. When you moved into the Marché Dauphine, I fought against my feelings for you. How could I be attracted to a man who made me so mad all the time? It was a losing battle. Every day my attraction grew stronger, and I had to admit there was something more there that needed exploring. Like you, I didn't know how to say it, whether to risk speaking those words out loud. I thought any other man would be a better choice, but my heart only yearned for you. Was it just some animal attraction? I felt like if I told you, we might have a fling and it would fizzle out, being based on nothing solid. I tried to think of you with my matchmaker hat on, and I knew I'd choose someone who I thought was more dependable. But that's the thing. You are dependable. You *are* all of those things. All of those and more. And as I've got to know you better, I knew you were the one for me. I've been writing to you in that diary secretly since that very first day.'

The diary is open to the first page, written the evening after *le scandale* when I had sadness in my soul but hope in my heart.

> *Today was the very worst day being confronted in the market square, but I locked eyes with a man with wild eyes. My heart and soul recognised his somehow. I feel silly even writing such a thing, but that's how it felt. A sense of the world shifting on its axis, so we'd stop and find each other. I've never felt such a thrill, such a longing for someone, and how can that be? I still had tears in my eyes from le scandale, and now this? Will I ever see him again?*

He pockets the diary and pulls me into his arms as the crowd around us lets out a cheer. When he kisses me, I'm sure I can feel the Wall of I Love You pulsate behind us, as if he truly loves me in every language.

EPILOGUE

Has Paris Cupid Found Love?

Here at Paris Daily we're all about love! We recently sat down with Lilou Babineaux AKA Paris Cupid herself and asked where she's at after admitting she's the mastermind behind the popular match-making site, where lonely hearts commit to writing love letters and partaking in slow-burn romance. Tell us, Lilou, what prompted you to confess that you're Cupid?

I wanted to take ownership of the site and with that came the risk of every choice I've made in my love life being judged and heavily scrutinised. It struck me that the mistakes I've made on the path to finding true love are mistakes so many of us make, and why should we be ashamed about it? I never did anything malicious; my intentions were always pure. I'm a heart-on-sleeve romantic who believes there's someone out there for everyone and all I intended to do was help others find love.

Why do you think the idea of writing love letters has appealed to so many Parisians?

The idea of romancing someone you've never met with words alone appeals because it's so different to the modern-day methods we use to find love. Writing to your match, you can't rely on your physical attributes, your outfit, your status. You have to unfurl layers of yourself, letter by letter. Matches have reported back that by writing love letters, they found they've opened up more, shared more intimate details because there was that safety of anonymity – if they chose, they could keep their identity a secret. All matches know about each other are first names and what they do for a job or hobby. With that comes a certain sense of freedom. They can be brave and bold with their words. They can go at their own pace to build a connection before they meet in the real world, if they feel a spark.

Speaking of sparks, is there any truth to the rumour you've been receiving love letters of your own and have recently found love?

We can report Lilou has responded to that question with a knowing smile that says everything, in our opinion! It looks like love is in the air for everyone including our very own Cupid! If you'd like to see what all the fuss is about check out https://www.ParisCupid.fr

ACKNOWLEDGEMENTS

A huge thanks to my editor Isobel for the patience, help and support while writing this book. You know why. To the readers who've been with me since day one, thank you – it means so much to me. And for those just finding me now, I hope you'll stick around for more Parisian adventures. Frankie and Belinda, what would I do without you? Lily, hurry up and get here! We've got ten thousand steps to do. Hilary, thanks for making the grey days blue and being a constant source of inspiration. To everyone at team Boldwood, thanks, you are all amazing and I appreciate every single one of you! As ever, my family do their utmost to support my work and help balance the long days when I'm locked away in my office. I'm so lucky to have the best support crew around and I love you even more than all the languages on the Wall of I Love You.

ABOUT THE AUTHOR

Rebecca Raisin writes heartwarming romance from her home in sunny Perth, Australia. Her heroines tend to be on the quirky side and her books are usually set in exotic locations so her readers can armchair travel any day of the week. The only downfall about writing about gorgeous heroes who have brains as well as brawn, is falling in love with them–just as well they're fictional. Rebecca aims to write characters you can see yourself being friends with, people with big hearts who care about relationships and believe in true, once-in-a-life time love.

Sign up to Rebecca Raisin's mailing list for news, competitions and updates on future books.

Follow Rebecca on social media here:

facebook.com/RebeccaRaisinAuthor
instagram.com/rebeccaraisinwrites2
bookbub.com/authors/rebecca-raisin
tiktok.com/@rebeccaraisinwrites

LOVE NOTES
LOVE IN EVERY CHAPTER

WHERE ALL YOUR ROMANCE DREAMS COME TRUE!

THE HOME OF BESTSELLING ROMANCE AND WOMEN'S FICTION

WARNING:
MAY CONTAIN SPICE

SIGN UP TO OUR NEWSLETTER

https://bit.ly/Lovenotesnews

Boldwood

Boldwood Books is an award-winning fiction publishing company seeking out the best stories from around the world.

Find out more at www.boldwoodbooks.com

Join our reader community for brilliant books, competitions and offers!

Follow us
@BoldwoodBooks
@TheBoldBookClub

Sign up to our weekly deals newsletter

https://bit.ly/BoldwoodBNewsletter

Milton Keynes UK
Ingram Content Group UK Ltd.
UKHW040704260624
444650UK00002B/6